Find
SHIP

™ MILLS & BOON®
Pure reading pleasure

*First published in Great Britain 2008
by Harlequin Mills & Boon Limited,
Eton House, 18-24 Paradise Road, Richmond, Surrey TW9 1SR*

ISBN: 978 0 263 85971 3

46-0608

*Harlequin Mills & Boon policy is to use papers that are
natural, renewable and recyclable products and made from
wood grown in sustainable forests. The logging and
manufacturing processes conform to the legal environmental
regulations of the country of origin.*

*Printed and bound in Spain
by Litografia Rosés S.A., Barcelona*

For Jim, who was my "salsa suicide" driver and, as always, helped with the punch lines

SHIRL HENKE

received her BA and MA in history from the University of Missouri and then worked at many different jobs, including running the circulation desk on a small daily, writing and editing "house organ" newspapers, administering a federal information programme for the elderly and finally as a university instructor.

Ever since she was a child she read avidly, everything from Robert Heinlein's sci-fi adventures to the big historical sagas of the 1970s and 1980s. She sold her first novel to Warner Books in 1986. Within two years, she was able to quit her day job. Now she can't imagine doing anything but writing for a living.

She and her husband, Jim, share their cedar house in the woods with an utterly spoiled and very geriatric tomcat. As with writing, life without cats would be unimaginable. For therapy when she's not at the computer, she cooks large dinners for their extended family, works in her garden and greenhouse, and still reads avidly. When deadlines permit, she loves to travel. Visit Shirl on the web at www.shirlhenke.com.

ACKNOWLEDGEMENT

This is my first venture into comedy/adventure. I think Bombshell and I were meant for each other! Lots of people helped make Sam and Matt's story possible, beginning with all the friendly residents of Miami. You are as sunny and warm as your climate!

My husband, Jim, drove on my research trip to Miami. Besides navigating the metro area, he helped gather information. A former navy man, Jim wore a cap bearing the logo of his ship that opened many doors for a writer. Former marine turned tour guide and boat captain, Juan F Campos regaled us with entertaining stories about the Intracoastal islands and suggested yachts and speedboats for the chase sequences.

At the US Coast Guard Station on Terminal Island, Joel Aberbach, SO-PS DIV VI, of the Coast Guard Auxiliary explained which causeways were closed for boat traffic, the height of each causeway, the ebb and flow of tides affecting when larger craft might slip under them and the procedure for raising drawbridges.

Detective Juan Delcastillo of the Miami-Dade Police Department, Media Relations Section, furnished us with essential background information on the Russian mob in Miami, gave us neighbourhoods where nefarious activities might take place and filled us in on all procedural matters regarding one of America's largest and finest police organisations.

Growing up on the Mississippi, Jim and I knew nothing about oceangoing crafts. Mr D Larry Deitch, owner of a Tiara, was so kind as to give us a tour of his yacht, explaining how various mechanisms worked. The folks at Florida Yacht Charters and Sales were most helpful furnishing us with ideas about yachts and chase boats – and they didn't even get to make a sale.

The experts furnished me with accurate information. Any errors are mine. If I fudged with a bit of literary licence, I hope they forgive me.

Chapter 1

"What a great set of buns," Samantha Ballanger said under her breath with a low whistle. It wasn't professional, but then this wasn't an ordinary job.

From the cover of her van door, she watched Matthew Granger bend over to pick up a beer can some litterbug had tossed on the sidewalk. He pitched it into a nearby trash can like a good citizen, then turned and continued walking down the opposite side of the street. He'd spot her in half a minute.

The photos didn't lie. He was tall as a church steeple, six-six if he was an inch, and looked like a young Tom Selleck. Very appealing, but his size might present some logistical complications. Brushing that worry aside, she pulled the other door to her Econoline van wide open and slid an oversize box halfway out. Then she pretended to struggle loading it.

At five-four, the curly-headed brunette was, as her Irish-Catholic mother euphemistically put it, "well endowed."

That's why she choose to wear a sprayed-on pair of hip-hugger shorts and a halter top that displayed her assets like an Excel spreadsheet. If this getup didn't grab his attention, he had an eyesight problem her research hadn't revealed.

As soon as he looked across the street, she could tell there was nothing wrong with his vision. Sam increased her exertion, even emitting a few ladylike swearwords to indicate she was in big trouble. A guy who cleaned up litter surely wouldn't refuse to help a damsel in distress. She watched him vacillate, obviously wanting to help her as he glanced down at his wristwatch.

Chivalry won out just as she hoped it would. Granger crossed the deserted street. She knew this wasn't the best neighborhood in San Diego for a woman alone, especially an attractive one whose least provocative article of apparel was the fanny pack strapped to her waist. The big brick complex of buildings where Granger lived was called Samaritan Haven, a place where people hid from their pasts, or ran from their futures. Not all of them were exactly hospitable to strangers.

"Need some help?" he asked, nodding to the box, half in, half out of the van.

"Yeah, I could use some. Thanks," Sam replied with a bright grin, stepping back so he could take the box in both hands. *Predictable as snow in Boston.*

"What've you got in here, rocks?" he asked, bending his knees to put some muscle behind shoving the box across the carpeting of the van.

Sam moved in close behind him, giving him a whiff of her perfume, a faint musky rose scent. Just for added measure, she let her breasts brush against his shoulder to distract him further. When he shoved the box all the way inside, she shoved the barrel of her gun sharply into his right kidney.

He grunted in surprise as she said conversationally, "It's exactly what it feels like, so don't get cute."

"You're the one who's cute, honey, or I wouldn't have walked my stupid butt across the street to be mugged," he replied.

"No mugging, *honey,* but this will be a prelude to a funeral if you don't spread your legs and lean forward into the van. Put all your weight on your palms."

"If you're a kidnapper, I have to warn you there's not enough in—"

"Just do it," she snapped curtly, pressing the gun muzzle harder into his kidney to emphasize her point. He was too big to take any chances with.

"Ouch," he muttered with an oath, leaning forward and spreading his long legs.

Sam tossed a small plastic nasal inhaler next to where his left hand pressed into the plush carpeting. "Squeeze a spray into each nostril, then snuff it up—good and hard," she instructed.

When he hesitated, she cocked the snub nose. He picked up the bottle and squeezed. She could see that he was trying not to get much of the spray up his nose, but with this new drug, that shouldn't matter. "Now inhale." She used the gun to emphasize her point. He complied with a noisy snuffle.

"What is that stuff? My nose's tingling," he said, trying to turn around.

"Stand still," she commanded him, jamming the snub nose harder in his kidney until she was satisfied that he wouldn't try anything stupid. Then she grabbed the back of his shirt with her free hand and balled it up tightly between his shoulder blades.

"Hey, you're choking me," he protested.

She ignored him. No time to fool around now, she thought,

eyeing the deserted street again. "Drop the bottle and put your hand back on the van floor."

"Okay, you're calling the shots." He coughed as his shirt collar bit into the sides of his throat. "For a little broad, you have a grip like a sumo wrestler. Now what?"

"We wait," she said. This was her first use of the new inhalator. Just her luck to experiment on a guy tall as a skyscraper. He coughed again. She imagined his brain starting to spin like the Seattle Space Needle.

His right arm buckled. He straightened it and shook his head. "Shit, that stuff wasn't Vicks, was it?" he muttered thickly.

Sam heard the slight slurring in his voice and swore silently. Jules had told her the nasal delivery system worked fast, but with a guy this big she'd never imagined it could work quite this fast. Damn! He was starting to puddle up real quick. She found it distracting enough that the man was drop-dead gorgeous. But did he have to be twice her size to boot? If he oozed beneath the van she'd be screwed. There was no way she could heft over two hundred pounds of male muscle from the pavement into her vehicle.

When his legs suddenly started to give way, she hissed, "Lock your knees. Stiffen your legs, for God's sake." A little panic was not all that unprofessional.

"Stiffen…stiff… My ass." The sibilant sound hissed between slack lips. "I cudn' get stiff for Julia Roberts."

Sam could see his legs were liquefying. She uncocked the .38 and slipped it into her fanny pack to have both hands free to work. She reached up between his legs to grab the front waistband of his Levi's.

"Doan get fresh!" It came out "fesh."

He grunted in acute discomfort as she levered her forearm up against his testicles. It was an old jujitsu move guaranteed to turn any man into a toe dancer. Any man not already higher than a satellite. His knees continued to wobble like Jell-O as she tried to shove him inside the van.

He muttered, "Hey, hey, tha's m…m' fam'ly jew'ls."

"Either you help me get your ass in that van or I'm going to liquidate a couple of the family assets right now. Got it?" Braced behind him, Sam cupped her left hand under his knee, trying to get him to lift it onto the floor of the van. She revised her estimate of his weight. He was the size of her uncle Declan's semi carrying a full load of sheet steel.

She tugged at his knee again, cursing as she became truly desperate. "Come on, throw your friggin' leg up there!" A quick glance up and down the street revealed no spectators, her only break so far. Finally, using her body weight against his rump, she bumped him hard several times until she was able to lever his knee high enough to slide it onto the van floor and roll him inside.

"Guy's 'posed ta do the h-humpin'," he said, collapsing, giggling in baritone as he flopped onto his back.

Now she only had one of his long legs and an arm dangling out the doors. "I can do this," she muttered to herself, leaning over him so she could pull the offending limbs inside.

"Ya got great k-knockers…ash, too," he murmured as his hand groped clumsily around her hip.

Quickly she bent the leg and shoved it inside, then threw the offending arm across his chest and slammed the door before it flopped out again. Sam could hear the crack of his elbow hitting the door panel but he was clearly feeling no pain. The giggling continued, a side effect of the drug she hadn't been warned about.

"Crap, 'happy hour' at ten in the morning," she muttered to herself. Relief made her almost giddy enough to giggle in return while she once again scanned the street. Not so much

as a window shade moved in any of the buildings. Southern
California. It figured. "I could've gone after him with a net
and trident and nobody would've noticed a thing."

Sam climbed into the driver's seat and turned the ignition,
then placed the .38 in the glove compartment before pulling
out and driving away slowly. In the back of the Econoline she
could hear soft male snoring as her new "retrieval" settled into
a deep, drugged slumber.

"Well, handsome, we sure as hell gave added dimension
to the term *tailgating*," she said, turning the corner of the
street and heading for a deserted strip mall next to the freeway.

Pulling into the back of the parking lot beneath a cluster
of blue gum trees, she shifted to Park, keeping the engine running while she climbed over the seat and quickly changed into
a loose set of pink hospital scrubs. After exchanging her
slides for a pair of crepe-soled lace-up shoes, she climbed out
of the side door of the Econoline and opened the back.

Changing Granger's appearance took a bit more work but
she'd had lots of practice. Still, her usual "snatches" weren't
built anything like this specimen. It took her twice the average time to get his big body trussed up in a lightweight straitjacket concealed by a large institutional-looking terry robe.
The faintest hint of a raspy black beard gave him a piratical
look. *More eyelashes than Liz Taylor.* She shook her head in
aggravation and slipped a sleeping mask over those wonderful eyes, then taped his mouth shut.

By the time she'd swathed his head with gauze bandages,
Sam felt her confidence return. She replaced his shoes with
bedroom slippers, then used the custom seat-belt straps attached to the floor to secure him safely for the ride. The belt
would also minimize any thrashing when he woke.

So far, so good, she thought as she climbed out of the van

carrying two oblong magnetic plates. After locking the rear door, she attached the signs to the sides of the vehicle. They read Fairview Hospital and gave a bogus address about five hundred miles northeast of San Diego on Interstate 15. When they neared there, she had other sets for the cross-country trip to Boston.

"Sweet dreams, gorgeous." Humming softly to herself, she pulled out of the deserted parking lot and hopped on the freeway. With any luck they'd make Utah by nightfall.

Funny, but he'd never gone blind with a hangover before. Matt blinked and tried to focus through the blackness, past the pounding inside his head. He'd been fading in and out of consciousness for an indeterminate length of time while someone was driving him someplace. He hadn't the foggiest who or where. His head throbbed so wickedly he didn't much give a damn. But then the vehicle came to an abrupt stop and he was forced into full and painful wakefulness.

Sam could see he was conscious if not exactly alert. She gave him an experimental shove. "Rise and shine, sweet cheeks."

Matt wished to hell he could choke the life out of whoever it was and just fade back into blissful oblivion. *Must've been one hell of a party.* He couldn't remember tying one on this badly since he was a freshman at Yale. The woman prodded him again. Shit, he was trussed up like a Thanksgiving turkey! What the hell was going on? No party, for sure. It started to come back to him when he heard that Boston accent again and smelled her rose perfume.

"Just sit up. You can do it," Sam wheedled, tugging on the robe covering the straitjacket that held his arms immobilized.

If only his head would stop the trip-hammer pounding so he could think. Did she work for Renkov? He asked but only mumbles came out. When he tried to talk he sounded like Bruce Springsteen singing. Then he recognized the tight burning feeling over his mouth. The loony bitch had taped it shut! And blindfolded him. His senses were starting to coordinate now, feeding his aching brain enough information to let him know that he was in trouble.

Big trouble.

For all he knew she intended to dump him in San Diego Bay. Yeah, she had to be working for that mobster Renkov. But how the hell had the bastard found out he was here? Had he compromised his sources and placed Tess and her son in danger, too? Matt swore to himself, frustrated, unable to think of anything he could do to break free.

Sam could sense the wheels turning in her captive's cunning mind. She knew he was going to make this difficult for her as she yanked his legs over the side of the van and pulled him into an upright position. He tried falling backwards into the van, but she applied pressure to a reflex point under his jawbone just in front of his ear that sent a nasty wave of pain shooting into his skull, which she was certain already pounded with agony from the nasal Mickey she'd given him. She'd studied martial arts since her early days with the Miami-Dade PD.

Matt wondered how long he had been out. Judging from the stiffness in his joints, he guessed hours. His bladder suddenly joined the circuit overload and informed him that he needed to take a serious whiz.

Sam knew he was achy and bruised, not to mention past due for using the bathroom. "You'd better cooperate and climb out of the van like a good boy or I'll have to apply more persuasion. I know the drug's worn off. If you want to be comfortable and get rid of the restraints, you have to cooperate. Then I'll explain everything. Oh, and you can use the convenience, too," she added as an afterthought.

Bitch. What choice did he have?

As if reading his mind, she continued, "Walk for me or I'll leave you wrapped up in the van while I get a good night's rest in the motel room."

His bladder made the decision for him. He sat forward and gingerly slid from the van to the ground with her guiding him. Maybe she didn't intend to kill him or turn him over to Renkov. Damn, but he'd never felt so helpless in his life, bound and gagged in pitch darkness. Not to mention the wretched drug hangover enhanced by her skillful application of torture to his jaw. He let her guide him across a sidewalk toward whatever fate she had in store for him.

Sam checked the parking lot of the Shady Acres Motel, a small sleazy place situated in a nothing burg in southern Utah. No one watched as she led her "patient" toward the door to the dingy room. The desk clerk had barely taken his eyes off a *Wheel of Fortune* rerun as he processed her credit card and handed her a room key. She was an R.N. transporting a burn patient to a special rehab facility in Salt Lake. Not half as interesting as Vanna White.

Desert heat seared them as they walked to the room. Sam could tell by his muffled curses that his feet burned through the thin soles of the slippers. He was uncomfortable but there was nothing she could do except hurry him inside. "Here, lean against the wall while I unlock the door," she commanded.

A blessedly cool blast of air hit her, never mind that it was dank and reeked of old cigarettes. So much for a nonsmoking room. "Here, let me guide you to the bed," she said to Granger, who shuffled along, forced to trust her.

He was the biggest man she'd ever dealt with and, frankly, he made her nervous for more than one reason. The skinny teenagers with shaven heads and body piercings she usually picked up were a piece of cake, mostly because they were usually too high on narcotics or theology to give her much trouble. Even if they tried, hey, there was a reason for those nose rings farmers put on bulls.

But Matt Granger was another story altogether. He was tall, lean and muscular. Not a thing had been folded, spindled or mutilated on this bod. She'd bet he went two-twenty and all of it was solid muscle. Her old partner Will "Pat" Patowski had asked her to put this guy on ice, but he never warned her she'd have to watch her libido while she worked. She'd deliver Granger safely to Boston or Pat would have her hide. Besides, the fee was too good to screw this up.

She removed the stun gun from her fanny pack and placed it on the bed opposite Matt's. Then she began unwinding the wrapping from his head, followed by the blindfold. He blinked several times and she noticed that his eyes were a gorgeous shade of golden brown. Kinda went with the black curly hair and darkly tanned skin.

Get over it, Ballanger. This is business. "Okay, here's the deal," she said without further preamble. The tape on his mouth would come off after she'd finished her spiel. Then he could argue. The head cases always did. She was sure this guy would be considerably more convincing. "Your aunt Claudia Witherspoon hired me to retrieve you from the cult you joined in San Diego. Here's my card."

He blinked, trying to get his eyes accustomed to the light in the scrofulous motel room which contained two saggy beds. They were seated on them facing each other. He was still trussed up and couldn't talk. Might as well read the damn card she was shoving in his face. It said Samantha Ballanger, Retrieval Specialist. How the hell had this dame hooked up with his aunt Claudia? She sounded south Boston while his aunt was a Brahmin from old and serious money. He didn't like the way this whole mess smelled. Then she started talking again, so he paid attention.

"I'm taking you back to your aunt. She's really concerned about your living in a Southern California commune and has the best psychiatric specialists waiting to treat you once you're safely home. As you can see—" she gestured to the bundle of gauze lying on the bed beside him, then pointed to the robe and slippers she'd dressed him in "—you're a burn patient and I'm your nurse. I'm transporting you to a rehab facility. At least, that's what anyone I tell will believe.

"One way or the other, we're driving straight through to Boston. I can get you there the easy way or the hard way. It's all up to you. I'll make you as comfortable as possible, but if you try any funny stuff, I'll have to use this." She picked up the stun gun from the bed and held it to his thigh. "Sorry about this, but I've found that one quick object lesson is worth a thousand warnings."

With that she gave the tiniest flick of the trigger mechanism and an incredibly sharp burst of what seemed like living flame shot up and down his leg. He nearly tore the tape loose cursing as she calmly replaced the weapon on the bed beside her.

"Like I said, sorry. But understand, that little jolt was only a love tap. If you try to jump me, I'll give you a shot that'll make you think you French-kissed a wall socket."

This broad's the one who needs "the best psychiatric specialists" in Boston! He glared at her.

Sam met his eyes. Had he bought her story? He knew he wasn't a head case living in a commune, but would he believe that she thought so? It would sure make it easier if he did. "Okay, now let me help you out of the jacket and make you comfortable. Then you can talk."

When he looked down at the nylon wrapping holding his

arms immobilized across his chest, she said, "Yeah, it's a straitjacket. Custom made for me by an outfit in St. Louis called Leather and Lace. Scoot over to the end of the bed but stay sitting," she instructed, slipping that vicious stun gun into her waistband.

He complied, desperate to get the damn tape off so he could ask if she ever planned to let him use the bathroom. Or, maybe the whole shtick was a ruse and she just intended to talk until his bladder exploded. But, she moved behind him and pulled the robe from his shoulders with one hand, then unfastened the straps of the straitjacket.

One of Matt's first assignments at the *Miami Herald* had been to write an exposé on abuses in a Florida mental facility. As he shrugged off the restraint, he knew regular hospital jackets weighed a hell of a lot more than this lightweight job. *Leather and Lace.* An uneasy thought crossed his mind. He just knew she was into serious S & M when she dangled a pair of handcuffs over his shoulder. When she yanked the tape from his mouth, his lips burned like they'd been basted in jalapeño juice. "Son of a bitch!"

"Click the cuff on your right wrist," Sam said, stepping back and moving around to face him again. He was big and angry and his eyes burned into her like lasers. She felt more uncomfortable than she had on her first snatch—hell, even on her first arrest as a rookie cop.

"You must be that S & M outfit's best customer. Get a volume discount?" he asked, waiting to see what she'd do. Maybe this would be his chance. Then again, maybe not. He eyed the stun gun held unwaveringly in her hand.

"I imagine you need to use the facilities," she said dryly, enticing his cooperation by nodding to the open door of a mold-encrusted bathroom.

His bladder did a couple of push-ups to remind him of how

right-on that was. "Yes, I do," he said grudgingly, clicking the cuff on his wrist.

"Get up slowly and walk inside, sit on the stool and attach the other cuff around the pipe beneath the bathroom sink."

If he hadn't had to go damn bad, he wouldn't have been so cooperative. But he did so he was. She stood in the doorway, watching intently. When he had cuffed himself to the pipe, she continued to check out the small room until he felt on the verge of gargling. "You gonna stand there and watch?"

Sam finished her inspection of the facilities and regarded the irate man seated on the commode. *He really thinks I'm some sort of sex pervert.* The idea amused her. She couldn't suppress a grin. "Water sports aren't among my favorites, Mr. Granger." She started to close the door.

"Turn on the television," he said.

"Why should I?"

He hesitated. "I don't want you listening."

She stared curiously at him. What now? His face was the color of Spanish roof tile. "Listening for what?"

"Bathroom…noises," he muttered.

She couldn't stop the sudden burst of laugher. Bathroom noises. Jeez!

Matt became enraged. "You damned pervert! Straitjackets! Handcuffs! Now bathroom bondage."

She held up her hands. The guy was serious. Sam didn't mean to humiliate him any more than essential for security. "All right, all right, I'll turn on the TV." She shut the door with good intentions, but then was unable to believe she was saying, "I could play one of my CDs instead—the Chamber Pot Concerto in PP Minor." She could hear him curse as she turned on the television, then flopped onto the bed and muffled her laughter with a pillow.

In the bathroom Matt thanked God for small favors. At

least she wasn't a nutcase looking for some cheap motel thrills. As he attended to the pressing business at hand—awkward as hell for a guy forced to do it sitting down—he considered his situation. Was she on the level with this "retrieval" stuff? Could he convince her that she had the wrong guy?

When she opened the bathroom door a quarter hour later, a pizza carton and two cans of Coke were sitting on the chipped particleboard table by the window. "Double cheese, pepperoni. Okay with you?" she asked, tossing the key to him so he could unlock the cuff from the drainpipe.

Matt sniffed the heavenly aroma of greasy spice and his stomach gave a growl of gratitude. "I'm happy starving your prisoners into submission isn't your M.O."

"You're aren't my prisoner, Mr. Granger. Now toss me back the key and take a seat."

He eyed the stun gun and held up the dangling handcuff. "Coulda fooled me." He sat on a rickety orange plastic chair and reached for a slice of gooey pizza.

"Eh, eh, eh," she scolded. "First click the cuff to your chair leg."

Scowling, he obeyed, then used his left hand to dig into the food. "Sure, I forgot. The handcuffs will keep me from falling off my chair and hurting myself. I'm a patient, not a prisoner. Say, can we talk about that?" he asked around a mouthful of pepperoni.

"You talk. I'm gonna eat," she replied, devouring the first food she'd had in well over twelve hours.

"You've got the wrong guy. I'm a reporter for the *Miami Herald*. I came to San Diego to research a human interest story. About women hiding from abusive husbands, mothers hiding their kids from fathers trying to kidnap them. That sort of thing. I haven't joined a commune." He wasn't about to mention Renkov and the Russian mob, the real story he was working on.

"That's not the picture your aunt Claudia gave me."

"Look, my aunt has a photographic memory—but no film. She's the one who needs a shrink, not me."

"I'll let the two of you work that out with your doctors."

"Call the *Herald* news desk and ask for—"

"Thought you said you were doing a human interest piece. The story you described is a feature, not news," she said, wiping her mouth.

"You have a dual major in jujitsu and journalism?" he asked, sinking his teeth into a slab of pizza and imagining it was Aunt Claudia's jugular.

She ignored his outburst. "Look, I've heard it all before. Everyone has a reason why I should let them go. Some of them are pretty good."

He took a deep breath, then said in his most intimidating tone, "I could sue the socks off you once we get to Boston. Even press criminal charges for kidnapping."

Sam remained undaunted. She tossed the paper napkin into the pizza carton, then walked over to her bag and removed a sheath of papers. "Believe me, I checked out your aunt's story and background quite thoroughly before I took the job. I always do. Read these." She handed him the papers.

Matt quickly skimmed down the pages, then crumpled them in outrage. "She swore out a bench warrant on me for stealing Uncle Harvey's engraved Rolex!"

Sam just looked at the expensive gold watch on his wrist, saying nothing.

"For your information, my great-uncle gave me this watch personally while his sister Claudia stood there beaming. It was a college graduation present, for chrissakes!"

"Something else to settle with your aunt when we get back

to Boston. She claims it's a family heirloom and you had no right to take it."

"This is false arrest. I'll sue you! Hell, I'll still sue her!"

"Lots of my retrievals threaten to sue me or have me arrested for kidnapping. Cult members—"

"Samaritan Haven is *not* a cult," he said through gritted teeth. "It isn't even a commune—at least, not the sort you yank brainwashed kids from. It's really more of a hiding place where people drop out of sight." Matt leaned forward on the table and combed his fingers through his hair in utter frustration. "I only moved into the place to check out a lead."

He hesitated. How much should he reveal? He couldn't endanger his source. That might get her and a number of other innocent people killed. Then again, if Samantha Ballanger had been hired by the Russian Mafia, she already knew that her targets were hiding in the complex. Finding them wouldn't be difficult. He reconsidered. No, if that were true, he'd already be dead. He decided to take a risk.

"You ever heard of Mikhail Renkov?"

Sam nodded carefully. "The KGB guy who defected to the West in the last days of the Cold War? A big feather in the CIA's hat, as I recall. Now he's some sort of import-export millionaire, isn't he?" *Play dumb, Ballanger.*

He nodded approvingly. "You read the newspapers. What they haven't said, yet, is that he hasn't exactly broken all his ties to Mother Russia. He's up to his eyeballs in all sorts of illegal stuff—playing footsie with the Russian mob, even dealing with Colombian drug cartels—and I bet he has some pals inside the Company or even in State who're turning a blind eye."

"Hang on, Mel," she interrupted, putting a hand up in dismissal. "*Conspiracy Theory* was a great movie—"

"And the nutcase Gibson played was right in the end,

wasn't he? Just let me finish. Remember reading about Renkov's son buying the farm last month?"

"Alexi, the golf pro? Yeah, he was killed in a car bombing. Cops suspect the wife did it—to keep him from divorcing her and running off with his starlet bimbo of the month. Mrs. Renkov dropped out of sight and they're looking for her."

"Yeah, the car bomb was her final project to get her electrical engineering degree. Come on, a woman car-bomber? Tess Renkov didn't kill her husband."

Sam shrugged. In her checkered career she'd been a cop, paramedic and even moonlighted running down bail jumpers. What he said about the Renkov case could be true. All Pat had told her was that Granger was getting too close to a joint PD-FBI investigation of Mikhail Renkov and they wanted the reporter out of their hair.

"Look, if a bad actor like old Mikhail thought you'd killed his only son, would you stick around and chat?" he argued doggedly. "I think his golden boy was killed by daddy's enemies. What we have here is a turf war with billions in Eastern Bloc cash at stake."

"Don't forget the drug cartels. They have lots of dough, too. But they're not paying me. Aunt Claudia is. Maybe you can convince her about all this—after I collect my fee." She shoved the key to the cuffs across the table so he could free his right arm from the chair.

"A one-track mind," he said with a sigh of resignation. Convincing this dame was as likely as riding a zebra.

Sam watched him unlock the cuff, then took back the key and motioned him to sit on the bed. She knew he was getting tired of taking orders, but he was too sharp to try and jump her—at least just yet. He did as she asked resentfully, then watched as she smoothed out the legal papers he'd crumpled and replaced them in the bag she'd brought from the van.

Stubborn as a stump in hard clay but one fine-looking woman, he thought. Under different circumstances... *Forget it, Granger. Remember how that stun gun smarts.* Then again, if he could soften her up...so to speak. What the hell, worth a try. It wasn't as if she was a dog or anything close. In fact, she was a looker. He'd only be doing what came naturally. And so would she, if her earlier reactions to him had meant anything. Usually he read women pretty well.

Sam approached him, holding a set of pajamas she'd taken from the bag. She could almost hear the wheels turning in his mind as she said, "Strip and put these on."

He cocked his head and grinned, tsking. "With you watching, Ms. Ballanger? You adding voyeurism to bondage?"

"I'm a trained medical professional," she said coolly. A little bit too coolly. Her indifference to the visions of Matt Granger's naked body was pure bravado. Sam tightened her grip on the weapon as she tossed the pj's at him. She was finding that pimply kids spaced out on cosmic visions were a lot easier to handle than one smart-mouthed newsman with a body to die for.

He caught the pajamas deftly, then extended the upper garment back to her. "I've always been a bottoms guy myself. Want the top?"

She could feel his eyes on her suddenly hardened nipples as surely as if he had X-ray vision. "No thanks. Never liked *The Pajama Game.* Just put on both pieces," she said with satisfaction when readily visible evidence of his reaction started to grow in his jeans.

"Well, what the hell, Ms. Medical Professional, you like 'The Bondage Game' well enough. And apparently the Chippendales."

He gave her another of those infuriating grins and kicked off the slippers, then pulled his shirt over his head...very slowly. She could see every muscle flexing. Tossing it carelessly to the floor between the beds, he started to remove his jeans. She was pleased when he paid careful attention to unzipping his fly. It must have been uncomfortable as hell, she thought smugly, but when he dropped the jeans to his ankles and kicked them away, her mouth was dry. Other places on her body weren't.

According to her cover story, his attic floorboards were supposed to be warped, but all the timbers below were in great shape. Bloody *Architectural Digest* quality, dammit! The most interesting one at the moment was the structural beam jutting straight out as he met her eyes and dared her.

"Gonna zap me?" he whispered.

She pointed the stun gun at the strategic place and replied, "If I do, we'll have a wiener roast, so don't tempt me." *More like a kielbasa roast.* "Just be a good boy and put on the pajamas," she managed to say with a level voice. He turned around and reached casually for the pj's, giving her a full view of that great set of buns. *Fits with the sausage.*

Looking over his shoulder as he slipped the bottoms on, he said, "Didn't mean to moon you, but I imagine a trained medical professional's seen it all, hasn't she?"

"Pretty much." She managed to leash her libido by reminding herself about the cool ten K plus expenses she'd collect from dear old Aunt Claudia. Right now that road was looking really long, hard and rocky. *Don't think long. Don't think hard. Don't think rocks, dammit!*

"Good night, Mr. Moonie." She motioned for him to lie down on the bed.

He stretched out and then folded his hands as if to pray with the open cuff still dangling from his right wrist. "Now I lay me down to sleep. I pray—"

"You'll have to do your nightly devotions hands unfolded.

Reach down and click the cuff to the bed frame." She pointed at the exposed steel bar beneath the box spring.

"I work much better with both hands free, darlin'," he said, grinning again as he patted the mattress.

"You'll only need one hand free to do what you need to do tonight." Sam couldn't help the snide tone any more than she could keep her eyes away from the tent pole under the sheet.

Muttering about feminine perversity, he clicked the cuff to the bed frame and closed his eyes. Sam flipped off the lights, undressed and slipped into her own bed. After a few moments, she heard him whisper.

"You know, a few times today, I thought I heard Cole Porter tunes."

She rolled on her side and stared across the darkness separating them. "I was playing an Ella Fitzgerald CD of Cole Porter's hits. I like his music." The minute she replied, she could've kicked herself. Not smart to get involved, especially in a snatch as unorthodox as this one.

"Me, too. My favorite's 'Night and Day.'"

Too late now. She replied, "Hmm. I'd never have taken you for a romantic. Mine's 'Love for Sale.'" His soft chuckle caught her by surprise.

"Certainly it is."

Damn the man. So she was mercenary. So what? A girl from South Boston didn't have all that many options, unless she considered driving over the road with Uncle Declan. But Sam would be damned if she explained herself to a preppy-turned-reporter like Matt Granger. In a few minutes she could hear the sound of soft male snoring blending with the wheeze of the air conditioner.

She lay in her bed staring at the ceiling, wide-awake.

Chapter 2

"Rise and shine, Prince Charming. It's time to hit the road for Boston."

Matt opened one eye and blinked at Sam, then pulled the pillow over his head, muttering through the feathers, "Go away, Fairy Godmother."

"My, aren't we testy this morning. You had a good night's sleep." She tried to sound self-satisfied but knew it ended up coming out with too much edge.

He tossed the pillow to the foot of the bed and stared balefully at her. Sam Ballanger looked like she hadn't gotten one wink last night. Maybe the advantage he needed? Matt decided to push the envelope. "Cranky as hell, huh? I offered to help, but nooo, Ms. Medical Professional, you had to stand on principle...or should I say lie on it?" He grinned at her and watched her seethe.

"Your snoring carried all the way to the Continental Di-

vide. That's what kept me awake," she shot back. "Believe it
or not, you're not that irresistible. In my book, no man that
badly in need of rhinoplasty is."

"Liar. I snore soft like a baby."

She tossed the key onto his bed and shrugged casually.
"Just get up and head for the bathroom."

He shoved the sheet down to his waist and rubbed his hand
over his right deltoid muscle. "You should try sleeping with
one arm cuffed to a bed frame sometime. I probably have a
dislocated shoulder. Now, if you were really a trained medical professional, you'd know how to kiss it and make it
well…"

"Very funny, Mr. Granger. Now please move it," she said
in what she hoped was a bored voice. "While you take care
of necessities, I'll get us some breakfast from the vending machines in the motel office."

"Sounds yummy," he groused, still lying flat on the lumpy
mattress.

"Beggars can't be choosers," she replied cheerfully.

"I thought I was a 'patient,' not a beggar."

"Quit stalling. We need to be on the road within half an
hour if we're going to make it anywhere near Denver by tonight." She waved the stun gun just to emphasize her point.
She could see him glance away from it to the table where
she'd laid out the sleep mask, bandages and a roll of medical
tape.

Matt could also see that the jim-dandy custom straitjacket
was draped over the back of the chair. One more day's ride
locked in solitaire and his reflexes would be so shot that he'd
never be able to take her. Still, there was the fitting on the
gooseneck pipe under the bathroom sink…

Sam pointed to a small vinyl zipper bag lying on the top
of the battered old television and said simply, "Toiletry items."

"How the hell am I supposed to brush my teeth, not to mention shave or take a shower, with my right hand cuffed to the drainpipe?"

"No showers, Mr. Granger. We'll both get a little ripe before we reach Boston. For the rest, you're a big boy. Be resourceful and you'll figure it out."

I'll be a hell of a lot more resourceful than you'd ever imagine, Sammie, babe. Matt let her lock him in the bathroom. He always thought clearer on an empty bladder.

While he was taking care of business in the other room, she peered through a broken slat in the blinds. No one in sight. Might as well go to the office and see what she could scare up for breakfast.

When Matt heard the outside door close, he fleetingly considered yelling his lungs out for help. But then he recalled that she'd told him they were the only customers in the fleabag. Probably true. Even if he could make himself heard over the blaring TV, it was doubtful a desk clerk in a dive like this would give a shit. Even if he did, "Nurse Ratchet" would make him believe her poor "patient" was having a seizure or a conversation with Bart Simpson.

Matt set to work on the gooseneck pipe. "Great. Everything in this dump is made of Lego blocks except the plumbing. Which is made of friggin' Swedish steel!" He grunted, red faced with strain, wrapping both hands around the connection to give it one last desperate try. No go. He needed something for leverage. "Not even a Boy Scout would carry a pipe wrench in his jammies," he muttered savagely as his eyes swept frantically around the small mold-encrusted room for anything he could reach that might help.

That's when he saw it. A rusty old C-clamp holding together the broken curtain rod over the window. It was partially obscured by the hideous blue-and-orange plastic ruffle and a generous layer of cobwebs. Matt Granger was a tall man with long arms to match his lanky frame. But stretch as he might, his fingertips could only come within six inches of the damn clamp. He yanked on the ruffled "window treatment," hoping to rip the rod loose from its mooring. No go, again.

With a sickening thwap the rotted brittle plastic flew off the rod, smacking him in the face with sticky cobwebs. Snarling an oath about spider spit, he threw the filthy monstrosity into the tub and pulled the shower curtain closed to cover it up. Then he wiped up the mess around the sink and in his hair, praying she wouldn't notice the missing plastic ruffle on the window. No sense giving Sam any ideas about checking out the next accommodations more thoroughly than she had these. Then he heard the front door open.

"Ready or not, here I come," she sang out.

Matt decided if he was ever going to get away from this single-minded broad, he'd better take his chance now. Just thinking of her little "object lesson" with the stun gun made him wince, but what the hell. She'd have to move in real close to use it—not that he doubted for one instant she'd hesitate. Still, he reasoned, he was a big man and she was a small woman. How hard could it be to overpower her before she got a shot at him? Trained medical professional. He snorted as the bathroom door opened.

"All I could get was a carafe of their coffee and a couple packages of cake doughnuts, artifacts that must've been in the vending machine since the dawn of automation." Sam glanced at his bare chest and the droplets of water dripping from his hair and face onto those broad shoulders. *No good, Ballanger.* Ah, not good, but beautiful. She tossed him the key and spun around, stalking out of the doorway to wait while he unlocked the cuff.

Matt noted the way she'd looked at him. Maybe he could

give good old lust one last college try before chancing the stun gun. "Coffee smells good," he said. In fact, it smelled like a blend of road tar and battery acid, but he was used to the stuff in the *Herald*'s newsroom, which was even worse.

When he reached for his clothes, piled in a heap on the floor, Sam said, "No. Leave them. I'll put them in the van later."

He gave her a quizzical look, then grinned. This was working out even better than he'd hoped.

"Put on the pj's again and slip on the robe and house shoes. It looks more convincing if a patient's not dressed in street clothes," she explained quickly, too quickly.

"So much for romance," he mumbled as he reached for the discarded pajamas and coarse terry robe, taking his time, letting her stare at his naked chest. After he'd belted the robe casually around his middle, he walked over to the table, never breaking eye contact with her. "Pour me some java?"

"Pour it yourself," she snapped, gesturing with the gun. As he did so, she watched the front of the robe gap open. He hadn't buttoned the pj top, either. She could see his chest again. Had he done that deliberately? Of course he had. *Ballanger, you have to be a moron to fall for this guy,* she chided herself, watching him take an experimental sip of the coffee and reach for a doughnut as he sat down across from her.

Smiling, he swallowed down the large Styrofoam cupful as if it were medicinal. "Ah, nothing like a jolt of caffeine in the morning."

"You must have a cast-iron mouth," Sam said as he poured a second cup and chomped into a doughnut.

"Newsroom habit. Reporters learn to drink this sludge like water. Only thing that redeems it is it's too hot to taste. I really do work for the *Herald*, you know."

"Yeah, well your aunt said you 'dabbled' at writing sto-

ries. Didn't say where. Look, I checked out Claudia Witherspoon before I took this job, believe me. She's a female War-
ren Buffet. We've been over this before, remember?"

Matt snorted in disgust. "She never approved of my career
choice. I was supposed to be a good little Yalie, stay in Boston and work for the family brokerage firm." He shuddered.

Sam looked at him with renewed interest. "Yale, huh? Figured you'd have ivy of some kind growing out of your ears.
Why not just chill out at the family manse, live off your trust
fund?"

"Would you like to sit around and do nothing?" he asked.

Sam shrugged. "Never had the option. It might be nice to
jet-set around though, you know, sipping martinis."

He couldn't help the frustrated bark of laughter. Oh, would
his great-aunt pay for this if he got dragged all the way to Boston right in the middle of the biggest story of his career! He'd
wring her scrawny, manipulative old neck! "That's what you
imagine the life of a Boston Brahmin is like?"

"It isn't?"

He knew she was humoring him. "It's boring beyond measure and filled to the brim with social obligations."

"No wonder you ran away and joined a cult then."

Matt sighed. "I did not join a cult." It came out through
gritted teeth.

"Not what Aunt Claudia said. You were living in that complex just the way she described it. I believe her term was 'a
pack of California coconuts.'"

He raised one eyebrow as a thought occurred to him. "I
wonder if the old girl's finally gone around the bend."

"You're the one around the bend. She sounded plenty sharp."

"Sharp she always has been." His eyes narrowed in cunning intensity. "She's paying you to bring me to Boston. How
about I pay you not to?"

Sam shook her head, wiping crumbs from her mouth with a paper napkin. "Against my ethics. If I took bribes it would wipe out my business." *And Pat'd put me in the slammer with Renkov and his pals when they arrest them.* "A girl's gotta think of her reputation, after all."

"Yes, I know, you are, after all, a 'trained medical professional.' I'll pay you...three thou to let me go." He measured her over the rim of his cup as he sipped.

Sam chuckled in genuine amusement. "You never give up, do you? Even if I were willing to stiff dear old Aunt Claudia—which I'm not—it wouldn't work. She's paying me ten K plus expenses. I get you back under her wing within the week, she even promised me a bonus. The old dame's loaded."

Matt swore beneath his breath. Last option closed. Three grand was all he had to his name unless he hocked his car and small sailboat, neither of which were exactly liquid assets. "She inherited a couple of mil from my grandfather and quadrupled it several times playing the stock market over the past forty years or so," he said glumly.

While he appeared deep in thought, Sam observed him. He acted nothing like a patient, but then he wasn't nuts, only a reporter messing around in a deal way over his handsome head. Her usual range of clients sulked, turned mute, whined or were so catatonic that she could've propped them up in a corner and slept through the night in perfect safety. Now and then one went ballistic. Once Granger found out the truth, he might, too. A good thing she carried the stun gun.

She'd never met a guy with half as much sex appeal as Matt Granger. Of course that was understandable, considering that her snatches were usually pimply teens or wealthy nutcases whose families spent a fortune to prevent scandal. Nothing like this dude. *He's out of your league, Sam. If you met him in Miami, he'd walk past you without a second glance.*

Samantha seemed distracted. This might be his only chance. Matt lunged against the table, overturning it into her lap and sousing her with coffee. She let out an oath of outrage as the scalding liquid splashed across her chest and legs. His long arms extended, big fingers biting into her shoulders. Her hand, still holding the stun gun, was pinned beneath the edge of the table. Luckily, the table was small and round, lightweight enough for her to kick at the center base of it and roll it off her as he moved in.

He was a big sucker and his grip was punishing as he tried to get her into a bear hug, immobilizing her arms. That helped get her to her feet, but before he could lift her off the ground, she hooked one ankle behind his knee hard. He lost balance and started to topple, still holding her. But his grip on her arms loosened sufficiently for her to raise the gun and press it against his rib cage. She gave him a short jolt.

"Son of a bitch!" He grunted through gritted teeth, but didn't let go, trying instead to knock the weapon out of her hand.

Then she let him have it, a full three-second burst. He folded up like an accordion at the end of a three-day Polish wedding. Granger slid bonelessly to the dirty carpet, now soaked with coffee and powder sugar. He was still conscious but his muscles were sending crazy jangled signals to every nerve in his body. Sam stepped quickly back as he twitched and flopped. A banked carp could've moved better.

His eyes, the only part of him still able to obey brain commands, glared at her in confusion while he tried to curse. At least, she was pretty sure he was cursing. His speech was too garbled to really tell.

"I warned you, Mr. Granger. Now look at the mess you've made. I'll have to charge Aunt Claudia extra to pay for the damages. And we're going to be late getting on the road." She affected a sigh of patient resignation to cover her acute case of nerves. Boy, would he be pissed when he found out how he'd been set up. Too bad, but all the better to get thoughts of sex out of her head. This charming little encounter definitely cured her of that. It had been a close call.

Sam had only been forced to zap a few of her patients and none with a maximum charge before. Then again, none had been his size. As she waited for him to come around, hoping it would not take too long, she soaked some towels with warm water and tried to clean him up as much as possible. A burn patient covered with powder sugar and reeking of stale coffee might just raise a few questions if anyone got close enough to notice.

After she'd done the best she could with Granger, she quickly changed into another set of scrubs. Considering how furious he'd be, she decided it might be prudent to put him in the straitjacket while he was still malleable. Getting the jacket on him was not easy. He was dead weight and groaning at every movement. As she worked, Sam explained. "Maybe I should've told you I'm not just a med tech, Mr. Granger," she said calmly. "I was a cop for seven years before I went into the retrieval business. I have a black belt in judo. *Ni-dan.*"

Great. Matt's brain felt like an egg frying on a Miami sidewalk on the hottest day in July. It could comprehend what she was saying, but refused to have anything to do with his autonomously spastic muscles. *I've been taken down by a woman—a woman half my size! Well, what next?* He decided it didn't matter. She probably had a nuclear device or two stashed in that fanny pack of hers.

By the time Sam had him propped up against the wall wearing his "custom jacket," his tongue had begun to unthicken. He tried it out. "Can you leave off the sleep mask? I feel disoriented enough without being blind, too." He paused, then added grudgingly, "Please?"

"Sorry, but you've just amply demonstrated that I can't trust you."

He cocked his head at her as she reached for the mask. "Guess there's no hope you won't gag me, is there?"

"Not a hope in hell, Mr. Granger," she replied, slipping it over his head, then starting to pull off a length of tape.

His tongue still did not work right. He spoke slowly, slurring his words. "You're being a bitch, Samantha. I could've hurt you, but I didn't. Now you're torturing me."

"Shut up," she replied, clamping his jaws together with one hand while applying the tape with the other, feeling guilty as hell. Why couldn't he just be another head case? Damn Sergeant Will Patowski and the whole Miami-Dade PD! Damn the FBI! She tried reminding herself that he had stuck his reporter's nose in a police investigation and brought this on himself. Even his aunt had agreed enough to pay her a fortune to get him out of the firing line. But Sam still felt rotten.

As she wound the gauze around his head he mumbled curses through the tape. This time she was certain he was cursing and that she was the object of his fury. She could practically feel his eyes burning through the sleep mask. He would be one dangerous customer if he got loose again. *This'll teach me to think with my hormones.*

"Okay. Time to hit the road, Mr. Granger."

He didn't move when she tugged at the collar of his robe. "I know the charge has worn off or else you wouldn't be able to talk so glibly. We really do have to go, so...unless you want me to demonstrate how my little gizmo works on your thigh again—only a short burst, you understand—I suggest you let me help you up and walk to the van like a good boy."

He climbed in the van like a good boy.

Chapter 3

By noon they were on Interstate 70 in eastern Utah. Sam could not stop thinking about his last words before she taped his mouth. He could have punched her but he didn't. He'd only grabbed her, trying to keep her from using the stunner. His plans had obviously not included using his fists. Unlike a number of rough customers she'd dealt with over the years—not to mention collars she'd made while on the force—he had not wanted to hurt her. And with those muscles, he certainly could have. He had every reason to be furious at the way she had treated him.

Dammit, his speech had been so thick from the stun, he must be parched by now. She knew how a shock like that messed with a victim's—no, dammit—a patient's electrolytes. Guilt was a bitch, she thought with a sigh. Maybe there was some way to make it up to him. That's when she saw the sign advertising Sam's Slurpee Stand. A message from God?

According to the billboard, the guy using her name served "the biggest baddest ice drinks this side of Death Valley. Only one mile off the highway." She watched for the exit and pulled off, following the arrows that pointed down a twisting blacktop road. "Sam's a damned liar," she muttered as the direction continued sending her deeper into nowhere. "I don't have time for this." Already they were hours behind schedule to make Denver.

Just as she was about to give up and make a U-turn, she saw the joint at a fork in the road. "Pays to advertise," she said, observing the long string of cars inching their way toward the drive-up window. Of course, it probably didn't hurt Sam's business that this was the only place within a hundred miles. She took her place at the end of the line and looked at her watch. Damn, the service had better be pretty fast or she was out of here.

Then Granger groaned again. Sam settled back against her seat with a sigh of resignation. After what seemed like half a day, although she knew it was only half an hour, she reached the window and bought two supersize strawberry Slurpees. Not wanting any company when she gave the treat to her "patient," Sam started to pull away from the small white clapboard drink stand. Suddenly the shrill bleat of a horn coincided with a nasty spray of gravel and the crunch of a fender. Hers.

No good deed ever goes unpunished. Sam rested her head against the steering wheel.

Some Utah yutz had just blindsided her. The rusty yellow pickup had pulled out from behind the stand and crashed head-on into the passenger side of her van. Great. Wonderful. Only Sam used stronger words for the situation as she climbed out to survey the damage. Already she could hear Matt making muffled noises from the back. Before he got it into his head to start kicking at the door, she rushed over to the wizened old man sitting behind the wheel of the pickup.

"I'm a nurse transporting a burn patient. He's really in pain. Could I just exchange insurance information with you and get back on the road?" she asked the codger. When he grinned sheepishly at her, she could see why he liked Slurpees. He had no teeth.

"Right sorry about this here leetle bump." He took a long swill of what looked like grape Slurpee, then pulled his wallet from his jeans and handed her his driver's license.

"No, I need your insurance card, not your driver's…" Her words trailed away when she glanced at the expiration date on the license. Damn! It had expired nearly ten years ago. Fat chance he'd have insurance. She handed the yellowed square back to him. "I don't suppose—"

"Nope. But Jasper Hopwell's good fer any damages. Jest ask anybody here at Sam's. They'll vouch fer me. Say, that there feller inside is sure raisin' a ruckus. He all right?"

Matt was banging his foot against the door like the Beast from Revelation trying to escape the gates of Hell. Sam nodded. "Like I said, he's in terrible pain. I have to get him to a burn center just outside Denver as soon as I can. Now, I wouldn't want to get you in any trouble for hitting me, so why don't we just forget about this little fender bender?"

"I'll be glad to pay once't yew git yer wagon fixed," Jasper offered sincerely.

Here she was letting him off the hook and he was too decent to take the offer. "No, really, it's all right. I'm fully insured through Fairview Hospital and my patient comes from a very wealthy family." Well, that was sure the truth. Aunt Claudia would have bodywork tacked onto her bill. "I won't get in any trouble." *Unless you call the local constabulary.*

Jasper appeared to consider her appeal as she smiled her most winsome smile at him. She held her breath until he nodded. "Reckon, if'n yew say it's all right. Tell yew the truth," he whispered conspiratorially, "Effie, my missus, she'll skin me and tack my hide to the barn door if'n she finds out I been drivin' whilst she wuz off visitin' her sister in Ogden."

"Good deal. You take it easy driving home, okay?"

"All righty. Say, yew take good care 'o thet feller. He don't sound too happy. Right strong fer a sick 'un, though."

Matt's muffled oaths had grown louder as she and Mr. Hopwell talked. So had the kicks at the door. "I'll sure do that, sir." She returned to the van and took off, heading toward the highway. Just as she turned off the back road, one of the big Slurpees tipped over, spilling thick red goo all over the passenger seat.

"Dammit!" she yelled, pounding on the steering wheel. Granger, whose protests had subsided once she was under way again, renewed kicking the door.

All right, she'd gone through hell to get him that big fat Slurpee. He would damn well drink it! She crossed the overpass and found a deserted rest area boasting the only shade tree in the state. Setting the emergency brake hard enough to nearly snap it off, she seized the oversize Styrofoam cup and stomped to the rear of the van. She yanked the doors open and glared at Granger, who glared back.

Oh, it didn't matter that he had gauze covering the blindfold, she knew he was glaring, damn his hide. She thought of Effie and stretching a hide on a barn door. Granger's would be big enough to stretch over the whole frickin' barn. Sam took a deep, calming breath. The Econoline still ran. The bent fender was nothing that a body shop couldn't take care of for a pittance, say a grand or two.

"Too bad, Aunt Claudia. You can afford it," she muttered as she unstrapped Matt. "Okay, swing your legs around so I can help you sit up," she told him.

He tried to talk through the tape, but she ignored the mumbling. "Look, I went to a lot of trouble to get you this. According to the ads, it's the best Slurpee in the state. You gotta be dehydrated and I know your electrolytes are messed up, so cooperate."

Finally, after considerable struggling, she got him propped against the fender well with his feet dangling over the edge of the fender. He was still pretty groggy in spite of his kicking fit back at the Slurpee stand—or maybe worn out because of it. She hesitated for a moment as she unwound the gauze and reached for the tape over his mouth, willing herself to chill out. Grudgingly, she added, "I owe you for not hurting me this morning. You were right. I was a bitch." Then she pulled the tape off, taking care not to pull his parched lips any more than necessary.

"Can't argue with that," he mumbled. His tongue felt like number-seven sandpaper and his head pounded like Ricky Ricardo's bongo drums. Then she took hold of his chin with one hand and thrust a straw between his lips with the other. He tried to suck but his mouth was so numb and the Slurpee so thick, nothing came through. He tried again. No go.

"I know you're dying of thirst. You gotta be," she said in exasperation, thinking of the red goo soaking into the passenger seat while she wasted time with him.

"Can't...get it...through the straw."

"Oh, for Pete's sake," she said, pulling on the straw to get it out of the small hole punched in the lid. It wouldn't budge. She tried opening the lid and it appeared welded to the cup. "Great! The other one opened like sesame. This one's sealed tighter than Brad Pitt's buns." She pried with her fingernails and broke one before the edge of the lid finally popped up, spraying her with thick red ice.

Matt could hear her swearing and only guessed about what was going on since she'd kept his blindfold in place.

He was half sitting against what he thought was the rear fender well inside the van, slipping as she scooted around. A small grin tugged at the corners of his mouth. "Having troubles, Sammie?" he couldn't resist asking in spite of how thirsty he was. Why did he provoke this woman? She could dump the whole bloody thing over his head and he'd dehydrate by nightfall.

Sam saw his smirk and nearly did just what he was thinking. "I'd love to give you a shower but it would be unprofessional—and worse yet, unprofitable."

"Anyone ever tell you you'd make a great Ferenghi?"

"What's that?" she asked. She figured it wasn't flattering. "Just drink, will you?" she demanded, tipping his head back and starting to pour the icy contents of the cup down his throat when he opened his mouth to answer her question.

The mouthful of Slurpee was thick, filled with shaved ice. And some of it went down the wrong pipe. He coughed and swallowed, feeling his face turning strawberry-red. "I hate strawberry," he mumbled ungraciously between coughs.

"Tough. I didn't have time to consult you about the menu," she snapped, pulling on his jaw so she could dump more of the wet stuff down.

He had to open his mouth to gulp in air as he coughed. That's when she hit him unsuspecting with another strawberry salvo. He tried to swallow it mid-inhalation. This time all of it went down the wrong pipe. He tried to lean forward but his butt was slipping on the plush carpeting and all he succeeded in doing was sliding more.

"Hold still, dammit! You're gonna choke," Sam said, setting the cup down and reaching out to pull him up while he coughed and gagged. "Boy, when you said you hated strawberry, you weren't kidding." *Ungrateful lout!*

He weighed too much for her to be able to pull him up-right, so she jumped out of the van and knelt to brace his feet on the smooth carpet and give him some traction. The open Slurpee cup tipped over when his knee brushed against it, splashing the contents over her shoulders and head. Sam let loose with a volley of curses, wiping the sticky liquid from her face. She stood up and combed ice chips from her hair while Matt continued to cough.

Damn, this was getting serious! She leaned inside and tugged on the straitjacket's straps to pull him forward. That's when he gave one great whooping cough and let loose with a stream of the trapped liquid. He looked like a big fire-breathing dragon as red Slurpee gushed from his nostrils and mouth. The spray of liquid "fire" caught them both.

Matt couldn't catch his breath. Every time he tried to in-hale, more of the confounded Slurpee shot from what he was sure was the bottom of his lungs to the top of his aching head. Damn, it was cold coming through his nose! And it burned! He could hear Sam cursing and yelling but at the mo-ment, he was too occupied trying to breathe to pay any atten-tion to her.

"Look at the mess you've made! I can't friggin' believe this! Jeez!" She pounded on his back until his coughing and spewing subsided and his face started to retreat from bright red to grayish tan. Then she left him propped against the wheel well and reached for a big roll of paper towels stored with her other gear. All she could do was soak up the worst of the goo from her new plush carpeting and dab at the mess on her scrubs. The scrubs were pink already, but that didn't help much with the deep crimson of red dye number two soaking them. As to the mess on Matt Granger, she figured since he spewed it up, he could live with it until tonight.

Then she remembered the front seat of the van, which

she'd intended to clean up as soon as she gave him a few sips. "Not bad enough I'm covered, you're covered and the back of the van's soaked—so's my passenger seat!"

"If you hadn't tried to drown me with the nasty stuff, none of this would've happened," he rasped out.

"That's real gratitude! I go miles out of my way to get you a cold drink instead of warm bottled water and all you can do is blame this mess on me. Even got smacked by a geezer driving without a license. I was worried about your reaction to the stun gun. Seeing you're back to your usual charming self, you must be okay."

Matt took a deep cleansing breath, relieved that his lungs worked. "Right now, that warm bottle of water sounds like nectar of the gods," he said through clenched teeth. "And for your information, there isn't a cell—an atom—in my body that doesn't hurt like I've been worked over by a pair of goons with ball bats. Who'd believe one little dame could inflict that much pain."

"I'm no ordinary dame, Mr. Granger." Looking at the wreckage of her van, she, too, spoke through gritted teeth.

"No kidding. You're Lucrezia Borgia with electrodes."

"You're funny. Oughta go on Letterman. Just remember you brought this whole thing on yourself."

"Yes, I'm prone to inciting people to kidnap and choke me. A shitty habit."

Sam ignored the last comment. Obviously her "patient" was recovered. Glumly, she surveyed what had been new carpeting in her van, then took the towels and did what she could to soak up the puddle in the front seat. At least it was vinyl. She disposed of the bonus-size roll of bloodred towels, tossing the whole mess in a trash Dumpster near the lone tree, then returned to the open doors at the back of the van.

"We're so far behind schedule we'll never make Denver

tonight." She tore off a fresh strip of tape and reached for his mouth.

Hearing the now familiar sound, he quickly said, "I could use some of that water. Please." He practically choked on the plea, but damn, that strawberry ick was about to close off his bronchial tubes again.

Muttering under her breath, Sam retrieved the bottle and shoved the straw in his mouth. "Think you can suck this up?"

He took several long thirsty pulls, then couldn't resist answering, "Sammie, since I met you I've sucked up a lot worse than warm water."

She smacked the tape over his mouth and added a second piece, even longer, just for spite, then secured him with the seat belts before locking him in and taking off. As she drove, the sickly sweet odor of strawberry filled the van. She felt like gagging but stifled the urge. *Aunt Claudia, get out your checkbook!*

They'd lost a good two hours between his dumb stunt this morning and the great Slurpee deluge. Sam pushed hard through the afternoon, keeping an eye out for highway patrol cars as she sped into Colorado. It was nearing dusk and she still needed to make another hundred miles in order to keep on schedule. But she was beat. Slurpee stained her clothes and made her brown hair stand up in strawberry spikes. She shuddered every time she caught sight of herself in the side-view mirror. If a cop pulled her over, he'd haul her straight to jail.

"I gotta have a shower," she muttered. What's more, if she didn't clean Matt, too, he'd dry stuck permanently to the carpet in the back of the van, her passenger forever. No Aunt Claudia. No money.

She considered what to do. According to her map, the next town was a wide place in the road around fifteen or so miles due east. "You better pray there's a motel in this burg com-

ing up, buster, or I'm gonna drag you through a car wash on
the end of a rope," she yelled into the back of the van.

She pulled off the highway and found just the kind of joint
she wanted.

The Mountain Dew Inn boasted indoor plumbing and that
was about it. Cheap and quiet, the small mangy hole-in-the-
wall would be a place where no one asked questions when
she requested a room at the far end of the building "so her
patient wouldn't be disturbed."

The desk clerk gave her a funny look and a sniff test, mar-
veling to himself over a customer who looked and smelled as
if she'd rolled in stale strawberries. It took all kinds and he'd
seen most of them. But Elroy Phleggi had no intention of asking about a paramedic's weird habits. Maybe it was burn
salve. Go figure. He'd let that snotty new maid Kimmie deal
with any mess they left in the morning.

He tossed the keys across the counter at her and gave directions to the last room on the left side. Then he turned back
to the TV and a rerun of an old Beatles movie.

Sam knew the paper towels hadn't done much to remove
eau de Slurpee from her vehicle. "Oh well, Aunt Claudia can
absorb the cost of new carpet, so to speak," she muttered as
she backed the van up to the door and guided Matt into room
thirteen. The moment she checked out the bathroom, she
knew the number had been an omen.

"Not a damn place in the shower to hook that cuff to."

Matt could hear her curses as she drew nearer. He would've
smiled if not for the tape over his lips. Now she was muttering something about the shower stall as she began unravel-
ing the bandages from his head. The sleep mask came next.
Then she removed the tape, not at all gently.

"Anyone ever tell you your bedside manner stinks?" he asked, blinking to get his eyes to focus.

"Anyone ever tell you that you just plain stink?" she shot back.

"That's your fault for dumping that gunk down the wrong pipe."

"The right pipe would've been a lead one—to beat you unconscious for the rest of this trip."

In spite of the red splotches and crisp hairdo, she looked kind of cute. He grinned. "You look like you have a wicked case of measles. Oh, and I like the 'do.' That Slurpee stand's in the wrong business. Oughta start marketing that stuff as hair gel."

"Amusing from a man who looks like Rudolph the Red-Nosed Reindeer, Mr. Granger."

"Don't you think you could call me Matt?" Why in the hell was he getting the hots for a woman who'd done him more bodily injury than a Jersey leg-breaker?

"Nope." Her single-syllable reply did not convey the cool certainty she had intended. *How can a man in this condition be wildly attractive to me?*

He stared at her breasts again, even though that was what had gotten him in this mess in the first place. *Think of something else, Granger.* He raised his head and looked at her face. In spite of everything, she was still one hell of a good-looking dame. He shrugged inside the straitjacket and grinned stupidly at her. "You going to keep me trussed up all night?"

"Nah," she replied grimly, removing the stun gun from her fanny pack. "But unless you want to do more break dancing, better pay attention."

"As Ross Perot said, I'm all ears."

That wasn't exactly the part of his anatomy her thoughts had strayed to, but she would definitely not share that with him. "There's no way to secure a cuff in the shower stall in this dump, so I'll have to bathe you myself."

He leered. "Now I'm all eyes."

"You won't be for long." With that, she slipped the blindfold back on.

"Hey, what's going on?"

"I'm going to remove your clothes and the jacket, then cuff your hands behind your back and guide you into the stall. You behave while I scrub you off—I mean, oh, hell, you know what I mean."

He grinned. "No fair. You get to watch and I don't."

"I'm the health-care professional, remember?" *Just keep reminding yourself of that, Sam.*

Chapter 4

Sam slipped the robe off of his body, unfastened the jacket straps and pulled the apparatus off of him. Every article of apparel on him was stiff with red ichor. Then she stood back and said, "Take off the pj's and then put your hands behind your back." Obediently, he unbuttoned the pajama top and shucked it.

But the bottoms were stuck to his legs. He said to her, "Okay if I bend down and peel these off or will you zap me again?"

"Do it—slowly."

He yanked the cheap cotton off with a hiss of pain when sizable clumps of his leg hair went with it.

"Now you know what a bikini wax feels like," she said.

He straightened up and glared at her through the blindfold. "Thank God I was born male."

Her mouth went dry just looking at his body. She was definitely happy he was a male, too! Now naked for her to admire, Matt Granger was quite a sight to behold. *Keep it professional, Sam.* She cleared her throat, then said, "Now, put your hands behind your back."

He did as he was told, holding his hands so she could click the cuffs on his wrists. Then he let her guide him toward the sounds of steamy water pouring from a shower nozzle. He could hear the soft rustle as she shed her clothes and visions of the two of them naked in the water flashed through his mind, sending signals to his body. Now he was sure there'd been no permanent damage from that stun gun. Thank God!

"Don't you think you could call me Matt, *now?*"

"Definitely not now. Get into the shower." Sam shoved him beneath the steamy downpour, but not before he backed up just enough for her breasts to brush against his arm. Damn, the man had some moves, even blindfolded and cuffed!

"No fair again. You have me buck-ass and you're still wearing stuff," he groused.

Since her bra and panties hadn't suffered during the accident in the van, she had left them on, body armor of a sort. *A Victoria's Secret chastity belt.* Ha! Somehow, Sam didn't figure it would do much good. "Quit bitching and stand still," she said sharply, lathering up a bar of soap between her hands. She stood stupidly, suds running down her arms while she stared at his water-slicked body, which filled the small shower stall.

She was afraid to touch him.

As if reading her mind, he taunted, "Come on, Samantha. Scrub me off."

You can do this. You're a trained professional. And he's worth ten grand! Sam repeated the words like a mantra as she reached up and began lathering his chest. God, the pelt of black hair felt good. Too good. She moved up his neck and said, "Close your eyes."

"Why the hell should I? I'm blindfolded."

She thrust her soapy hands into his hair and started scrubbing.

"Yeow! That burns!"

"I told you to close your eyes. Soap's dripping inside the mask." He was handsome even when his face squinched up, dammit! After that she was forced to move to those broad shoulders and then let her hands glide down his biceps. Odd that she'd never before realized the similarities between bathing someone and foreplay. "Turn around so I can get your back."

"But you haven't finished with my front," he said, chuckling as his erection nudged her right in the belly button. "Bull's-eye," he crowed.

"Nope. High, twelve o'clock," she managed to say before all the breath left her body. Stepping back, she seized his shoulders and forcefully turned him around. "Raise your arms so I can wash your armpits."

"What do I look like, a contortionist? Lady, you have my hands cuffed behind my back. Now, if you'd care to unlock them…"

In response, she took the bracelets by their connection and yanked them up. He yelped in surprise. Then when she reached two soapy hands to scrub his armpits, he tried to clamp his arms to his sides, hunching over, sliding away. "That…tickles," he gasped, fighting not to laugh out loud, failing as she continued forcing her soapy fingers higher into the sensitive cavities.

His whole body convulsed with helpless laughter and he leaned back against the shower wall. Sam couldn't help her broad grin, unable to resist playing the game in spite of its inherent dangers. "I don't need a stun gun to control you— only my fingers," she said, knowing the laughter in her voice was unmistakable.

"Anyone...ever tell...you...you're vicious?" He finally managed to get the words out through rumbling chuckles that echoed in the small confines of the shower. Her fingers moved across his bent back, tickling the sensitive skin at his nape. To reach his neck, she had to press her body over his and lean into him on tiptoes. Matt could feel her breasts, still clad in a nylon bra, feel the nipples' nubby distension through the thin fabric.

Damn, Granger! What the hell are you doing? Quit now. But his body overruled his mind. Her panties were a wisp of lace under his fingers and her body was as slick with soap as his. It didn't take much to tug those panties down, even with his hands cuffed. He slid the briefs over the curve of her hips before she could stop him—if she wanted to, which he was beginning to doubt. At least, he sure hoped she didn't want to stop.

When her panties dropped to her ankles, Sam let out a squeak of surprise and slithered off his back. "How the hell did you do that?" she gasped, struggling not to lose her balance with her feet practically tied together.

He turned to face her with a lopsided grin. "Lots of practice. Wanna see me unhook a bra blindfolded?"

"No. If I want slight-of-hand, I'll watch David Copperfield." She tried to sound cool, but leaning against the shower wall with her panties around her ankles made it difficult. There wasn't enough room to bend over and pull them back up so she kicked them off, again stumbling against the wall. Matt glided in quickly, pinning her with his body.

"Careful you don't fall and break that delectable keister," he murmured in her strawberry hair. "I'm not the only one who needs a shower," he purred. "I could give you a shampoo..."

"No way," she said breathlessly, seizing the soap and giving her head a quick lather and rinse. "God, that feels better."

"Yeah, it sure does," he said, rubbing his pelvis against her belly.

Sam's hips instinctively hitched forward. Lord above, even rigor mortis couldn't make flesh that rock hard. But the guy certainly qualified as a big stiff! Suddenly she wanted to touch it, wanted to very much. "You were right—I haven't finished washing your front," she managed to get out.

"Please, be my guest," he replied, his voice no steadier than hers. Stepping back, he allowed her to put about three inches between them.

She reached for the soap again and lathered her hands, then lowered them to the pole probing her navel. All she could think was, *Lower, just a little bit lower...*

The minute her hands took hold of his cock he let out a guttural oath of sheer desperation. "You know, we gotta do something about this."

"Yeah. Wash your legs." She let go, teasing his balls before sudsing down one long hairy leg, then moving back up the other leg, pausing to cup those small tight male buns. They'd looked great the first time she saw him. They felt even better. Damned if he wasn't right. No stopping now. Some small voice of sanity tried to reason with her. This was dangerous as hell—not to mention a gross breach of ethics.

But her hormones won.

"Okay, Houdini, let's see you unhook a bra with your hands cuffed," she whispered, slithering her body against his as she turned her back to him.

"Don't think I can, eh?" he dared her.

Matt turned and bent his elbows, running his fingers over the delicate indentations of her spine until he reached his destination. As he took the bra hook in his hands and freed it, he rubbed his head against the shower nozzle, catching the elastic band of the sleep mask on it and pulling back. The mask popped free and dropped to the shower floor.

By the time Sam had shrugged the bra off, and turned around, he was facing her wearing nothing but a wide lascivious grin and a serious hard-on. "Damn, you're gorgeous," she breathed, not really registering that his eyes were making a sweeping inventory of her wet naked body just as hers were making one of his.

"So are you, Sammie." Before she could react, he bent forward and took one nipple in his mouth and sucked on it until she moaned.

The blindfold was gone and so was she, the instant his mouth made contact with her breast. Now Sam was the one unable to see. Her eyelids fluttered down and she concentrated on how good it felt.

If only his hands weren't cuffed. But, hell, he could improvise. He backed her against the wall of the stall and used his mouth to very excellent advantage, working on one breast, then the other until she was hanging on to his shoulders and quivering like Jell-O.

Someone said, "The bed." Maybe they both did. But it was Sam, with her hands free, who finally ripped back the shower curtain and stepped out of the stall. Matt was right behind her, prodding her with his erection as they slipped and slid on wet feet across the tile floor, leaving puddles of water...and the shower still running full blast.

The ancient air conditioner alternately groaned and hummed, filling the musty room with frigid dehumidified air that quickly dried them, although the heat burning beneath their skin probably helped. Matt bent down and took her mouth, opening his over it, plunging his tongue inside after rimming her parted lips. She held tightly to his shoulders, tiptoeing to return the savaging kiss as she melded her body into his, working her hips over his erection.

When they started to tumble onto the mattress, Sam broke off the kiss long enough to yank down the faded blue chenille bedspread and blanket under it, revealing a decently white set of sheets on the twin bed. Impatient to continue, Matt leaned over and ran his tongue along the ridge of her spine, thrusting between the cheeks of her delectable ass with his rod until he overbalanced and they both went sprawling headfirst onto the lumpy motel mattress with Sam squished beneath him.

"Mmmumph!" she wheezed as he rolled off of her. "Jeez, you weigh more than a Peterbuilt Engine."

"An apt comparison, considering," he murmured, his brain scrambling for a way to consummate their passion with his hands cuffed behind his back. Some subliminal instinct warned him not to ask her for the key. He sat up on the edge of the bed, his erection now becoming acutely demanding as she wriggled over to the opposite side and knelt. She patted the bed, indicating that he should stretch out beside her.

He obliged. His shoulders felt as if they were being pulled from their sockets and the cuffs bit into his wrists when he rolled onto his back. All that barely registered when Sam swung one slender tanned thigh over his hips and took him in her hands. "Let me in, baby," he groaned.

She obliged. Her hips slowly lowered until the head of his shaft touched her. That was it. She lunged downward just as he thrust upward. Oh, sweet lord, was it good! Unable to stop herself, Sam rode like a rodeo champion, wanting it to go on for hours…glorious hours. But, desperate as they both were, it was over in minutes. As soon as the first spasms began deep in her belly, he thrust harder and faster, driving her to the most mind-blowing orgasm of her life.

Matt felt her muscles tighten around him like a velvet fist, squeezing him until he let go, pumping uncontrollably until

he was blissfully drained. Sam's hair tickled his chin as sh
collapsed on his chest. Those sensational breasts pressin
into his pectorals felt nice. Real nice. He wanted to hum wit
the warm comfort of it and just lay there melded together wit
her like two pieces of licorice, softened in the noon heat.

The window unit's compressor groaned back to life afte
a catnap, pummeling Sam with a sudden gust of frigid ai
Goose bumps marched down her spine, drying her swea
slicked skin and abruptly cooling the mad ardor of a momen
ago. Bliss was gone and conscience had returned.

With a vengeance.

What the hell had she done? Talk about sleeping with th
enemy! This was a hundred times worse. She had violated on
of the most sacred trusts of her profession—she'd taken ad
vantage of a helpless prisoner, cuffed and blindfolded...wel
maybe he had lost the blindfold, she amended, peekin
through her damp, tangled hair to glimpse his face. When ha
that happened? Back in the shower?

Damned if she knew. But she did know she'd done the un
thinkable and now she'd have to face the consequences. Apo
ogizing to an arrogant bastard like Matthew Granger wa
going to be pure hell. And they had another four days on th
road together. How the hell was she going to get through i
Well, Sam, old girl, only one thing to do. She had to look hi
directly in the eye and get her P.C. guilt out in the open.

At least he wasn't some poor mentally unbalanced cu
member. Small consolation, but it salved her conscience ju
the slightest bit. Damn if she wouldn't kill Patowski when th
was over. After she collected the ten K from Aunt Claudia.
girl had to keep her priorities, after all, she reminded herse

Stalling, Ballanger. Just do it.

Taking a deep breath, she sat up and stared down into his fac
He looked beatifically content. Not exactly smug. Just...happ

She cleared her throat and he opened his eyes, grinning at her like a large spaniel who's just been given a good scratch behind the ears—after woofing down a pound of hamburger.

"Thank you, Sam," he said simply, then grunted when she moved slightly, shifting her weight so the cuffs bit into a place where his wrists weren't already numb. Sharp pains radiated like pulsar beams from both shoulders when he instinctively tried to jerk his arms into a less agonizing position. He let out an involuntary oath.

"Oh, Matt, I'm so sorry," she practically sobbed, now guilty beyond endurance. He must realize what a terrible thing she'd done to him.

"Well, I'm not—at least not about this," he said, raising his head so his eyes could travel down to where she still sat astride his cock. "But could you please move so I can get up before my shoulders separate from my collarbones?"

Sam jumped off of him as if a bucket of ice water had just been dumped over her head. The air conditioner picked that instant to release another icy billow directly on the limp remains of his privates, which quickly shriveled to far less impressive dimensions.

"Aah, crap," he muttered, rolling onto his side so he could sit up and turn his back to the infernal machine torturing the most sensitive part of his anatomy.

The compressor chose that moment to kick off, allowing the sound of pounding water to filter through from the bathroom. "Ohmigod! We left the shower running and the curtain open," Sam croaked, dashing naked toward the bathroom. Before she got halfway to the door her toes began to squish over soaked carpet. The tile floor was covered with water, lapping gently over the doorsill.

Grumbling some of Uncle Declan's better oaths, she sloshed to the shower and shut it off. The motel would charge quite a bit for damages. How the hell could she explain that one to Aunt Claudia on the expense account? Thoroughly chastened, she began throwing the excess of towels from the rack onto the floor to soak up the water.

"I hate to interrupt a woman in a housekeeping frenzy, but I could use a little help here," Matt said with a grunt of pain in his voice.

He was still sitting on the bed, hands cuffed behind his back. And she was...buck-ass naked, bent over mooning him as she picked up towels! "I told Pat this was a lousy idea," she muttered to herself as she made her way across the wet carpet to the open case where she kept her clothes. She stuffed her arms into her robe, then fished frantically in her fanny pack for the key to the cuffs.

My God, his shoulders must hurt like hell! His hands were as white as her Econoline. Ugly red indentations bit deep into his wrists. The circulation in his hands could be permanently impaired and it would all be her fault!

Without saying a word, she knelt behind him and unlocked the cuffs. "Move your arms in front of you—slowly," she cautioned as he started to stretch them forward, only to curse sharply and let them drop to his sides. Still careful to stay behind him, she began rubbing one wrist, chafing it until the pinkness of circulation returned to his hand. After repeating the process on the other hand, she began massaging his shoulders until he let out a contented, "Mmm."

As she worked, Sam rehearsed her apology. Better to make it while his back was turned. *Chicken shit, Sam,* she chided herself. But it would be easier. Just as she started to open her mouth, he broke into her guilt-wracked thoughts.

"Now can we head back to San Diego?" he asked.

Chapter 5

Sam shot off the bed and seized the stun gun from the chest of drawers. "You think…you think just because…" she sputtered, uncertain of how to express her combination of outrage and guilt. "I know I took advantage of you—"

"No, you didn't, babe," he interrupted. "I wanted it as much as you, hell, even more. Look what I had to go through," he said with a grin, illustrating by rolling his shoulders stiffly and holding out his still cuff-abraded wrists. "You have to know now I'm not a cult weirdo. Hell, I'm not even a Hare Krishna. I'd look lousy with a shaved head."

"What you are is my patient, a sick man who's been brainwashed into joining a commune and whose aunt has requested that I rescue." *Keep repeating it and maybe you'll convince yourself, Sam.*

"For ten K and expenses," he added, disgusted that they

were back to square one now that the itch had been scratched scrubbed, or whatever.

"Plus a bonus," she shot back without missing a beat. *Try apologizing to a preppy newsman and you get what you de serve, Sam.* Damn, what the hell had she been thinking of Or with? She knew the answer and it made her madder than ever. Leveling the weapon, she stepped closer, feeling secure not only because she was armed but also clothed while he was still mother naked.

"Time for beddy-by. Put the cuff on your right wrist—"

"I know you get off on having me in your clutches, baby but the next time we take a roll in the hay—"

She stamped her foot and cursed the way her Uncle Declan did when his rig had a blowout, although the stamp ing foot sort of undermined the effect of the cussing. "I mean to sleep—alone!"

"Not until we have some food. I don't know about you, bu after a good…" Something in her eyes made him pause, o perhaps it was the sight of the stun gun in her hands. Jeez, he didn't have a stitch on. She wouldn't…would she? One look at her blazing eyes and he decided not to chance it. "Oh, hell it's only six at night and I'm starving. Please? You can lock me to the sink while you go out," he wheedled.

Another chance at a gooseneck pipe. He waited expec tantly.

Sam finally shrugged. "Why not? Can't have you com plaining to dear old Aunt Claudia that I starved her darling nephew." She dug a clean set of pj's out of her bag and tossed them to him. He caught them deftly. So much for his hand being permanently injured! Sam refused to watch his mus cles rippling as he pulled on the sleepwear.

"Do I get a clean robe?"

"I'll bring one from the van when I come back," she said

"It's the last extra large in stock, so don't spew gooey crap over it, okay?"

"You're the one who bought the 'gooey crap,' remember?" She was still attracted to him and mad at herself for it. He liked the idea. Liked it a lot.

Ignoring his leer and the reminder about her ruined van, she said, "Just head for the bathroom."

They repeated the drill of the night before. But as she backed him over the wet tile floor and had him use the cuffs to lock his right hand to the gooseneck pipe under the sink, both of them were aware of a charged difference after the sex. Her guilt amused him, but since she still wouldn't release him, he was more frustrated than ever. The thought of spending the next four or five days trussed up like Hannibal Lector while his lead in San Diego went cold made him want to strangle Aunt Claudia. How the hell had she hooked up with Sam Ballanger—and why?

Maybe the thought of sleeping in the same room with sexy Sammie from here to Boston didn't set too well, either, but he shoved that to the back of his mind. *Enough complications in your life already, Granger.* What he needed to do was unscrew the pipe on this sink and give Sam a surprise when she returned with dinner.

No luck.

Frustrated, he sat in a fresh robe, gnawing on a chicken leg so tough that the bird must've died during a race, not at a packinghouse. He continued to think of a way to convince Sam to let him go.

Sam was still embarrassed about their little "afternoon delight" and shoved a mound of gray slimy coleslaw around her plate, her chicken portion almost untouched. *How could I have been so dumb!*

"Better eat. You need to keep up your strength." He took

another bite off the leg and nearly lost an incisor. "Didn't know they raised racing chickens in Kentucky. On second thought, don't eat. You might break a tooth and cost Aunt Claudia another thou for a crown."

"In case you forgot, this wasn't the location where we were scheduled to stop for the night," she snapped, tossing her napkin over the mess of chicken and biscuits with a side of slaw.

"Now it's my fault you nearly caused me to choke to death," he said with a grin.

Sam was not buying his lame attempt at humor. Silently she got up and paced over to the window, careful to stay on the dry part of the carpet. She stared through the grimy blinds at the sunset, arms crossed over her chest.

"Fowl most foul," he said, failing to suppress a nasty burp. The dinner was definitely not setting well on his stomach. "I hesitate to ask, but could you uncuff me so I can use the convenience?"

Sam forced herself to look him square in the eye. "Never let it be said I abuse my patients," she replied, tossing him the key and watching, stunner at hand while he unlocked himself from the chair. Resignedly he tossed the key back to her and she laid it on the dresser.

Once she cuffed him in the bathroom and closed the door, Sam quickly shoved the uneaten food into a plastic bag. She was just preparing to take it to the Dumpster outside when a knock sounded on the motel door. Sam peeked out the blinds and saw a girl dressed in a Scout uniform, clutching a box of cookies.

"Friggin' unbelievable. What responsible parents would let their kid go door to door at a dump like this?" Then she considered the size of the town and decided the kids probably had to throw themselves in front of semis if they hoped to make their sales quota in this burg. Shrugging, she placed the stun gun in her fanny pack with the .38 and zipped it shut, then opened the door with a smile.

The grave-faced little girl didn't make a sound, just turned and walked toward an expensive dark green SUV parked out front. Two figures dressed in jeans and sweatshirts, wearing ski masks, materialized from their hiding place against the wall. They waved pistols under Sam's nose and backed her into the room. Then the taller one grabbed her and shoved her onto the bed while the other trained her weapon on her.

"Where's Granger?" the shorter one demanded in a squeaky voice.

"Check the bathroom," her companion said gruffly, backing away from Sam.

It was apparent in spite of their bulky clothes, masks and attempts to disguise their voices, that both were female. Sam was not certain what to make of this bizarre turn of events. Women with kids? They sure as hell weren't the Company... were they? Miami-Dade Homicide and Pat's pals at the FBI would kill her if the CIA got Granger. Then an even worse thought occurred to her. What if they were Renkov's goons? That sent cold chills down her spine.

The shorter woman strode quickly across the small room and yanked the bathroom door open, then jumped back and slammed it, sputtering in embarrassment. "Excuse m— I mean, hurry up!"

Sam watched them warily. No way could these female bozos be pros—spooks or Russian Mafia. She tried to gauge the distance to her fanny pack, which she had carefully zipped shut. *How could I have been so careless?* These female versions of Laurel and Hardy were obviously rank amateurs, waving those antique guns around like they were Cracker Jack toys. But when it came to a loaded weapon, nothing could be more dangerous than a pair of nervous neophytes.

"Look," she said reasonably, sitting up on the bed, "I'm a licensed health-care professional transporting—"

"Just give me the keys to the handcuffs," the taller woman ordered her, holding out a well-manicured hand.

"If I could only explain," Sam said, edging toward her fanny pack, "you see—"

"Please, just tell us where the key is and you won't get hurt," her companion said.

Before Sam could think of a stall, the shorter woman saw the key laying on the bureau and seized it with an exclamation of delight, her attempt to appear "masculine" forgotten. Damn, normally Sam kept that key in her pocket. While she was deciding whether or not to risk trying to take the taller, more aggressive woman while her pal was freeing Matt, the object of her speculation picked up the fanny pack and hefted it experimentally.

"A medical professional, huh?" she said gruffly. "You carrying a ventilator in here? Or maybe a gun?" She didn't try to open the pack but studied Sam with eyes narrowed through the round holes of the ski mask as she tossed it into the far corner, well out of reach.

Double damn! Sam could see that ten K plus expenses—not to mention her bonus—going down the tubes. She'd even have to pay for the water damage to the motel room herself. These nutseys had to be from the commune. They must have believed his cover and come to rescue him. By then Matt was free, walking out of the bathroom and grinning like a Cheshire cat. "You're making a mistake," she began carefully. "I represent Mr. Granger's aunt—"

"Put a sock in it, lady," the taller one said, shoving Sam back onto the mattress and sticking a small white gym sock into her mouth when Sam opened it to protest.

Matt grinned broadly now. This was more like it! He didn'

know who these two wacky dames were, but he would soon be back on his story. As he discreetly slipped into his clothes, he watched his tall rescuer order Sam to lie facedown on the bed and place her hands behind her. When Sam complied, the woman tied her wrists and ankles with strips of her own surgical tape and had her roll onto her back. Then she strapped her victim to the bed with what looked suspiciously like two cords of twisted panty hose, one across her upper body, one across her legs. Whatever it was, he hoped it was strong because Sam Ballanger looked as pissed as David Banner just after he started turning green.

In moments Sam was secured. The final touch was using her own tape to hold that sock in her mouth. He was thoroughly enjoying the show. "Now, Samantha, you be a good girl and go nighty-night," he said with wicked relish, then turned to his saviors. "Nice work, er, ladies. Might I ask to whom I owe my very timely rescue?"

His smile erased itself when the taller woman trained her ancient machine pistol on him and said coldly, "Mr. Granger, I'll need you to put your hands behind your back so I can handcuff your wrists. You're our prisoner now."

"Wait a minute, dammit! I'm a reporter for the *Miami Herald*. You can't kidnap me and expect—"

His protest was cut off when another of those damnable little white socks was stuffed into his mouth. Panty hose? Kids' socks? What the hell was going on here? He was as baffled as the infuriated Sam, who thrashed impotently on the bed. He would've loved to ask her how she liked playing "the patient," but he couldn't talk any more than she could answer.

Then the taller woman leveled her gun directly at him and said to her companion, "Lock the handcuffs on him."

The shorter woman approached Matt, grabbing his cuffed hand, then the other and pulling them behind his back. He felt

the old familiar grip of steel on his abraded wrists. Then she
tore off a strip of tape and sealed his mouth just like she'd
done with Sam.

"Start the car. I'll bring the prisoner," the tall woman said.

Utterly perplexed and more than a little frightened by this
weird turn of events, "the prisoner" watched her leave the
motel room and climb into the driver's seat of a big GMC
Yukon parked next to Sam's white Econoline. As the engine
growled to life, the tall woman motioned a bit too casually
with that ancient machine pistol, for him to follow.

By the time he was being shoved into the backseat of the
SUV, Matt wasn't altogether certain whether he'd been tossed
from the frying pan into the fire. Climbing up was not an easy
feat with hands cuffed behind his back, but the shorter,
slightly stocky woman gave him a push of encouragement,
boosting her shoulder against his tush. He overbalanced
against the backrest of the front seat, then flopped backward
with a loud "whump" onto the rear passenger seat. Behind
him the back of the vehicle was piled high with what looked
like gym bags and backpacks.

He nearly toppled into two little blond moppets who
watched him with large overly bright eyes. Not good at guess-
ing the ages of kids, he thought the older one, dressed in a
Girl Scout uniform, must be around eight or so. Her companion, wearing shorts and a Tommy Hilfiger T-shirt, appeared
to be two or three years younger. She was sucking on a gooey
string of red licorice.

What the hell was going on? Was the Russian Mafia using kids as decoys now? At least he could detect no traces of
Slavic features in either of their faces and took some small
measure of consolation in that. He sure wanted a gander at
their ski-masked adult companions. They wouldn't execute
him with two little kids watching…would they?

The vehicle turned out of the nearly empty parking lot and onto the service road leading to the highway. It appeared that his latest kidnappers might be heading back toward San Diego. He didn't know if that was a good or bad sign. Damn, the way things had been going for the last couple of days, he wouldn't have had the faintest idea what was a good or bad sign if it were painted in eighty-foot gold lettering across the sky.

"Are you a famous newspaper reporter?" the Girl Scout asked.

Matt shrugged, wondering how they knew he was a reporter. *Definitely not a good sign, Granger.* He nodded. Not exactly famous, but with a sock in his mouth, there was no way to add the qualifier.

"No, he isn't, either," the smaller Goldie Locks pronounced solemnly, clutching her licorice in one grubby fist. Then her expression turned gleeful as she whispered, "He's our captive and we can torture him if we want to."

With that disconcerting pronouncement, the little devil shoved the last of the licorice in her red-stained mouth. Looking like a dwarf Dracula on estrogen, she climbed agilely over her companion and thrust two sets of sticky fingers into his midsection.

He tried to flinch away, but in such close confines with his hands cuffed behind his back, there was not much he could do. She tickled him mercilessly, sensing with the unerring instinct only small children possess, that he was deadly sensitive to that particular form of "torture." Damn, the kid was more diabolical at this than Sam had been! He made a muffled grunt of protest, wondering if a person could die of some sort of internal rupture from unexpelled laughter.

"Mom, Mellie's bothering Mr. Granger," Scout said in a singsong voice, making no attempt to rein in her smaller cohort.

"Mellie, stop that right now," the woman driving the car admonished, concentrating on the road and paying little attention to the mayhem in the backseat.

The kid ignored her.

Between grunts of pure misery, Matt wondered how they knew his name and what they planned to do with him. Of course, he might not survive long enough to find out if little Mellie didn't stop pretty soon. At least they seemed on course back to San Diego. If only he could ask—shit! If only he could stop the infernal tickling, which now—in direct violation of her Scouting pledge—the older girl was joining in on. He cursed through the tape and sock, his face turning the same shade of red as the smaller kid's licorice-stained hands.

"Mom, Mr. Granger's turning a funny color and I think he said a bad word," Scout dutifully reported.

The tall woman in the passenger seat pulled the ski mask from her head and shook out a thick mane of shoulder-length auburn hair, then turned toward the culprits with a stern expression and said, "Stop that right now, Tiffany and Melanie or no Happy Meals when we stop for dinner."

Girl Scouts? Happy Meals? *I've been kidnapped by a pair of soccer moms!*

Sam worked the strips of panty hose—yes, they'd actually used panty hose to tie her to the bed—loose enough to wriggle her way beneath the ones holding her upper body to the mattress. But the ones binding her ankles were secured more tightly to the bed frame. Could she roll off the bed and kick free? Even if she did, that still left her hands and feet separately bound with tape they'd borrowed from Sam's bag, not to mention the gag in her mouth.

Nothing ventured nothing gained. With every minute that passed, her snatch was another mile farther away and so was her ten K. She levered herself to the edge of the bed and used her bound hands to push off, tumbling her upper body to the floor and nearly braining herself on a nightstand in the process. How the hell could a sagging motel mattress be that damn high up?

She hit the thin carpet covering the concrete beneath it like a sack of potatoes dropped from the steeple of Old North Church. Her head throbbed wickedly from the glancing blow off the nightstand's drawer handle. The room started to spin. If that wasn't bad enough, her lower back felt like a chiropractor trained by Dr. Mengele had just given her an adjustment. She lay twisted in a heap, blood rushing to her head while her bound ankles were still strapped to the mattress above. Her right arm would be black and blue by morning.

So will Matthew Granger when I get my hands on him.

She gritted her teeth against the pain of her twisted spine and tried scooting her body across the carpet at a right angle from the bed, all the while working her legs to loosen the bindings holding her feet to the mattress. One thing about panty hose. Even pulled really tight, they always had a little more give in them. She thanked whatever small lucky star might now be smiling down that they weren't control tops.

When she could feel the nylon finally began to slacken, Sam gave a really hard kick and the end fastened across the opposite edge of the mattress gave way. Exhaling through her nose heavily, she rolled her legs off the bed and lay flat on the floor. Blessed relief, even though her hands were still tied behind her back. A quick vision of Matt Granger lying with his hands cuffed behind him on that very mattress flashed into her mind.

She squashed it.

This was worth ten K. The hell with a sexy interlude with a hunk like Matt. After a brief break, she tried sitting up, hoping to be able to stand, then hop to the door and unlock it. But every time she got as far as her knees the queasy dizziness returned with a vengeance. After studying the distance from the bed to the door, she considered that hopping might not be such a hot idea. She could topple over and brain herself again. It might be a safer bet to roll to the door and then try standing up. Of course, part of the carpet she was forced to roll over was rather damp, thanks to the radiating moisture from the overflow. Goat cheese left in the sun for a week smelled better than the motel's carpet.

Great.

Ignoring the odor, she slithered up the side of the cheap wooden door, getting a few splinters in her arms in the process. But she could not turn the knob with her hands tied behind her. After several attempts that nearly resulted in another fall, she gave it one last try—and overbalanced, landing like a felled redwood on very damp ground, her head mere inches from the nasty corner of the bureau housing the television.

Utterly enraged, she slammed her feet against the door in frustration. It was hollow and made a loud thump. If there was anybody around the joint they'd hear her—wouldn't they? Cleaning staff? She looked around the moldy room and rejected that idea as laughable. With the stench of wet carpet still suffocating her, she abandoned that as a long shot. Still, there might be other customers checking in. Given the location and condition of the joint, ironically the very reasons she'd chosen it, she had little hope.

But Sam gave another resounding kick with her bound feet. Harder. Harder…

Think of the ten K. Think of the expense account. Think of what Patty Patowski will do to you if Granger gets away. Think of your goddam medical bills if you survive this place!

"Anyone in there?" a timorous voice asked from the other side of the badly battered door.

Sam's muffled cry elicited the sweetest sound she'd heard since Uncle Dec used to dress up like Santa when she and her brothers were kids and ho ho ho his way down the hall on Christmas Eves—the click of a key in the door lock!

In the five minutes or so it took for the skinny, frightened maid to find scissors and cut her free, Sam calculated how far down the road Matt and his captors could have gotten. Luckily a kid playing outside had seen a man hustled into a large SUV that had shot out of the motel lot, turned right on the service road and headed up the westbound entrance ramp. They were most likely taking him back to San Diego. Whoever the hell "they" were.

Sam paid the bill, giving the sleazy manager carte blanche with her credit card to cover the water damage. Dangerous, she knew, but so was having her client in the hands of women who might be working for Renkov. Sam had never lost a snatch yet and she definitely didn't intend for Matt Granger to be the first. Aunt Claudia had agreed to pay for her nephew to be delivered to her safe and sound. At least, Sam tried to convince herself that pride and money were the only reasons she was so desperate to retrieve him.

She fished her spare key from its magnetic hiding place beneath the front bumper on the van and was hurtling down the highway in less than a quarter hour. When she spotted the dark green sport utility, they were cruising along as if they didn't have a care in the world. She would have roared on past except she was sure the driver was wearing a ski mask. Who the hell were these wackos? Not only were they armed, with Matt as hostage, but they had two innocent kids in the vehicle with them.

A game of bumper cars was for sure not an option. Following until they made a pit stop was. She dropped back, allowing several cars between her and her quarry so they would not spot her van. Being the oldest in a family with six brothers, a situation she likened to being raised by wolves, Sam knew two kids that age would have to pee sooner than later. When they did, she'd make her move…whatever it would be.

Chapter 6

Matt sunk back against the seat, trying to catch his breath and get a look at the vaguely familiar auburn-haired woman as she said to the driver, "For heaven's sake, Jenny, take off that mask before we get pulled over by the highway patrol."

Her companion did so, revealing a short cap of sand-colored curls. Releasing one chubby hand from the steering wheel, she waved at Matt sheepishly, saying, "Hi, Mr. Granger. Remember me?"

He did. Jenny Baxter, Tess Renkov's sister. She was the lead he was supposed to meet when Sam had snatched him. He'd seen her at a commune rap session several days before arranging to meet her privately. And her taller companion must be her sister, Alexi Renkov's widow, Tess. The news photos didn't do her justice. Old Renkov's dead son had had great taste in women.

"I apologize for the rough exit from the motel, but we

wanted to make it look as if we were actually kidnapping you," Tess said, reaching over to remove the tape from his mouth and pull out the sock.

"Yes, we wanted to make it look like we were bounty jumpers," Jenny interjected.

Tess rolled her eyes. "The term is 'bounty hunters,' honey."

Through a cottony mouth, Matt croaked, "Bounty hunters?"

"You know, like in those books about the woman who's always getting her prisoners stolen away from her," Jenny explained.

"She means a bail bondswoman, like Stephanie Plum," Tess said.

"Whatever," Jenny replied with a shrug. "We wanted her to think we were taking you to the guy who paid her to kidnap you. You know, so we can collect the reward? That way, when she gets loose, she'll chase us east, not follow us back to San Diego."

Matt didn't know Stephanie Plum from a Sunsweet Prune but he was pretty sure a dame as smart as Sam Ballanger wouldn't chase them to Boston—even if they had known about Claudia, which they obviously didn't. He was still choking from the aftereffects of the gag, trying to clear his throat when Tess reached over and offered him a sip from a warm can of Coke. Ambrosia.

"We saw that woman abduct you from the front of the building complex just as we were picking up Jenny's girls from their school," Tess explained. "I called a friend at Samaritan Haven to watch my son and we took off after you."

"Ski masks and guns?" Matt questioned dubiously. Sam Ballanger accused him of being crazy? These dames were nuttier than Boston brown bread.

"Oh, we stopped and bought the masks last night after following you to the first motel," Jenny said. "Then we had to figure out a plan. Lucky for us, we already had the guns."

"Why not? What conscientious mom would be caught without her machine pistol?"

"We have to carry them in case..." Tess stopped, casting a quick glance at the girls, who had ceased squirming and were listening avidly now. "I'll explain when it's safe to pull over, but it might be best if we put a few miles between us and that woman back at the motel, just in case she doesn't fall for our ruse."

"Not a bad idea," Matt replied with grim amusement, thinking of Sam gagged and tied to that motel bed. "Soon as the maid hits the motel room early tomorrow morning, she'll be after us."

"Only if she's hitchhiking," Jenny said with a laugh, dangling the keys to Sam's van from her finger before tossing them back onto the seat.

"Not bad," Matt conceded. That would surely have to slow her down.

"Mom, I have to go," Tiffany whispered loudly, holding her hand so as to shield her message from their male passenger. Mellie quickly chimed in.

"There's a rest area a couple of miles ahead," Jenny said, looking at her sister.

Tess nodded. "I suppose it's okay. Please don't worry about the guns, Mr. Granger. They're perfectly harmless, not even loaded. Mr. Zandski from the commune gave them to us. Everyone calls him Uncle Hugo. He's the one watching my son Steve. We trust him completely."

"No gun is ever 'perfectly harmless,'" Matt cautioned, uneasily eyeing the Chinese machine pistol lying on the seat between Jenny and Tess.

Jenny turned the car into the deserted rest area and pulled

up in the scant shade offered by a pair of olive trees. Turning off the ignition, she said, "Don't worry, it's a World War II antique. See?"

With that she picked it up and thrust the weapon at Matt, barrel first. The muzzle was only inches from his face, and he was only a sphincter spasm away from messing up the car seat. "Jeez! Lady, lady, don't ever point a gun at somebody like that!"

In a tone of voice Jenny reserved for her daughters, she assured him. "These guns are relics, Mr. Granger. They really are safe. Look." Smiling, she pointed the pistol at the roof and squeezed the trigger. A sickening click resounded and Matt flinched in spite of the fact the weapon was aimed at the roof of the vehicle. "See?" But before Jenny could release the pressure of her finger, the weapon seemed to come to life in her hand, jerking violently as it spewed a hail of bullets, tearing ragged holes through the roof and leaving everyone's ears ringing from the deafening noise.

She dropped the pistol to the floor with a cry of terror, frantically looking back to see that her children were uninjured. "Oh, shit, shit—what have I done?" she wailed as Tess tried to console her. The two girls looked stunned for an instant as their ears rang from the ungodly racket, then broke into giggles as if a brush with death was as much fun as a trip to Disneyland.

Matt was absolutely certain these dames and the kids were more than a fry or two short of those Happy Meals Tess promised. How the hell did he get himself into these messes? Maybe Aunt Claudia had the right idea. He ought to return to Boston and be a stockbroker. No retrieval specialists or gun-toting soccer moms did business with Lodge, Asher, Witherspoon & Fiske.

From her vantage point on the opposite side of the rest stop where she'd concealed her van behind a thicket of bottlebrush, Sam watched the roof of the SUV suddenly erupt as gunfire tore through it. Damn! She jumped out of the van, gun in hand, only to stop short after a couple of paces. The automatic pistol had fired through the roof, not a window or door. If they wanted to kill Matt, this was certainly not the way to do it. Something about the whole deal stank as bad as the soggy carpet back at "Motel Hell."

She studied the lay of the land around the rest stop. A typical small brick building with accommodations for men and women, divided by a vending machine, map and concessions room. One of the women and the two little girls were approaching the building. A smattering of stubby trees and brushy shrubs provided cover. It would do. She darted from tree to bush, trying to get close enough to decide on her next move.

When Jenny took her pair of dragons-in-training to the rest shelter to use the ladies' room and buy soft drinks from the vending machines, Tess nervously unlocked Matt's cuffs. He rubbed his hands as Tess apologized.

"Mr. Granger, you must be ready to kill us all. I'm sorry about what my nieces did, and for having you gagged and handcuffed."

"Don't worry about it. I was sort of getting used to bondage games," he said with a grin, as visions of Sam naked and straddling his body on that bed flashed through his mind. *Concentrate, Granger,* he reminded himself.

"But what about Jenny's awful accident?" She looked up at the bright dots of sunlight streaming in through the roof and shuddered. "Uncle Hugo assured us that the guns were unloaded. We were too afraid of them to try opening them up to check."

"I will admit to not being crazy about the fireworks." Now

it was his turn to glance at the ruined roof. "But it's over and no harm done that a good body shop can't fix, though you probably ought to have it done before the next rainy season. For now, how about we take both weapons and lock them in the glove compartment until we get back to San Diego?"

Tess nodded and did as he asked. Then he suggested, "I could use a little walk, kinda stretch my legs. Okay by you?"

She took a deep breath. "After that horrific shooting, I'd like nothing better than to air out the SUV. It stinks like firecracker smoke."

They both climbed out. After Tess opened the vehicle's rear hatch, they strolled in the opposite direction from the restrooms and Jenny's dragons. "You were going to explain about the guns?" he prompted.

"I didn't want to in front of the children. Tiff and Mellie have been through enough trauma with that bastard of a father they have. Uncle Hugo has really helped them adjust after Jenny got them back. He's a disabled World War II veteran and the dearest old guy. When Jenny confided our circumstances to him, well, he offered her two trophies of his and insisted we each carry one, just to scare off her ex-husband.

"My sister is terrified Len Baxter will abduct his daughters again—he did it once already and it took the authorities nearly a year to get them back. That's why Jenny went into hiding with the girls."

"And your story?"

Tess sighed, shifting on her seat and combing her fingers through that great mop of hair. "It's long and ugly, I'm afraid."

"Try me. I tracked your sister in the hope that she'd know where you were hiding. Figured there was a chance you knew some dirt on your father-in-law. I'm investigating Mikhail Renkov's connections to the Russian Mafia."

Tess paled. "I don't want to become another statistic just

so you can have your story, Mr. Granger. I have a son to think of. Jenny said you wanted to help us so we couldn't let that woman kidnap you. I thought she worked for Mikhail."

"I did, too, at first, but that's another story. Just consider this—if I could find you so easily, don't you think Renkov can, too? He has considerably better resources at his command than I did, believe me. Your only hope is to give me everything you got and let me nail the bastard."

"You haven't urged me to go to the police," she said with a cynical twist of a smile.

"Other than the fact that they might not be able to provide sufficient protection, is there any reason you have an aversion to talking to them? There have been hints from that direction indicating they think you offed your husband."

"I had motive," she conceded. "If you know anything about Alexi, you know he was a player and I don't just mean on the golf course."

There was a tight defiance in her voice. Alexi had hurt her and probably their son, too. Matt could figure that much by her tone and body language. "I heard he was quite the lady's man, yeah," he coached, waiting for her to tell the story in her own words.

"It didn't stop after we were married." She looked away, studying the horizon for a moment. "He'd make promises...but always break them. Steve worshipped his father. How many sons can say their dads play in the Masters? I stuck around for his sake, but now he's old enough to read the stories splashed across the tabloids—about his father's coke parties with bimbos and booze. My God, they rack those rags right at the checkout counters in the supermarkets. Mikhail's tried to keep it quiet, but even he can't control the paparazzi."

"I bet he didn't like the attention drawn to the family."

Tess nodded. "Several weeks before Alexi died, I overheard him and his father having a terrible argument in Mikhail's office. I'd come over to pick up Steve and was surprised to see my husband's car outside."

"So you eavesdropped. Good for you. What were they fighting about?"

"Mikhail didn't care about Alexi's unfaithfulness to me, just the attention in the international press it was garnering," she said with disgust. "That was bad for business."

"Which seems to indicate that Alexi was more than just a golfer. He was part of his father's international criminal network."

"I think he was. My husband always liked living on the edge. He thrived on danger. Ever since he was in school he did rock climbing, white-water rafting—any kind of extreme sport, you name it. Mikhail said he'd disinherit Alexi if he didn't act 'with more discretion.' Alexi usually deferred to his father. They were really a traditional Russian patriarchy, but apparently when he'd been summoned to his father's place, Alexi had been drinking—another thing they fought about— Alexi's penchant for DUIs."

"Dutch courage?"

She nodded. "Alexi told Mikhail that he had hidden evidence worth a fortune to someone named Pribluda. He said Mikhail could take the family money and jam it." She swallowed. "Only that wasn't exactly the way he said it. I was shocked that he'd speak that way to his father, but as I said, he'd been drinking."

"You know who Valentin Pribluda is?"

"Some gangster from New York, Brighton Beach, isn't he? I've read about him in the newspapers. I never imagined my father-in-law was in the same business." She shuddered.

"What happened then?"

"My husband stormed for the door and I ran for cover,

ducking into the little library adjoining Mikhail's office...
Nancy was there and it seemed pretty obvious to me that
she'd been listening, too. The door between the two rooms
was ever so slightly ajar and she'd been standing by it when
I slipped in the hall door."

So the trophy wife was picking up info, too. He filed that
away for later. "Any idea what this evidence Alexi had collected was?"

"No, only that when Alexi made the threat, Mikhail was
furious. Whatever it was, it must've been really important...and damning."

"You still don't think the old man intended to kill his son?"
Matt asked.

Tess shook her head. "No. Alexi was his only son, only
child. He was very old-world that way. He might punish him
in some way—Lord knows he whipped him when Alexi was
young. To 'make a man of him.' But he'd never kill him—
intentionally."

Matt reserved judgment on that. "Why do you think Nancy
was listening in?"

"She was always nosy. The yelling must've caught her attention. She's a slut who only married Mikhail for his money.
I think...no, I know she and Alexi had a brief fling. I caught
them coming off our yacht. He claimed he'd just taken her
out to show her how fast the new twin engines he'd had in-
stalled could go. He was into boat racing, too, and always
souping up engines so he could fake out his competitors."

"There was a news story a week or so before he was killed.
About his leaving you for some Hollywood chick, one of the
ones who can't tell the difference between scavenger hunting
and shoplifting. Nobody ever figured Nancy might be one of
his lovers, did they?" Matt asked rhetorically. The case for

Mikhail offing his son had just moved up another notch in his book.

Tess's expression was tight, cynical. "The cops are speculating—a crime of passion, woman scorned, that sort of thing. I should put my life and that of my son in the hands of guys who reason like that?" She scoffed. "I consulted my attorney the day after the escapade you mentioned turned up in the tabloid headlines. Steve has been more and more reserved here lately. His father's lifestyle was hurting him. I couldn't let it continue. That's why I intended to divorce Alexi and never look back. Our marriage was over years ago. The starlets—and Nancy—can have him." She looked tired now, massaging her temples with her fingertips.

Matt believed her. He was good at reading people and seldom made mistakes. *But you made a beaut with Sam Ballanger. Didn't think she'd use that stunner.* "Okay," he agreed, brushing away thoughts of the furious woman they'd left tied up in the motel room, "but if you didn't kill Alexi, and Mikhail didn't do it either, then who did?"

"Oh, I think Mikhail killed him."

"Come again?" Matt's head was spinning now.

"Oh, he didn't intend the bomb to kill Alexi. I said he wouldn't kill his son *intentionally.* Alexi was driving my car that day. He'd forgotten to put gas in his Ferrari and needed to be in Palm Beach for a game, so he took the Lexus."

"According to the cops, that's also his. You drive a Town Car."

"The transmission was slipping on it. I'd started using the Lexus a few days earlier. Mikhail knew that."

"Okay, why would he want to have you killed? I don't figure it was just to keep sonny boy from having to pay alimony."

Tess shook her head, pressing her fingers together over the tip of her nose and trying to gather her thoughts. "That's not it. It's all so…sordid."

Sam crouched behind a clump of wild rosemary bushes and listened to their conversation, trying to piece it together with what little Patowski had told her about the case. She could bust up this little party right now and take him back, but the information she'd gather if she sneaked along for the ride could turn the case for Pat.

What the hell? Pat's FBI contacts here in Utah could retrieve her car for her. She'd retrieve Granger after she got the dirt on Renkov for the authorities. There might even be an additional reward in it for her.

She dashed back to the Yukon and waited as a convoy of semis whizzed past, drowning out Tess and Matt's voices… and what little noise Sam made as she slipped through the opened back hatch of the SUV. She burrowed beneath the mound of backpacks, sleeping bags and other kid droppings just as the sister and her daughters came out of the building. No one saw her.

Matt waited for Tess to go on, but then he heard Jenny and her dragons returning to the car. He and Tess retraced their steps and joined the crew. "I can handle sordid," he said gently to her. "We'll talk later."

Tess nodded, then walked back and slammed shut the rear hatch of the GMC.

In her nest, Sam relaxed. Peeping out, she could see the kids climb in, dripping bright red Sno-Kones and making loud slurping noises. Ugh. She'd noticed Matt had messy red stains on his shirt and knew they weren't from the Slurpee. For a minute, she was afraid he'd been shot before she realized it had to be something the kids must've smeared on him.

"That oughta hold them until we stop for the night," Jenny said with an apologetic glance at Matt whose jeans already bore several drops of sticky liquid in addition to the red licorice. "Oh, unless you want to ride straight through to San

Diego? We could take turns driving. The girls are used to sleeping on the road," Jenny offered.

"Mom, you promised McDonald's," Scout whined. The lead tickler joined in the protest.

The thought of being cooped up with two miniature Torquemadas for the long drive made Matt give serious consideration to stopping, but he really needed to get back to San Diego. "If you're up to it, I'm game—and we could stop at the next McD's along the way," he added quickly when Melanie and Tiffany narrowed their eyes dangerously at him.

"Hey, you took his handcuffs off," Scout said, suddenly noticing their victim was not only no longer mute but no longer defenseless, as well.

"Mr. Granger was never our prisoner, Tiff," Tess explained. "We only made it look that way so we could throw that bad lady off our trail."

As they pulled out of the rest stop and headed down the road, "that bad lady" seethed in the rear of the car. The air-conditioning from the front didn't reach her hiding place. Being labeled "bad" while she crouched in sweaty misery with every muscle and bone in her body aching didn't help, either. Aunt Claudia wasn't the only one who would pay when this deal was over. Patowksi was going to owe her big-time. The thought made her smile.

Chapter 7

Jenny pulled the GMC into the McDonald's parking lot and took the girls inside to place their orders. Matt and Tess opted to stretch their legs and climbed out of the car, leaning against the frame as they talked. It was full dark now and the temperature had cooled appreciably. From her hiding place, Sam could hear as they resumed their interrupted conversation at the rest stop.

"So why does your father-in-law want you dead? The threat of divorce?"

Tess sighed. "It's Steve."

Comprehension dawned. "You mean if you took him away, the Renkov dynasty would end with Alexi."

"Yes. And Mikhail knew with me out of the way my family would have no chance of winning a custody battle. Look at poor Jenny, hiding from an abusive husband. The only other kin we have is an elderly aunt up in Michigan. Mikhail has always been devoted to Steve—as if to make up for the way he messed up with Alexi, I suppose. I know he intends to train him to take over the family business." She shivered.

"He knew you'd talked to a divorce lawyer." It made sense.

"Nothing goes on in Miami that he doesn't find out about. If only I'd known he was a criminal before I married his son…" Her voice faded before she took a deep breath and went on. "Mikhail can be incredibly charming when he wants to be. I thought he was a highly successful international businessman dealing in imports and exports. And Alexi…well, he was successful, too—maybe the next Tiger Woods according to the sports commentators. I was dazzled—and dumb."

"I can see how you could make the mistake," Matt said sympathetically. "The media has all but forgotten Mikhail's KGB activities since he defected and became the State Department's darling. He's supposed to be going straight, but a turkey like him never does."

"I had my first inkling of that over a year ago."

"What happened?" he prompted.

She smiled thinly. "I suppose I have to trust you, don't I, Mr. Granger?"

"Call me Matt and yes, you can trust me. I won't write anything until Renkov's behind bars and you and your family are safe. My word on it." Even though he could smell Pulitzer now, he would keep that promise. The lives of two innocent women and their children depended on it.

She studied him in the flickering lights from the fast-food building, then nodded. "Last year Alexi and I were at their house in Aventura during the holidays. I overheard Mikhail and Nancy arguing."

"I'm surprised he'd let his American trophy wife in on his business interests."

"I imagine she found things out the same way I did, by accident—or eavesdropping. The conversation was through a closed door, so I couldn't catch everything, but the gist of it had something to do with offshore accounts in the Caymans."

"Money laundering for the Ruskies is my guess," Matt said.

"I assumed that, but I didn't actually hear much. Then Alexi caught me and steered me away. I…I don't know if he told his father." She shuddered. "After all that's happened now, I think he did."

"When Alexi was drunk and threatened Mikhail, you have any idea what kind of evidence he had squirreled away that he could sell to Pribluda's crowd?"

"Somehow it was related to Alexi's traveling in Europe. He mentioned his last golf junket to some eastern countries bordering on Russia and the Ukraine. That seemed to set Mikhail off."

Matt considered a number of scenarios related to what he'd dug up about Renkov's illegal international activities. The possibilities were endless but evidence was damned scarce. For some reason he had yet to penetrate, the CIA seemed to be covering for the bastard. "Any idea where your husband might've hidden his cache?"

"He said something cryptic. Remember, he'd been drinking, and he was muttering as he came toward the door. Mikhail couldn't have heard him but as I opened the door to the library to hide, I caught part of it. He said…" She paused and tried to remember his exact words. "Something about 'a clear channel straight to Pribluda.'"

Matt puzzled over that. "Anything else that might help me find out who killed him?"

"Alexi was threatened a few days before he was killed, told if he didn't throw a game in Santa Barbara, someone in his family would pay the price. He dismissed it as some sort of crank call. Celebrity athletes get them now and then. He played and won. But Mikhail insisted he inform the police about it."

"Did he?"

"Yes. Ironic, isn't it? Then he ended up dead in my place."

"Because he was killed in your car instead of you. Hmm." Matt considered the puzzle pieces, stroking his chin. "If you're wrong and Mikhail did kill his son, he may have arranged the threatening phone call as a diversion. That's a possible angle to check."

Sweating beneath a ton of kiddy refuse, Sam committed everything they said to memory. If only she could keep it straight until she had the chance to talk with Patowski.

On the way back to San Diego the three drivers were tired and tense. After the girls fell asleep, Tess gave Matt everything she could think of about Mikhail Renkov, his blond trophy wife and a long list of associates. Matt figured the best way Tess and Steve would be safe was for him to expose Renkov as a criminal, perhaps even the murderer of his own son. Tess had been present when Alexi received the threatening phone call and described that in as much detail as she could remember. Right now, it was the most solid lead he had, barring any new inspiration Tess could come up with about the hiding place for whatever Alexi had threatened to sell Pribluda.

Listening in the back, Sam wished Mrs. Renkov knew exactly what was going on in the Caymans and what her dear Alexi had been up to while he was touring in Eastern Europe. He'd threatened to sell something to Mikhail's worst rival, Pribluda. If the cops and fibbies could find Alexi's evidence, she would really put money in the bank with them. Considering the cloud under which she'd left the force, that was a good thing.

Sam desperately wanted to filch a pen and paper from one of the kiddies' backpacks and take notes as Tess and Matt talked. Of course, before she gave Pat anything, she had to recapture Granger and put him on ice. As the hours went by she began to feel the same sort of acute discomfort Matt had the day she snatched him. But she couldn't slip out of the SUV and relieve herself at any of the rest stops because the adults and kids never all left the vehicle at the same time.

Tandem peeing. What a concept! Why the hell couldn't they all get out at once and take care of business? Just when she was certain she couldn't hold off another minute, they pulled off the highway and everyone piled out of the car at a neon lit sign advertising "Eats! All Nite!" As soon as they hit the diner, Sam hit the bushes behind it.

After taking care of business, she realized she was parched and starving. She'd always been a skinny kid with a high metabolism. In a big Irish family, everyone learned to wolf down food, much and often as it was available. It would be hours until they reached San Diego. Sam knew it wouldn't be wise to chance eating or drinking anything. She settled for a few swallows of lukewarm, rusty water from a drinking fountain in the diner's restroom hallway, then slipped back into her hiding place.

It was going to be a long hungry haul back to San Diego. She prayed her stomach didn't growl and give her away.

As the SUV finally approached San Diego, Matt said to Tess, "If Renkov's after you, he'll likely have someone watching your place by now."

"Thank God they don't know about Uncle Hugo," she said. "But if we lead Mikhail's people to Steve, they'll kidnap him." Tess clutched the steering wheel with whitened knuckles. "I have to get my son out of there!"

"Call Uncle Hugo right now," Jenny said with a hint of panic in her voice as she glanced at her sleeping girls.

Then a news bulletin on the radio cut short their discussion. An announcer's voice droned, "This breaking news on the car-bombing death of golf's golden boy Alexi Renkov. His widow, Teresa 'Tess' Renkov, wanted for questioning by Miami-Dade Police, may have a three-million-dollar motive. The Renkov family has alleged that their daughter-in-law killed her husband to collect on a three-million-dollar life insurance policy—"

Tess quickly clicked off the radio, then said, "Alexi didn't have a life insurance policy—at least, that I know of. And I wasn't the beneficiary of anything. By terms of the prenuptial agreement I signed, his whole inheritance goes to Steve."

"It looks as if that devious KGB bastard's setting you up to take a big fall," Matt said. "Maybe you ought to give a heads-up to this Hugo Zandski."

Tess pulled off the road, shaken by this latest revelation. She quickly placed a call to the old man, alerting him to watch out for strangers who might attempt to kidnap the boy. After signing off, she managed a weak smile. "He says Steve's fine and he has enough weapons to hold off the whole Russian army."

"My turn to drive," Matt said, seeing how shaken Tess had become. As they switched places, he continued, "It's only a matter of time until the cops track you to San Diego." His mind whirled with various possibilities. Could Sam be working for the Company? They had the resources to figure out Tess's location and send Sam Ballanger to get him out of the way. Then Renkov could do what he wanted with his daughter-in-law while the CIA looked the other way, but that left too many loose ends. They'd just let Renkov's goons kill him, too. Of course, there was Aunt Claudia. The old broad had a lot of clout in some pretty high political circles... *Even the Company wouldn't dare kill her only heir.*

"We can't let the police find us," Jenny said, interrupting his chaotic thoughts.

Damn straight on that. "We have to get you out of Samaritan Haven until I can figure out what's going on." Matt tried to put the pieces together. Sam Ballanger sure didn't fit the profile of a spook. And what about his aunt? He'd have to call her as soon as he saw that Tess and her loony sister and the kids were safe. His head felt as if it were stuffed with cotton candy. No one had had much sleep except the two girls since the three adults had taken turns driving through the night.

"How can we get to Steve if my father-in-law or the police are watching Samaritan Haven?" Tess asked.

"I have a map of the complex," Jenny said. "Hugo gave it to me when we moved in because the girls kept sneaking off to play with friends in the next building and they'd get lost and I couldn't find them." Jenny climbed halfway over Tess and opened the large glove compartment, which was crammed to the brim with everything from Uncle Hugo's guns to fossilized Girl Scout cookies. After rooting around for several moments, she said, "Here it is," then unfolded the map.

Tess took it and began scanning it, then pointed to one spot, saying to Matt, "Look here. If we approach by way of Alvard Street, we can park the van, then cut across the common ground—"

"The woods are full of poison ivy," a suddenly alert Tiffany announced.

"Tiff, you were supposed to be sleeping. How long have you been awake?" her mother asked suspiciously, swiveling her head around as she remained perched between the front and backseats.

"Are we going to be spies like in *The Bourne Identity*?"
the girl countered, ignoring Jenny's question.

"How did you see that movie, young lady? It's not rate
for kids." Then before her daughter could reply, Jenny sighe
and once more turned her attention to the glove compar
ment.

Sam thought Jenny never won an argument with either ki
She tried to resettle herself beneath the lumpy cover of back
packs and duffels. But her misery was quickly forgotten whe
Tiffany said, "I have some gunk for poison ivy in my ge
someplace back there." She started rooting dangerously ne
Sam's hiding place. *What the hell do I do now? Pull my stur
ner and scramble a couple of kids and soccer moms?*

Jenny saved Sam the decision. "Never mind, honey. I sa
some in the glove compartment." She pulled out a small spra
bottle of poison ivy repellant.

"Be prepared. Isn't that the Scouting motto?" Matt aske
grinning as he exited the highway and pulled into a gas st
tion. While Jenny paid cash and filled up her SUV, Matt ar
Tess continued studying the map. From the corner of his ey
Matt noted that Tiffany was regarding him with grudging r
spect. He might be in trouble.

Within a quarter hour, they had a game plan. "I think
would be smart for you to spend the night someplace in tl
complex where no one can find you. Zandski will probab
know a hidey-hole if he's been living here for years," Ma
said.

"Then we can backtrack to Jenny's SUV in the mornir
and take off." Tess nodded.

"We're going on the lam," Mellie said excitedly, clappir
her hands.

Didn't either of the little dragons ever sleep, Sam wo
dered. Probably too busy watching forbidden movies.

"We just have to be careful for a few days until the police arrest the bad people," Jenny said soothingly to her daughters.

"But Steve's granddad says Aunt Tess killed Uncle Alexi and we know that's not true. Is he a bad person?" Tiffany asked logically. "Will you find out, Mr. Granger?"

Matt was impressed with the kid's logic although he hated to admit it. "I'll try, Tiff," he promised gravely. Then, turning to Tess, he said, "We need to keep in touch. I'll give you my cell number. Check in with me at irregular intervals and if I don't pick up, don't leave any messages. Just try again later."

"Believe me, I'll be careful," Tess replied. "I'll give you my cell number, too, just in case."

As they exchanged numbers Sam listened, committing both numbers to memory. It was time for a quick exit. She knew their plans and how she could retake Granger. She was within an hour of San Diego, an easy if expensive cab ride back to Samaritan Haven. Lucky for her she didn't have to sneak in the back way and risk poison ivy. As bad as her reaction to the stuff was, not a product on the market would save her from weeks of looking like a refugee from the "Creature Cantina" in *Star Wars*.

While the rest of the passengers in the Yukon used the gas station's restrooms, Sam slipped out the back hatch and paced in front of the Quik Mart as she speed-dialed Patowski. She had a lot to arrange before tomorrow morning, she thought as she watched the SUV pull away. Her first call was to the cab company. Then she reached Pat by way of his beeper and gave him an edited version of what had happened since last night.

"Yeah, so I need a pair of drivers to pick up my van and make like kamikazes back to San Diego." She listened to the

anticipated outraged rejoinder, then said, "Look, you wan
Granger on ice or not? You give me the van, I give you Tes
Renkov." She paused a beat, then added another enticement
"Alexi stashed some kind of evidence about his father's op
erations. Threatened to sell it to Pribluda if Daddy didn't ge
off his case."

That got his attention big-time, just like she knew it would

"What'd he do with it?" the cop asked.

"Don't know yet. But it has something to do with his gol
trips this spring to a bunch of Eastern bloc countries near Rus
sia and the Ukraine." She could hear the wheels in Pat's hea
turning long distance. "Let your fibbie friends run with tha
one."

Pat wasn't happy about making the arrangements for he
car but did it just as she anticipated. She gave him a street nea
Samaritan Haven where her van should be deposited. It wa
a tight timetable. Could Pat's FBI connections deliver th
Econoline to her before she had to snatch Granger again? A
she could do was make a backup plan.

Uncle Hugo was one of a kind. So was the arsenal hangin
from every wall in the front rooms of his living quarters—a
the guns were either World War I or II, or earlier vintage. Ma
imagined many were souvenirs the old man collected durin
deuce. *No wonder he gave Tess and Jenny those damned re
ics. He probably didn't have a clue they were still loaded!*

A squat stocky man with an arthritic everything, Hug
Zandski's narrowed dark eyes studied the younger ma
shrewdly. Noting the obvious seal of approval Tess, Jenn
and "his girls," as he called Tiff and Mellie, had placed o
Granger, he smiled broadly, revealing the worst-fitting set o
dentures Matt could imagine, barring the wooden one
George Washington had worn.

"Welcome to my home, Matt Granger," he said, extending one bearlike paw and pumping Matt's hand with vigorous enthusiasm.

Then young Steve Renkov came flying down the hall and into his mother's arms. He was a tall, gangling kid with his father's golden good looks but his serious demeanor aged him well beyond a mere twelve years. "Mom, what's going on? I just heard on the TV—"

Tess shushed him imperceptibly, brushing a straight lock of blond hair from his eyes as she said, "It's going to be all right, Steve." Her glance at his younger cousins tipped him off not to discuss the dire situation they were in. "Can you take Tiff and Mellie and show them that new video game you got last week?"

He nodded gravely, warmed with the "adult responsibility" being accorded him. "Sure thing, Mom. Come on, girls. *Auto Heist* really rocks."

After the trio disappeared into the television room down the hall, the adults sat around the scarred oak table in the center of Hugo Zandski's dirty and cluttered living-dining area. Besides the weapons on the walls, which Matt noted were at least placed high enough a kid couldn't reach them without using a stepladder, the large double room was filled with other relics from the past.

Polish nesting dolls perched on rickety little tables, tattered old handmade afghans and quilts were spread or piled on the lumpy sofas and armchairs crowding the room. An enormous hutch and two smaller cabinets were filled with a mismatched array of chipped and faded dishes. Granger imagined they must have belonged to his wife and sisters, long dead according to what Jenny had volunteered.

The old man shuffled into the big old-fashioned kitchen and soon had tea steeping. After retrieving four cups from the

mound of dirty dishes piled in the sink, he scrubbed them out
dried them and brought the refreshments to the table. The stuff
was strong enough to strip varnish off white pine. Matt added
another heaping teaspoon of sugar in futile hopes of killing
the taste as he listened to the old man.

"So, those Renkovs say Ta Ta here killed that good-for-
nothing husband for insurance, eh?" he asked rhetorically.

"It's a way to discredit her so the police won't believe anything she says," Matt replied.

"I fought Nazis in Poland until our 'Soviet liberators' arrived." Zandski removed a red cotton handkerchief from his
back pocket and blew his nose noisily. "Never trust a Russian
He'd lie over his own mother's grave. Especially old KGF
like Renkov. Once you belong, always you belong."

Matt nodded in agreement. "That's why most of them
ended up in the Russian Mafia."

Tess explained their plans for eluding the police and the
Renkov family by finding an isolated place in northern
California where they could hide until Matt figured ou
how to nail Mikhail. "We cleaned out both our bank ac
counts at an ATM in Utah. I only hope it'll stretch until thi
is over."

"I have money, too." He shushed Tess and Jenny's protest
as he withdrew a large wad of bills cleverly concealed in on
of the nesting dolls. "You will use my truck," the old man sai
in a tone that left no doubt that they must obey. "The polic
and Mikhail's people, they will know that Yukon."

"Besides, there might also be a problem if it starts to rain,"
Matt said. "And the cops'll be curious about the bullet hole
in the roof, too."

Hugo turned to the red-faced women in alarm. "Someon
tried already to shoot at you?"

Jenny stuttered until Tess said, "It was our fault—I mea

about the holes in the roof. We had an accident with one of the guns."

Matt produced the two weapons which he'd confiscated from the women when they got out of the SUV. The instant the old man saw the machine pistol his eyes widened in horror. Seizing the weapon, he opened the breech.

"I already removed the bullets," Matt said.

Hugo's shoulders slumped in relief. "How did you get this?" he asked the women.

"You told me to take that one from above the window," Jenny said, pointing to the opposite wall, "but I couldn't reach it and you were busy finding one for Tess. So I just took one from above the sofa instead. It looked almost exactly like the one you said for me to take. I didn't know there was any difference," she added weakly.

"Difference was, one I offered you was unloaded. This one always I keep loaded."

"Oh," Jenny said with a gulp.

"My fault. I should be more watchful." The old man shook his head. "My little ones could be hurt." He sighed mournfully.

"Luckily, no one was, but now everyone is tired. Is there somewhere in the complex where they could spend the night?" Matt asked Hugo.

The old man nodded, pointing above him. "End of third floor. Old Mr. Tucci died last week. His place is vacant. Come," he said, motioning to the women. "I give you clean bedding."

"Good plan. You ladies get some sleep while I stash the Yukon," Matt said. "Then you slip out before dawn tomorrow in Hugo's truck, but first have him drive it over to Alvard Street for you. You cut through the woods just the way we came in."

Hugo grinned. "That way, no one sees you leave."

"With Miami-Dade's chief suspect out of sight, I should have some time to find out what's going on," Matt said.

"How can we ever thank you, Mr. Granger?" Tess asked.

He grinned. "You wouldn't happen to know anyone on the Pulitzer committee, would you?"

Chapter 8

Matt hid the SUV on the basement floor in a large but ill-attended parking deck in the worst neighborhood around downtown San Diego, then removed the plates. By the time the cops located it, it'd be stripped so bare there'd be nothing left to trace. He took a bus back to Samaritan Haven and used a side entrance to his own building, not expecting any trouble.

His first order of business was to call his aunt in Boston. He was pissed but not terribly surprised when her secretary informed him that the old bat was off for a few days at Martha's Vineyard. Incommunicado...unless she deigned to check up on him.

Whoever had convinced his aunt to sic Sam on him wouldn't be looking for him until darling Samantha got loose and reported his escape. He reconsidered and grinned. Nope. Sam would never admit she'd let a prisoner—oops—"a

patient" get away. Once she was released from that motel
room and made her way back to San Diego, she'd come looking for him again. He was sure Sam wouldn't fall for the soccer mom ruse about being bail bondswomen who were taking
him to Boston. But it would take her quite a while without
wheels. He grinned. Two, three days or so…if he was lucky.

He slept like a baby.

Sam didn't. With her cabby's meter running, she cased the
Samaritan Haven complex and located Hugo Zandski's apartment. No way to overhear what was going on in the joint, but
she felt pretty sure the happy crew inside would not be going
anywhere before the following morning. She waited until
Matt emerged and followed as he hid the shot-up GMC, then
followed him back to his digs in the complex. He looked as
beat as she felt.

"No rest for the wicked," she muttered to herself as he
climbed the stairs to his room. With Matt getting his beauty
sleep, she would have time to check on the arrival of her van.
If she couldn't use it, that would greatly complicate the
snatch. This was the most pain-in-the-ass assignment she'd
ever taken. Matt Granger was the most pain-in-the-ass retrieval she'd ever met, too. Also the best looking. *No, don't
go there.* That interlude in the motel was very unprofessional,
she chided herself.

But she couldn't help remembering how great they'd been
together in bed. And she couldn't help considering how much
better it would be if he had his hands free the next time. *No! No
next time.* This was business and if there was one thing Samantha Ballanger took seriously, it was business. She would collect her fee from his aunt, give the info on the Renkov case she'd
gathered to Pat and walk away. Let the Miami-Dade homicide
detectives and the FBI take it from there.

The Russian mob and Matt Granger would be out of her life. Odd, but somehow she realized that of the two, Matt was a lot more dangerous—at least to her. And once he found out the real reason she'd snatched him, he'd never want to see her again. Forcing herself not to think of that, she directed the waiting cabbie to take her to a small, dingy motel room nearby. She collapsed on the unmade bed after she set the alarm, then dozed off instantly.

Late the next morning, Matt was awakened by the jangling of his phone. Overturning the nightstand groggily, he reeled in the receiver and growled, "Granger here."

"Mr. Matthew Granger?" an officious female voice inquired.

He could hear voices, the swish of elevator doors and other clacking sounds in the background. Busy joint. "Yes. Who is this?"

"My name is Vivian Vitelli, Mr. Granger. I'm a nurse at Alvarado Medical Center. I'm calling for a Mr. Hugo Zandski. He gave me your number and insisted I phone you."

Matt sat bolt upright in bed. "He's a patient? What happened to him?"

"He was admitted to emergency about an hour ago with severe contusions, broken ribs and the fingers of his right hand have been…severely damaged. He appears to have been the victim of a vicious attack."

"Is he going to be all right?" *My God, where are Tess and Jenny and the kids!*

"He's an amazingly tough old gentleman, Mr. Granger. Kept saying something about Russians while they were sedating him to sew up the cuts and set the broken bones. He was in the Second World War," she added with youthful awe in her voice, apparently astounded that anyone from that era was still alive.

"I need to talk to him—it's an emergency." Matt held his breath.

"I'm afraid that's impossible right now. He's still in recovery. Amazing, but he wouldn't accept treatment until I practically swore a blood oath that I'd contact you."

Matt combed his fingers through his sleep-tousled hair and tried to unfog his mind. "I'm heading straight to the hospital. Give me directions." As he jotted down her instructions, his mind raced. The old guy had been tortured for information about Tess. This stunk of Renkov.

"Mr. Zandski should be out of the E.R. and waiting for admission to a room on a floor within an hour or two, although I wouldn't vouch for how coherent he'll be after the doctors give him pain meds."

Matt chuckled grimly. "Knowing Hugo, I'd bet my last buck they'll have to strap him to a gurney before he'll accept any more pain medication before he talks to me."

Matt was dressed and out of his room in the Samaritan Haven complex within five minutes. He raced down three flights of stairs rather than waiting for the antiquated elevator that ran strictly on whim—when it ran at all. He hit the pavement, checking both directions and seeing no one, then made a dash for his car, parked half a block down the street. He was just putting his key in the door lock when he felt a familiar pressure against his right kidney.

"Miss me, Matt, darling?"

He muttered an obscenity beneath his breath as he leaned his head on the car roof. "This can't be happening. How the hell—"

"How the hell did I escape your pals' neat little wrap job? It wasn't easy," she replied grimly. "Only took pounding my feet against the door until they were bloody stumps. And that was after I nearly brained myself falling twice. The maid heard me or else I'd still be sucking on a damned sock. That dump only has maid service three days a week. Lucky for me yesterday was my day."

"Today sure as hell isn't mine," he said with a sigh of resignation as she shoved him into the driver's seat and pulled open the rear door, taking her place behind him.

She stuck the stunner over the console and jammed in into his ribs. "Now, drive very carefully and make a left at the corner. Follow around the block to where my van is parked. You do remember my van, don't you? Just follow your nose. Have any idea how sitting for hours with the carpet marinating in strawberry Slurpee made it smell?"

"They locked the van and took your keys."

"Yeah. Real cute. But I always carry a spare set." She wasn't going to enlighten him about her little "hitchhike" in the back of Jenny's Yukon. "Get this hunk of junk revved up. And so help me God, if you try to pull anything, I'll scramble your antenna but good!"

He might have known she was that resourceful. Matt made a mental note not to make the mistake of underestimating Sam Ballanger again. "Look, Samantha, you have to listen to me. I was on my way to Alvarado Medical Center to see Hugo Zandski, a friend of Tess Renkov's. Seems her in-laws got to him last night and busted the old guy up pretty good—trying to find Tess and her son. The Miami cops are trying to pin a murder wrap on her and Renkov's goons may have captured—"

"Save it for Aunt Claudia, Matt." *Patty, I'm gonna kill you when I get back to Miami.* But only after she collected her fee and expenses from the Witherspoon broad, she reminded herself. "Ah, here we are. Pull over. There's a parking space right behind the van."

"How bloody convenient," he snarled in frustration, seriously considering ramming the cheesy hunk of tin. But there wasn't a soul on the street and in this neighborhood he knew damn well no one would call the police. Remembering what it felt like to wake up with a stun-gun hangover had a lot to do with his restraint, as well.

She hadn't been lying about the sickly sweet stench inside the van. It was nearly noon and the sun had raised the temperature inside the vehicle close to that of a fresh lava flow. "You can't expect me to lay in there!" he said in outrage. She'd spread a cheap plastic tarp over the ruined carpet.

"Don't see why not. You made the bloody mess."

Her voice sounded positively cheerful. She was enjoying this. "*I* made it! You kidnapped me, used a stunner on me and then tried to drown me in strawberry Slurpee—and now you blame *me!*"

"Slurpees under the bridge," she said sweetly. "Use the inhalator. Then you won't be able to smell it. I still have to stay awake and drive."

"Look, whoever's paying for this—I mean really paying for this—I'll get my aunt to pay you double. She's good for it. I have to talk to Hugo Zandski and find out who those goons are who're after Tess Renkov. This is a matter of life and death for a couple of innocent women and their kids." He tried to keep cool, to think. Who the hell could this dame be working for?

Sam knew he was telling the truth—at least as far as he knew it—but she did not show it. She prodded him with the stunner. "Be a good boy."

The inhalator lay by his hand. Her free hand—the one not jamming that infernal torture device in his kidney—was now grasping the seat of his jeans in a very strategic place. Seeing no way out at this juncture, he capitulated and picked up the inhalator, being careful to get as little as possible up his nostrils

Although he did better than the first time, it still wasn't good enough. The stuff hit him like the kick of a mule. Before he could get out a coherent expletive, she was hoisting his woozy body onto the sticky van floor. His last thought before drifting off was that he might asphyxiate before she made a pit stop. Considering how the last few days had gone, the thought held no genuine alarm. He almost giggled again.

Sam was worried. Her old partner had placed her smack in the middle of a turf war involving not only the Feds but the Ruskies, and now, if Granger was telling her the truth, Renkov's daughter-in-law and her family were in danger. Once she had Matt secured and was on the road, she made a phone call to Sergeant William Patowski, Miami-Dade Homicide.

"Yeah, now that you got your snatch all safe and sound, you give me what I need," he said as he jotted down Tess Renkov's cell number and the address at Samaritan Haven. "We'll get an agent over to the hospital for a little talk with this Zandski guy—if he's really there like your newsman says."

"Just make sure you get those women and their kids under protection before Mikhail Renkov's boys reach them," she countered.

"The APB on Renkov's widow was only a smoke screen to throw old Mikhail off track." Sergeant Will Patowski's voice sounded like he'd just swallowed a mouthful of gravel. That had more to do with his four-pack-a-day habit than a poor phone connection.

Sam held her cell away from her ear while he hacked up a lung, then asked, "How long until you wrap this thing up?" She had the CD player's rear speakers turned up in case Matt was alert enough to overhear her end of the conversation.

"Just gimme a few more days," Patowski said. "The New York Ruskies have been crowding Renkov's action here in

Miami. After they blew his kid into orbit, Mikhail had Pribluda's number-one boy in Miami whacked—Niki Benko. My officers and the fibbies are sweating his shooter even as we speak. We're gonna break up this whole nasty turf war and expose the CIA's darling Mikhail. The Company gets a black eye and Renkov goes up twenty to life for killing Benko. End of the Ruskie mob in Miami."

"Better make it quick. I don't want to be responsible for anything happening to Tess Renkov and her kid. And I don't want my tits in a wringer if your case goes south and my 'patient's' aunt comes after me. In Boston the Cabots may talk only to the Lodges and the Lodges only to God, but all of them bow to Claudia Witherspoon."

"Don't sweat it. Tess Renkov knows more than she's telling about the family business. That's another reason we've got that APB out on her."

"From what I overheard, I don't think so."

"Could've been feeding Granger a line. The fibbies will put her in a safe house 'til we nail her daddy-in-law. Find out what she really knows."

"I don't like seeing an innocent kid involved," Sam argued.

She could imagine Pat's fatalistic shrug as he replied, "Hey, the FBI can protect the kid. His mom married the mob. No one held a gun to her head at the altar. I seen the wedding pictures in the society pages of the *Herald*. Speaking of which, how's your newsman holding out?"

"He'll live safely if not happily ever after. His aunt wants him on ice. She gets what she wants. So do you." But what about what Sam Ballanger wanted? Even if he walked out on his aunt when this was over and returned to Miami, Sam knew the odds of her seeing Matt Granger again were long. *What the hell did you expect for ten K? A stroll down the Miracle Mile?*

No turning back now, not after all she had invested in this caper. Let Pat's FBI buddies locate Tess Renkov and her family. The only thing she could do was beat feet to Boston and collect her money from Aunt Claudia. Maybe by that time the whole mess would be over and Mikhail Renkov cooling his heels in jail.

Sam glanced uneasily into the rearview mirror. No one following...that she could spot. From here on out, she'd be super careful. No more surprises from crazy soccer moms flashing guns and for sure, no Slavic-looking types were coming within fifty yards of her and Matt Granger.

Insidiously, the thought hit her. Once this whole mess was straightened out, she could collect her money from Aunt Claudia, then kidnap Matt for herself... *Think of something else, Ballanger.* Like how long it would be until Miami-Dade Homicide had Mikhail Renkov wrapped up with a sweet pink bow tied around his rotten ass.

One thing she'd put money on: The CIA wouldn't get his collar away from Patowski unless the president himself called and demanded it. "Nah. Not even then." She remembered how pissed Pat had been over the 2000 election results in Florida.

Sam kept her eyes on the rearview more than usual that afternoon. A big old '89 Lincoln dripping with chrome kept pace about a half-dozen cars back on the busy interstate. She slowed, letting the rest of the cars pass, but the Lincoln never did. "Probably just some little old lady from Pasadena," she muttered to herself, pulling off the road into a rest stop. But if she remembered the Beach Boys' lyrics, that gal burned rubber.

Much to her relief the Lincoln drove serenely on. Its windows were tinted so she couldn't see inside. Not all that unusual out here in the desert...or in the intense Miami heat. The

car had Florida plates. "Shit, I'm getting as paranoid as Matt."
He started kicking the van door again. Speak of the devil....
A good thing the area was deserted. The racket sounded worse
than some creature from the Book of Revelation trying to
break out of confinement. Remembering her ordeal with the
motel door yesterday, she wasn't all that inclined to rush.
Then again, what if he had to take a whiz? Cooped up lying
on that sticky carpet might make him feel he had nothing to
lose. Still watchful of the black Lincoln, she pulled off the
road and unlocked the van doors.

"Okay, Matt, darling. Time for a potty break?"

He tried his best to scowl through the damned bandages,
knowing so little of his face was visible that it was useless.
Damn this pigheaded female. How the hell was he going to
get away from her? Maybe tonight a loose piece of plumbing? Nah, too much to ask. She helped him climb out of the
van and stand between the doors, then unzipped his fly. As
her agile fingers aided him in conducting his business, he fu-
riously mumbled curses through the surgical tape.

*Samantha Ballanger, you will pay for this. And so will that
old battle-ax Claudia. I swear it.*

It was well past dark and Sam was exhausted when she
pulled off the road. God, it seemed like she'd been driving up
and down Interstate 15 for at least seven years. Her head
pounded as if one of the Three Stooges had just applied his
mallet to it. Still keeping her gritty eyes peeled for that black
Lincoln, she drove toward a flashing neon sign with over half
the bulbs burned out. Instead of STRATFORD LODGE, the
lights read RAT OR   LO G.

Just the sort of joint she was looking for. No one driving
a Lincoln would be caught dead here. Now if only she and
Matt weren't. Other than blowing smoke from an unfiltered

Camel in Sam's face, the blue-haired harridan behind the check-in desk barely glanced at what was probably her only customer of the night. Within minutes Sam had Matt inside the room.

He stumbled over a chair, still mummy-wrapped and barely able to keep his balance when Sam released him. "Stand still. I gotta check something out."

Matt could hear her shut the door and vanish outside. Great. Here he was utterly helpless and she had to run off on some fool errand. The door was directly behind him. Maybe he could... He'd heard the lock click shut as she left. Then again, maybe he couldn't. Of course, he still had his feet free, but somehow the idea of kicking his way out of the room while straitjacketed, blindfolded and unable to utter an intelligible sound seemed an implausible plan.

There was always the gooseneck pipe, he thought wistfully as Sam returned. Without a word, she guided him to sit down on the bed so she could begin the process of de-mummifying him for the night. She was going out of her way to act impersonal, as if their little interlude in the shower the other night hadn't happened. Damn if he'd let her off the hook on that one. She felt guilty. Good. Maybe he could figure some way to use that.

Sam could see that he had the drill down now. Once she freed him from the jacket, he reached up to take off the bandages, tape and blindfold. By then she stood well out of reach with her stunner trained on him, dangling the cuffs. She tossed them to him wordlessly, motioning for him to go into the bathroom.

"You think the silent treatment will work, huh?"

"What silent treatment?" she replied, preoccupied by what she thought she'd spotted outside.

Matt knew this was more than just embarrassment over

their having sex. He could see her eyes flicking toward a broken slat on the window blinds. A nasty feeling started crawling around in his gut. "You've seen someone following us? These boys don't play nice, Samantha. We could both end up dead. What they did to Hugo Zandski wasn't pretty."

Sam wondered what the fibbies had found out when they talked to Zandski, but all she said was, "More conspiracy theories, Mr. Granger?"

"What happened to 'Matt, darling'?" he asked, grinning in spite of their predicament.

"You know the drill. Click the cuff to the drainpipe." Now her full concentration was back on him. She had to put him on ice, then check on that Lincoln. This wasn't looking good. She knew Matt would figure something hinky was going on, but right now she had more on her mind than reassuring him. Especially when she needed reassurance herself.

Dutifully, he went into the moldy bathroom and did as she commanded. The instant she heard the click of the cuff around the pipe, Sam stepped inside the room with him and slammed the door. He watched, amazed and more than a little bit scared shitless, as she cranked open the rusty window behind the toilet and climbed outside, saying tersely, "Stay quiet if you want to stay alive."

That's when he saw the .38 she'd withdrawn from her fanny pack. Things were definitely not looking good. "You need my help, Sam," he protested. She only shushed him, then vanished into the darkness. Frantically, his heart thudding in his throat, Matt began twisting the pipe.

Chapter 9

Sam slipped around the side of the building, hugging the wall in the darkness. Since she'd followed her usual pattern and taken the end-row unit, the hike wasn't long. Peering carefully around the corner, she saw two thuggish-looking types standing in front of the door. They actually wore sharkskin double-breasted suits and snap-brim hats.

Retro gangster! She'd have laughed out loud if their craggy faces hadn't looked cold and mean as a Russian winter. One gunsel was attempting to look through the broken blind into the darkened room while the other kept a lookout for any curious soul who might chance to wonder what they were doing.

No danger of that since her Econoline was the only car on the lot, standing out like a white elephant under the mercury vapor light at the edge of the Tarmac. Luckily that light had also bounced off the oversize chrome bumper on the Town

Car. She could see it more clearly now. It had been well concealed behind a clump of cottonwoods dividing the motel lot from that of a dry-cleaning establishment next door.

Sam sized them up. She was sure both were armed although only the stocky one had his piece in his hand while his taller companion fiddled with the door lock. They were on the shady side of forty and overly fond of their vodka by the looks of their swag guts. But big-boned heavyset men could take a lot of punishment and still keep coming.

Pat, I hope Uncle Declan beats you to paste at my funeral.

Sam waited until the lookout turned his back to her. Seizing the instant, she jumped him, .38 in her right hand and the stun gun in her left. She shoved the stunner in his gun arm and squeezed. His Glock dropped from nerveless fingers. He grunted an oath and thrashed around, facing her just in time to receive another blast in the gut. His companion, who had by that time succeeded in opening the door, turned just as the shorter guy tumbled into him en route to the pavement.

The tall fellow was knocked against the door frame, trying to jerk a .45 from his shoulder holster. "Uh-uh," she said, shaking her head as her .38 pointed perilously close to his nose. "Drop the piece with your left hand—slowly, very slowly." When he hesitated she wondered how the hell to say it in Russian.

That's it. I'm finished.

But then he complied. Breathing a silent sigh of relief, she scooped up both guns and stuck them into her fanny pack where she'd dropped the stunner, then motioned for him to back through the door into the room. "Sit down on the bed," she instructed, feeling in control now.

Sam waited until he did as ordered, then moved into the room. "With your pal there down for the count, you and me are gonna have a little talk, Ivan. What say?"

He stared at her with eyes like two pale gray marbles, his thin mouth a stubborn slash set under a bulbous red-veined nose. "*Nyet*" sounded very final.

What? Had she expected this to be easy? The turkey probably understood and spoke English but wasn't talking…at least not yet. Knowing his companion would be coming around sooner or later, she dug in her fanny pack and came up with a spare pair of cuffs. First things first. "All righty then. If you don't wanna have a chat, I assume you're familiar with these," she said, dangling the cuffs. "Put one on your right hand and click the other to that table leg."

She tossed the cuffs on the bed beside him. Again he hesitated as those unnerving gray marbles rolled in his head, studying the room, gauging his chances. Then he picked up the cuffs and clicked one over a brawny wrist, scooting glacially toward a wall writing table that looked as battle scarred as he was. Just as Sam was about to exhale, the bathroom door swung open and Matt emerged, brandishing a gooseneck pipe as he yelled, "Behind you, Sam!"

The stocky guy tackled her just as she turned and they went down in a tangle of arms and legs. Her .38 skidded beneath a bed as both of them thrashed around while struggling to reach the cache of guns inside her fanny pack. Ignoring the cuff on his wrist, the taller thug took a swing at Granger. And missed.

Grinning like a crazed chimpanzee who'd just peed into a Sunday crowd at the zoo, Matt swung the pipe with all the frustration built up over the past four days. It connected solidly with the side of his opponent's head, dropping him instantly. A good thing since his pal had just succeeded in getting his paw over the .45 in Sam's pack. Without breaking stride, Matt turned and swung his weapon down, whacking the back of the thug's thick neck so hard they probably heard his vertebra popping in the next county.

Sam crawled out from beneath the bruiser, who out-
weighed her by an easy hundred and fifty pounds. She struggled to catch her breath while scrambling across the floor to
retrieve her .38 from beneath the bed. As she climbed onto
the saggy mattress and sat panting, she looked down at the
guy she'd stunned outside and shook her head. "I gave him a
direct shot in the gut. All that body fat must've absorbed the
shock," she said, looking up at Matt's lean torso—and stiff-
ening in shock.

He held the big Russian's .45 in one hand, the pipe in the
other. Now his grin focused on her, shifting ever so subtly.
He looked like a German shepherd eyeing a juicy hunk of
steak. "I've been fantasizing about this for days…"

He paused and licked his lips, then glanced at the men on
the floor. "First things first. Toss your gun down, Samantha,
darling. You have to believe my 'conspiracy theories' now,
don't you? And no shit about Aunt Claudia."

Knowing there was little point in carrying on the charade,
she did as he asked. "Yeah. I suppose so." She waited, wondering what he was going to do after he closed the motel door
and relocked it.

"Let's secure these guys and then play twenty questions.
Oh, I'll need that stunner." He motioned to her pack. "Just lay
it on the bed and scoot away."

Sam eyed him uneasily. He wasn't crazy but he sure as hell
was pissed and, she admitted, had every right to be. She'd
badly misjudged the situation and endangered both their lives.

He sighed. "Much as it would serve you right, I don't intend to use the stunner on you."

Sam looked down at the two sprawled, unconscious bodies of the Russian mobsters. She unfastened the fanny pack
and laid it on the bed, moving away. "Okay, twenty questions
with the stun gun. I thought of it, too. Great minds run along

the same course," she said with a cheeky grin. "That was my plan...before things got out of hand."

He snorted. "Looked to me like that goon had things pretty well in hand—a .45 caliber Smith & Wesson." He glanced down at the gun he had taken from the unconscious Russian, then stuffed it into his belt and reached for the stunner.

"You know guns?" she asked.

"Four years in the Army. Don't look so surprised," he said, remembering her comments about being a cop back in Miami. "Help me drag the tall fellow onto that chair."

As they worked at the arduous task, Sam couldn't resist asking, "Why would a rich preppy type join the military—is ROTC a college requirement if your family landed on Plymouth Rock?"

Matt shrugged after depositing the goon on the chair. "Nope. I enlisted. To piss off my family."

Sam grinned. "Bet it worked."

Not wanting to discuss his family's quirks—or his own—he looked at their Russian captive slumped on the chair. "I don't think he's going to come around anytime soon."

"Don't be too sure of that. It's what I thought about the fat one. They must be tough as fried round steak," she said, trying not to shudder as she recalled the mobster's sweaty body pressing the breath from her while he pinned her beneath her. He stank of cabbage and garlic.

As she secured his companion with the straitjacket, Matt said, "If I'm going to intimidate Russian mobsters, I think it'd work better without the robe and slippers." She had little choice so she didn't argue. He went out to the van and retrieved his clothes.

By the time Granger had dressed, the tall goon was groaning his way back to consciousness. Meanwhile, Sam had cuffed his companion's wrist to the bed frame and left him lying on the floor.

"Let's take a look at their ID," Matt said, quickly going through both men's jackets and removing their wallets. "Nice tailor, guys," he commented as he tossed the heavy suit coats on the bed.

"Whaddya wanna bet they're from Miami?" Sam interjected, checking the label on one smelly jacket.

"Wouldn't bet against it," Matt replied, flipping open the unconscious one's wallet. "Yep. Florida driver's license. Yuri Garzenko, Coconut Grove." He opened the other. "Vassily Kuzan, Bal Harbor."

"The addresses don't fit with the tailoring," she commented. "Bet they're phony."

As he riffled through other materials, he grunted agreement. "Probably, but I wouldn't be surprised if their boss lives in a high-rent district." No photos or personal mementos, just a big wad of cash and an Allstate insurance card. He looked over at Sam, showing her the cash.

"Enough to pay my rent for a year," she replied.

Matt gave her a quizzical look. "Where do you live—Liberty City?"

She gave him a cutting glare. "On NE 110th just off Biscayne. I wasn't born with a silver spoon in my mouth like some people I know."

"Or a brain in your head. A woman alone—"

"I know how to take care of myself," she interrupted.

"Yeah, I could see that," he replied wryly, then turned back to business. "Now, give me that key." She complied and he removed the cuff from his hand, then turned his attention to the gunsel slumped in the chair.

"You stand behind him and be ready to do your version of the Vulcan nerve pinch if he tries to squirm too much." He paused as she walked behind the prisoner, making sure the guy was coherent enough to understand. "After all, having that much voltage flowing through his cock and balls might make him just the tiniest bit twitchy."

The Russian was either a damn good actor or just naturally stoic. Given the world the man had come from, Matt didn't doubt he'd be a lot tougher than your average Jersey leg-breaker. What the hell did old Vassily have to lose? He'd find out soon enough once Matt zapped him in the nuts with the stun gun. Leveling a hard stare directly into the mobster's expressionless gray eyes, Granger showed him the stunner.

"You know what one of these babies can do? Now your pal over there—" he jerked his head in the direction of the still-unconscious man lying on the floor "—he could give you a real vivid description. I'd bet on it, and my friend didn't even use it anyplace strategic."

Matt paused to see if this was sinking in. No dice. "I know you're the bastards who beat Hugo Zandski—tortured an old man so he'd tell you where two women and their kids were. How long'd you work on him before you figured out he wasn't going to talk? You leave him for dead or did somebody interrupt you before you could finish him? Believe me, even if he knew, he'd die before he'd let you kill them." He watched the thug's eyes, praying his faith in Hugo wasn't misplaced.

The Russian just returned his stare without a trace of emotion.

"If their bodies turn up, I will personally see that you get murder one. I have friends in the San Diego D.A.'s office. You'll be so deep in the gulag they'll be feeding you with a slingshot." He was almost sure these apes wouldn't have had time to get rid of the women and kids and then follow him. But what if he was wrong?

"Did you find Tess Renkov?" Still no dice. Matt placed the

stunner on the outside of Vassily's thigh, then gave him a short blast. Kuzan yelped and writhed inside the straitjacket, his whole face now as red as his nose. Sam kept one hand on his neck and when he tried to lunge up at Matt she applied pressure to just the right spot. That slowed him down—combined with the stunner which now was jammed in his right nostril.

When he settled back in the chair, Matt lowered the stunner to his crotch. "Now we go down and dirty, Vassily, my friend." He looked into Kuzan's eyes and read emotion for the first time. Stark terror. "Do I have to repeat the question?"

"*Nyet!* Old man tells us nothing. Woman and boy are gone. Then she—" Vassily glared at Sam "—she takes you away before we can get you. So, we follow."

Matt was inclined to believe him. Maybe it was wishful thinking, but it made sense. Now that he had the men who put Hugo in the hospital, the women should be safe for a little while.

"Okay. Who sent you after Tess?"

"Is difficult…you will not believe…" Kuzan's voice faded and he shivered.

Matt jammed the stunner into Vassily's crotch with enough pressure to elicit a sharp intake of breath. "Talk or howl, my friend. Up to you."

"*Da, da,* I talk! I talk." Staring in horror at the stunner, which was strategically placed to shatter his family jewels, Kuzan looked as if he'd either faint or toss his cookies. "Yuri and I, we are hired by someone we do not know—I swear it on my mother's grave!"

"Funny, but that tough old man you worked over said a Russian would lie on his mother's grave."

Sam applied pressure to the nerve cluster at the base of their captive's jaw. "I don't think you had a mother, ace. Wadda you think, Matt? Did this lizard hatch or crawl out from under a rock?"

"Personally, I'd vote for the rock," Granger replied as Yuri groaned, once more, incredibly regaining consciousness. "His associate for sure is made of stone." He turned his attention back to Vassily Kuzan. "Let's go over this again. How could someone hire you without you knowing them?"

"We never meet person who pays. Only a voice over phone. We do not know who," he entreated, those marble-cold eyes bulging out, his expression desperate.

"You freelancing for somebody local, Vassily? Too afraid of him to talk?" Matt taunted, jiggling the stunner between his captive's thighs.

"If I were you, I'd be more afraid of this guy," Sam said with an evil grin.

The gunsel's eyes were glued to the weapon held against his crotch. Taking a deep breath he plunged in. "We work for Valentin Pribluda's man in Miami, Niki Benko. Renkov has him killed. We have no boss. Then Yuri gets phone call saying we will be paid to get rid of Renkov's daughter-in-law and her son. Money is good."

"Kill the kid, too!" Sam was aghast.

Kuzan nodded, suddenly realizing he may have made a blunder.

"For sure it's not Mikhail. He'd never kill his only grandson," Matt said.

"*If* this goon's telling the truth," Sam replied. Her eyes were hard as glass when she looked at a man willing to kill a mother and child. "Who else would want Tess and her son dead?"

"Pribluda in New York?" Matt speculated. "It'd sure as hell send a message to Renkov for offing Benko in Miami."

Sam shook her head. "I'm Irish, remember? Trust me on the vengeance thing. We do it as good as the Russians. Killing his grandson would set Mikhail Renkov out for blood.

He'd declare full-scale war from Miami to Little Odessa in Brighton Beach." She looked at Kuzan. "My people and yours have long memories."

Kuzan nodded. "*Da,* but Renkov, he already opens the war. He kills Benko. Maybe is Pribluda after Renkov's family." He nodded, happy with his answer.

"What do you know about Alexi Renkov going 'boom'?" Matt asked.

The Russian looked blank.

Shrugging, Matt pressed the gun hard against Kuzan's sausage. "Trying to suck it up into your body won't work, you know," he said conversationally, starting to press the trigger.

"All right!" the Russian gasped. "I tell you rumors. Maybe true...maybe not."

"Smart man." He withdrew the stunner a few inches and asked, "What about Alexi?"

"P-Pribluda. Maybe he tells Benko, kill Alexi."

"But Benko was already dead, right?" Matt asked logically.

The Russian nodded dumbly. "Old Mikhail hears this and kills Benko first," he suggested hopefully.

"Good mob reasoning," Sam said.

"Did you set that car bomb?" Matt asked Kuzan.

The Russian shook his head no. "We do not know bombs."

"I believe him. These goons couldn't set an alarm clock without help," Sam said.

"Why kill Alexi or his wife and kid? Why not hit Mikhail if Benko's New York bosses wanted to take over Miami?" Again, Matt applied more pressure with the stunner. "Was that bomb really intended for Alexi or for his wife?"

Kuzan's thought processes were obviously not exactly swift. "I do not know...only..."

"Yeah?" Granger prompted.

"Benko hears rumors before he is died. That Mikhail's son tries to make deals for weapons. From Kazakhstan."

"Now we may be onto why Alexi was wasted, but it doesn't explain who'd be after Tess and their son," Matt said.

Changing tack, Sam asked, "Tell us more about Alexi's deals. If you and Yuri weren't the guys who offed him, who was? We'll sort through rumors," she added with a sarcastic smirk.

The Russian shrugged inside the straitjacket helplessly. "Lots of weapons, bombs in old Soviet countries for sale. Maybe when he travels for golf, he sets up deal for nuclear device."

"In Kazakhstan?" Matt prompted.

"Is all we hear. Know nothing about how he is died. We are to kill wife, son. Is all we know."

"And how did rocket scientists like you track down Tess Renkov?" Sam inquired, already anticipating the answer and exchanging a knowing look with Granger.

"We follow you from Miami," Kuzan mumbled, looking worriedly at Matt.

"And you never imagined it's your dead boss's boss who hired you until now?"

The expression in the Russian's eyes now was a combination of utter confusion blended with fear. Sweat ran down his face in rivers, soaking his whole body, even through the straitjacket. The room stank of it.

"Use these to lock him to the other bed, well away from his pal," Matt said, tossing the cuffs he'd taken off to Sam. "Let's adjourn for some fresh air and think things over." He picked up her fanny pack, stuffed the stunner and her .38 inside, then opened the door, waiting while she did as he instructed. It felt good to be in command for a change.

"You believe him?" Sam asked once they were outside.

Matt shrugged. "He's scared shitless. And, Lord knows, he's dumb enough to take a job by phone and not have a clue who hired him. The part about Alexi and arms sales is interesting, though. I need to talk to Tess. First to be sure she's all right. Then to see if she can corroborate any of Vassily's story."

"I'd say Vassily made it up but he doesn't have enough imagination," Sam replied.

"What'd you do with my cell?"

"It's in the van."

He scrutinized her, an unreadable expression on his face. "Can I trust you not to try anything, Sam? No bullshit now."

"Hey, I just got a demonstration that proved you aren't paranoid, remember? Of course you can trust me." She wasn't crossing her fingers behind her back, but she felt as if she should. How the hell could she explain about Patowski and the Feds? Darling Matthew would wring her neck—or use her own stunner on her. But on the other hand, how could she let go of ten K? She had a lot invested in this enterprise already. Not all of it was material, but Sam wasn't going there right now. The time to sort out her feelings about the sexy Mr. Granger was later.

"Let me dig the phone out of the van for you. You have Tess Renkov's number programmed in?" She knew it, but she wasn't about to tell him that.

He still didn't trust her, but what the hell could he do? Muttering, "Keep your friends close but your enemies even closer," he strolled after her, watching as she unlocked the van and dug around in the backseat until she came up with the cell she'd relieved him of that morning. She handed it to him, then waited. He pressed a speed-dial number, praying. "Pick up, please, Tess."

After two rings Tess answered and Matt began to breathe again.

Sam wanted to eavesdrop, but he placed his hand over the mouthpiece and said to her, "Go inside and check on our boys. I'll be right with you." It wasn't a request. And he had all the guns. Grudgingly, she complied.

In moments he called her back outside. "I told Tess about Hugo. She's calling the hospital to make sure he's okay and tell him they're safe."

"Yeah, I guess you were worried about the guy—now that I know your story's legit," she admitted grudgingly. "What's she say about Alexi?"

"Tess doesn't know jack about Alexi dealing black market arms, but agreed it was the kind of risk he'd get off on. Seems our playboy liked skating on the edge."

"He skated over the edge big-time," she said.

"Tess is still convinced that old Mikhail intended to kill her from the minute she started talking divorce. Didn't want to lose his grandson. She still thinks Alexi's death was an accident because he was driving the car she'd been using."

"Then Pribluda and the Brighton Beach crowd aren't involved." She sounded skeptical. "I don't trust our Ruskie goons, but I can't believe a dim bulb like Vassily could think up those 'rumors' on his own."

Matt scratched his head. "Good point. None of this adds up. Let's take a look-see at our boys' wheels," he said, holding up the keys he'd taken from Yuri's jacket.

Sam led the way through the cottonwood thicket to the big Town Car. They searched it thoroughly, but as they did, Sam was careful not to leave her prints. They were still on file from her days as a Miami-Dade cop and that was one can of worms she for sure didn't want opened. "Zilch," she said in disgust, tossing an empty pack of short Camels onto the pile of junk-food wrappers and other debris littering the backseat floor of the luxury sedan.

"Kinda renews your faith in the power of American mer chandising, doesn't it?" Matt said with a grimace, dropping a bag filled with soggy French fries. Then he suddenly reached down and fished out a grease-stained carryout menu "What have we here, hmm?"

"That looks familiar. Joe's Catch 'O the Day. It's a dine on Palm, right next to Hialeah. You suppose our boys like to play the ponies?" she asked.

"For a dame from Boston, you sure seem to know a lo about Miami," Matt said suspiciously.

Sam shrugged. No use fibbing on that one. "I was raise in Boston, but I moved to Miami after dropping out of col lege."

"Then how'd Aunt Claudia find you?" Now his radar wa on full alert.

Dammit! She thought fast. "A referral. Happens all th time in my business. Believe it or not, I do have friends a over the country, especially in my hometown. Benny Hilton he's a Beacon Hill shrink now, but he went to school with m in south Boston. He set me up with your aunt."

Matt didn't look entirely convinced, but chuckled hu morlessly. "He should have set you up with another shrin in Miami."

"Real funny, Granger. What are you thinking about Joe' place? A lead?" she asked, trying to divert him.

"Could be. A pair like those bozos, somebody might re member. Speaking of them, we have to get them off ou backs. If we leave them in the motel sooner or later they' find someone to release them."

"I have an idea," Sam said with a grin. "Just leave every thing to me."

He followed her back inside with a dubious expression o his face. *After I get rid of them, what the hell am I going t do about you, darling Samantha?* The first thing he had to do after disposing of the thugs was to call Aunt Claudia and get her "retrieval specialist" off his back. He might learn a few things about who sicced Sam on him from his aunt while he was at it.

"First of all, we'll have to take the jacket off Kuzan, the cuffs off Garzenko, then tie them up good. I have tape in the van."

"How well I remember," he replied with a grimace.

She dashed out and retrieved the tape. By this time Yuri was grunting in pain, fully conscious. He glared at them and his cohort in the straitjacket with equal venom. "Something tells me Mr. Garzenko here might not have been as talkative as his pal," she said as Matt held Kuzan's gun on the thug. With professional dispatch she quickly trussed him up and secured him to one of the beds.

Granger scoffed. "He may think so, but he was never threatened with a shot in the nuts from a stunner."

"If you'd done it, you might've killed Kuzan. Looks like he's overly fond of vodka. Could have a bum ticker." Sam studied Vassily's paunchy midsection as she unfastened the straitjacket. "Would you have risked it?"

He grinned sharkishly. "They'll never know now, will they? Neither will you."

"Matthew Granger, International Man of Mystery," she muttered while she tied up Kuzan on the other bed. "We have to leave their guns here in the room. And make sure their prints are on them."

"Why?" The moment he asked the question, he had an inkling of the answer. "Devious Samantha," he said with a chuckle, shaking his head. He cleaned their prints off the weapons, then fit each man's gun in his hand so his prints would be clear on it. While Sam dialed the local cops, he placed the guns carefully on the table beside the window. It was quite a treat watching her work.

"Officer, this is Miss Edna Jean Cather. I want to report an assault." Her hoarse, breathless voice half convinced Matt she was some terrified, helpless old lady as she spun her tale. "Two big foreigners attacked me. Why, I don't know whatever would have happened to me if three nice young American gentlemen in a pickup truck hadn't come to my assistance. They're tying up those awful miscreants... Where? Oh, I'm calling from the Stratford Lodge just off the highway...yes, that's the place. Room twelve. Please hurry."

She put down the phone. "Do I get an Oscar?"

He shrugged. "An Emmy might be more appropriate," he said, glancing at the battered fifteen-inch television set chained to the wall.

"We'd better get the hell out of Dodge before Deputy Dawg comes rolling in and starts asking questions we don't want to answer," she replied, miffed at his lack of appreciation for her skill.

"What if the desk clerk gives the Highway Patrol your van plate number?"

Sam grinned. "Who says I gave the right numbers at the desk? These kinds of places for sure never check."

Matt was forced to nod in grudging approval. Damn, this dame was slick.

Chapter 10

As they cleaned up all traces of their presence in the room, Sam said, "Let's just hope the local gendarmes are sharp enough to check these guys for wants and warrants."

"They must have records. Guns are a definite no-no, even if these guys are tied up and the good people who reported them aren't here to contradict whatever story they concoct." Matt eyed Yuri and Vassily with grim amusement. "Think fast, you silver-tongued devils."

"Rehearsing your lines is gonna be a bitch gagged the way you are," she added cheerfully before closing the door to room twelve.

Sam drove and Matt took the passenger seat. They passed the county sheriff's cruiser just before they pulled onto the highway. Matt kept her fanny pack with the .38 and the stunner, just in case she got any funny ideas about trying to haul him off to his aunt again. "We have to talk, Samantha.

Seriously. My aunt really hired you to drag me back to Boston?"

His eyes bored into hers and she could see he held his cell phone in hand, no doubt ready to call dear Claudia and verify her story. Well, that would check out. But how the devil was she going to play this now that Pat's whole scheme had gone south? "Yep," she said, keeping her eyes on the road. "Give her a call and see if she didn't."

He looked skeptical as he dialed the cell and waited until the familiar voice of his aunt's social secretary came on the line. "Grace, this is Matt. I need to talk to her. It's urgent."

Sam waited anxiously as he and his aunt argued, something she gathered they did with regularity. She could only hear his side, of course, but it appeared that the conversation would end in her favor.

"I'm as sane as you are—no, scratch that. You've always been a head case... Yes, I think you were set up, too... My editor's name is Manny. He'd take it real bad if you accused him of wearing a dress... I already told you, the Renkov story is my ticket to a Pulitzer and I'm not quitting...."

There was a long pause on Matt's end of the cell as his aunt talked. A sudden idea came to her. Claudia Witherspoon was supposed to be sharp in spite of her advanced age. What if she just wanted Matt out of the Renkov investigation because he'd be in danger? She could've called the FBI. Possible. Or maybe when they told her Matt had joined a cult, she just played along. For all Sam knew, the director himself might have approached Claudia with this deal. Sam smiled inwardly. Then Matt started speaking again.

"Yes, I'll be careful.... Yeah, she did...twice..." Grudgingly, he said, "I guess. Look, I'm going to fly home...no, no Boston, dammit! Miami where I've lived ever since I got out of the Army.... Yes, I promise...."

Finally, he broke the connection and turned to her. He didn't look ready to throttle her. That was a good sign. "Well, what'd she say?"

"It seems a woman posing as the news editor at the *Herald* called her, all worried about me. Said I'd dropped off the face of the earth a couple of weeks ago after being sent out on an assignment to cover a cult in San Diego. She convinced Claudia that I'd been brainwashed into joining and wasn't coming back. Told her that I'd quit my job and said I sounded as if I was on drugs."

"That's pretty much what she told me when she hired me," Sam said, which strictly speaking was true. Pat had been her old mentor when she was a cop, but he knew she didn't work for free. He'd set this up with the FBI somehow so Claudia would pay Sam to keep Matt from stirring things up before the FBI and the Miami cops busted the Renkov mob. "I did some digging around San Diego and located you without much trouble."

"So did those goons who followed me." He was in over his head but damn if he'd admit it to Sam Ballanger. "They could've killed Tess Renkov."

"Yeah, but they didn't. She's in the clear for now and so are we. Question is, what are we going to do next?"

"We, Kemo-Sabe?" He cocked an eyebrow at her. "Sorry as hell, Sammie baby, but you aren't getting the ten K from my aunt. She understands I'm not going to sit this one out in Boston."

"Okay, what *are* you going to do? Go after Mikhail Renkov?" She paused, then answered her question before he could. "You buy Tess's story enough to beard her father-in-law in Miami? That really *is* nuts, Granger. You'd end up fish bait off the keys inside an hour. I know how dangerous the Russian mob in Miami is."

"Do you now? It seems like a hell of a coincidence, you're getting a referral to handle a case originating in Boston, and my aunt, who's nobody's fool, being hoodwinked by Miami mobsters and used as a cat's paw. Why didn't they just kill me and be done with it? This whole mess stinks like Jose Samora's bait shack."

"But you're going to get to the bottom of it, I know." Sam nodded, pulling off the highway as they approached an exit on the outskirts of Vegas. "Why not stop and get something to eat, then talk about this?" She'd had an idea percolating in her mind ever since he dialed Boston. Bold as brass but it just might work. She'd done the math and knew her expenses for this caper were way too high for her to throw in the towel without a fight.

He studied her with a speculative look in his eyes. She knew more than she was telling him. No way was he trusting her, but could he afford to turn her loose? "I'm taking the next flight I can book from Vegas to Miami." He waited for her response.

"Suit yourself." She shrugged, turning the wheel and making a right onto a street glowing with a mixture of cheap casinos and bars. The world was neon in Vegas. Even the wedding chapels had blinking signs advertising their wares. Bypassing one she chose a Denny's next door and pulled into the parking lot. "Steak and fries for me—and a large pot of coffee. How about you?"

He was so tired superglue wouldn't have held his eyelids open much longer. An injection of caffeine was a good idea. It also might help him think this whole mess through. A lot was riding on how he handled things, including the lives of innocent women and children. And just maybe even Sam Ballanger's. But he'd bet a Pulitzer she wasn't as innocent as she claimed. "Coffee sounds good," he said as he locked the guns in the glove compartment and pocketed both sets of her keys for the van. He considered frisking her for a third, but realized that might lead to hormonal complications he didn't have time to deal with right now...or ever.

Once seated in a booth at the rear of the crowded restaurant, Sam ordered a twelve-ounce filet, loaded potato skins, a large caesar salad and a wedge of pecan pie to go with the coffee. Matt looked over at the small, trim woman and shook his head. "How the hell do you eat like a stevedore and stay so slim?"

"Wrestling crazy people burns calories like you wouldn't believe," she said, handing the waitress her menu.

Matt suddenly realized he was ravenously hungry, too. "I'll have the porterhouse and a baked potato, house salad and..." He perused the desserts, then selected the cheesecake. "Hurry that coffee along, could you?"

The waitress, an emaciated woman with olive skin and silver-blond hair gone black at the roots nodded tiredly and shuffled off, calling out the orders in a cigarette-roughened voice as she went.

"Hold my seat while I visit the ladies' room," Sam said, starting to slide out of the bench.

He reached out and took hold of her wrist. "Are you sure that's all you're going to do?"

She tsked at him. "You have the van keys, Matt. And a clear view of it through the window. Besides, I thought you wanted to ditch me."

"Maybe, but not until we get some things settled."

With a swift flick of her wrist against his thumb, she was free, walking calmly across the floor to the restrooms. Before he could debate what to do, his cell rang and he picked it up. Tess Renkov's voice on the other end made the decision for him. He leaned back against the seat and said, "Is everything okay?"

"Just checking in as ordered," Tess replied, trying to keep the stress from her voice. "Hugo's going to be all right. He refused any pain meds until he heard from me after you didn't call. I explained why."

"That's good," Matt replied. "You all set up?"

"We've found a small place in an isolated area where we should be secure for a few days. What are you going to do about those men...the Russians?" she added, whispering now.

Matt grinned. "I don't think they'll be bothering anyone for quite a while. Sam Ballanger took care of them."

"Do you think you can trust her?"

Good question. "Jury's still out on that one," he said as he watched the subject of their conversation wend her way across the room. "Keep checking in. I'm on the way to Miami to follow up on some leads."

While Matt was on his cell, Sam ducked into the alcove beside the restrooms where the pay phones were and placed a call to Pat. She quickly filled him in on Kuzan and Garzenko, explaining the jurisdiction where they'd presently be residing. "Figured you might want to tip the local fibbies to pay a call. Oh, yeah, they parked their wheels in the dry cleaner's lot next door to the Stratford Lodge. Big black Town Car they can examine, too. Maybe if the fibbies pull rank on the local gendarmes, they can sweat more out of them than we had time for. Pair of tough bozos. Too bad the Bureau doesn't issue stunners."

"Yeah," Pat said in his gravelly voice. "From what we've seen of Renkov and his New York counterparts, it might take a jolt or two in the nuts to help refresh their memories. But since this is all pretty hush-hush, maybe they can be a little creative after they relieve the locals of their prizes and go over that Lincoln. Thanks for the tip, Sam."

"Just remember, you owe me, Pat. Big-time. I'm running up a fortune on my phone card."

He gave a rusty laugh. "Oh, I have faith you'll get 'her ladyship' to cough up for every last dime."

After signing off, she dialed another long-distance number...in Boston.

By the time she returned to the table, Matt had completed his talk with Tess and put the cell away. Sam's expression when she slid across the vinyl seat and looked him in the eye made him distinctly uneasy. "For a dame who's just lost ten thousand plus expenses, you look awfully pleased with yourself. I can almost see the Tweety Bird feathers on your lips. What gives, Sam?"

Her grin broadened. "Oh, on impulse—I'm an impulsive gal, in case you never noticed—I decided to call Aunt Claudia and let her know how much danger you're still in, working on this story."

His frown was thunderous as he clenched the heavy coffee mug so tight it looked ready to shatter. "Oh, and what pray tell did my aunt say then?" He could well imagine how Sam could embellish the tale.

"She's hired me to be your bodyguard. Three K a week until this case is over and all the bad guys are in jail. If you don't believe me, just call her back."

"Bodyguard, my ass!" he ground out.

"And a sweet one it is, too." Her eyes swept suggestively downward as if she had X-ray vision and could see beneath the table. "Admit it, Matt. You need help. Two soccer moms snatched you once and I snatched you twice. I was a cop on the Miami-Dade force for seven years. I know the city and now I have a vested interest in seeing that you stay alive to write your story."

"You're conveniently forgetting those two soccer moms also overpowered you and left you trussed up like a Thanksgiving turkey."

"Only proves how resourceful I am that I got away and came back after you."

"What about Yuri and Vassily? You'd be dead meat if I hadn't gotten free and saved your pretty little ass." He was starting to grin in spite of himself. What was it about this woman?

"You'd be meat right alongside me, big fellow, just remember that. We make a pretty good team…in more ways than one," she added, telling herself she was only coming on to him because of the money. *Who are you kidding?*

The slovenly waitress, whose name tag bore the unlikely moniker Cassiopeia, plunked down their orders. "Speaking of dead meat, this looks halfway decent." He cut a juicy slice of steak and slowly raised it to his mouth.

Sam watched him chew, her own mouth watering…but no longer for food. His dark eyes never left hers as he swallowed, then grinned wolfishly. *He knows what I'm thinking.* Furious with herself, she snatched up a potato skin and shoved it into her mouth. Sour cream and green onions oozed down her chin. She seized a paper napkin and wiped off the mess. Shit! She'd burned her tongue, but refused to stop eating. Damn if she'd give him the satisfaction of seeing how he affected her.

"No sense in letting perfectly good food go to waste," he said reasonably as he slathered butter over his baked potato and ate a huge forkful. "But by the time we finish off dessert, we'll need to work off all these calories…."

They didn't make it to dessert.

By the time Sam was halfway finished with her steak, Matt shoved his plate away and motioned to Cassiopeia to bring the check. As he peeled off bills from his money clip, he asked, "Where's the nearest motel?"

The waitress raised one black eyebrow and gave a knowing

smirk. "Right down the road on the left, two blocks." She pointed to a flashing neon sign that indicated it rented by the hour.

"Classy, Granger," Sam hissed at him as the waitress sauntered off. "A hot-sheets joint."

He shrugged. "Just so they change the damned things. Besides, we need some sleep before our great adventure," he said innocently, glancing at his watch. The night sky was obscured by the neon glow of Vegas, but it was past midnight.

"That mean you're taking me with you?" she asked, suspiciously. No way was she losing the heavy coin his aunt had promised her...or the time she could spend with him before he found out about her connection to Pat and the deal with the fibbies. Beyond that...well, she'd figure out something in the morning.

"We'll see," was his noncommittal answer as he extended his hand to her across the table.

She took it and they walked out of the restaurant into the smoggy heat of a Vegas night. Cassiopeia's recommendation looked bad enough that both of them were willing to scout a little farther in spite of raging hormones. A half mile further, they found a Days Inn. It took Matt minutes to register while Sam parked her van by the long row of units. She paced impatiently until he appeared, dangling a room key like a Christmas candy cane. Sam seized it from his hand.

"Right down there—first floor." He pointed to the third door. She had it unlocked in a flash. Just as she shoved the heavy door across the carpet, he surprised her by scooping her into his arms. "Now...I've had this fantasy about showers the past couple of days," he murmured as he kicked the door closed and lowered his mouth to hers.

The kiss was long and slow and incredibly sensuous. "You

taste like sour cream," he said, not particularly concerned as he nibbled small kisses down her chin and throat.

He tasted like every woman's fantasy, Sam thought. Her mouth was ready for complete meltdown, scorched by his lips as if she'd just chugged a jar of Tabasco sauce. Her heart pounded like a Cubano drummer playing "Flight of the Bumblebee." She ran her fingers through his black curly hair, digging in to pull his mouth back to hers for more of the utterly delightful fire.

When they reached the bed, he let her slide slowly down his tall body. He kicked off his loafers and discarded his socks while she unlaced her tennies with clumsy fingers. By the time she was barefoot, he pulled her back into his arms, resuming the kiss while he started to raise her T-shirt over her head. Sam returned the favor, tiptoeing up, then raising her arms to yank the tee away before she started unbuttoning his shirt.

Shoving the garment wide and tugging it free from the waistband of his slacks, her fingers dug into the luxuriant pelt on his pectorals. Lord, his chest was hard and sexy! *This is crazy, Sam. You're gonna regret it.*

She ignored the voice of reason. What woman with a working libido wouldn't when she had a tall, dark, gorgeous hunk like Matt Granger doing maddening things to her breasts? In seconds he had her bra unclasped and his big, warm hands cupped their prizes. Sam thrust her body forward and felt his thumbs circling her hardened nipples. Exquisite! "You… mentioned something…about the shower…" she finally managed to get out between moans and kisses.

"Yeah," he muttered, sliding her jeans over the curve of her hips with deft hands. "Only this time, Sammie baby, no cuffs."

Hadn't she wondered how it would be if he could use those wonderful big hands? Now she was finding out. He'd read her mind! Reality was even better than imagination. She unzipped his fly and shoved his slacks to the floor. They kicked their pants away and began moving slowly toward the bathroom door, kissing and caressing eagerly.

"This doesn't look like it came from Leather and Lace," he whispered hoarsely as he slipped his fingers into a tiny triangle of silk that served as her panties.

She wasn't coherent enough to tell him she ordered sexy underwear on the Internet at discount prices. "Didn't," came out in a breathless murmur as she yanked his briefs off while one of his large hands cupped her. Oh, heaven! She threw her arms around his neck and kissed him.

He had intended to make it into the shower, but when she jumped on him like a hungry lioness on a wildebeest, he lost his balance and they tumbled backward onto the queen-size bed. This time he was determined to come out on top.

When he slid her panties down, Sam had not the slightest interest in protesting. In fact, feeling the pressure of his erection only added to her excitement. She let him roll her under him, then guided him home as if they'd been made to do this together...always.

Amazing how much easier this is without my hands cuffed behind my back.... That was Matt's last coherent thought for quite a while.

Only after the earth, moon and all the stars erupted, spinning her wildly into bliss, did Sam even *try* to think.

She thought about the shower.

As he pressed her into the mattress, she held him tightly, her arms and legs locked around him in a grip tighter than any Leather and Lace straitjacket. When she could finally breathe enough to speak, she whispered, "We're kinda sweaty, you think?" She could feel the rumble of his chuckle as he rolled off her.

Matt pulled her up with him. "Yeah, we are. Let's see what we can do about it, hmm."

He was really good with a bar of soap, too. A woman could get used to this kind of lovemaking. Downright habit-forming, Sam thought as they climbed back into the rumpled bed, leaving a trail of damp towels and scattered clothes decorating the small room. He was much bigger than her but she fit perfectly spooned with her back to that wonderful broad chest. He nuzzled her neck and fell instantly to sleep.

Once again Sam Ballanger lay awake, feeling guilty. He wasn't her patient anymore, but she had deceived him and knew he'd be angry about it. How angry? She wasn't sure. But that was the only thing she was sure of as a thought haunted her: *He's out of your league. In the Ivy League. With a fat trust fund.*

But no matter how hard she tried to convince herself that they had no future together, she couldn't give up on the idea that a poor kid from south Boston just might make the cut. Uncle Dec always said the Ballangers were fighters. Sam intended to fight as hard as she could for every minute she could have with Matthew Granger.

Chapter 11

They awakened just after daylight to the screech of the semi shifting into second gear. Sam had briefly noted the cab when they'd arrived, an inferior rig to her uncle's, parked just down from them on the big lot. Matt planted a quick kiss on her neck, then rolled to the edge of the bed and sat up, running his fingers through his hair.

"God, I need coffee," he muttered.

"Well, good morning to you, too," she said, pulling the sheet up to her shoulder as she propped her head up on her hand, laying on her side. Not exactly romantic.

But then he turned around and gave her a grin that melted her heart like butter in a microwave. "Sorry, it's just that I hate mornings. And that grinding racket outside is about as soothing as a dentist's drill."

"He's in fifth gear now. Transmission needs an overhaul,"

she said as the sound of the semi rumbled by and melded into rush hour traffic.

Matt gave her a quizzical look. "How the hell could you tell that?" Lord, she looked adorable, tousled and as all-American as a cheerleader. Quite a switch from the "trained health-care professional" who'd abducted him at gunpoint twice.

"My uncle Declan is an over-the-road trucker. I used to spell him on long trips back when I was in high school and college. But I guess you guys on Beacon Hill wouldn't know about anything bigger than a Beamer," she added defensively.

Matt threw up his hands, scooting back on the bed beside her. "As a matter of fact, when I was in the army I had a pal named Rizzo who could make a ten-year-old junker purr like a Porsche. I learned how to change the oil in my Crown Vic."

"You oughta, with a dipstick that size," she quipped, trying for a lighter tone. No sense wearing her heart on her sleeve—if she had a sleeve instead of lying there naked beneath one thin sheet.

He yanked it back and lay beside her, pulling her into his arms. "Then I should check your oil, you think?"

She wasn't thinking at all when she replied, "Yeah. Oh, yeah!"

That was when their wake-up call came, a sharp ugly series of brrings from the phone on the laminated nightstand beside the bed. Matt smothered an oath and knocked it from its cradle, then returned to what he'd been doing.

"They'll hear us," she murmured.

"Those things are automated," he said. "Nobody there."

But the spell was broken. All the past night's insecurities and guilt nagged at her. "We really have to hit the road for Miami, Matt."

Thinking of Tess and Steve, he sighed in resignation. "Much as it pains me to admit it, Samantha, darling, you're right."

As if to reinforce his resolve, his cell beeped. He rolled off the bed and searched in the dim light trickling from behind the drawn blinds until he found his pants and fished the cell from the clip on the belt. "Granger," he said.

"I'm sorry to call so early in the morning, Mr. Granger," Jenny said nervously.

Matt recognized her voice immediately. "Where's Tess? Steve? Is anything wrong?"

"We're on the beach at—"

"Don't tell me your location," he interrupted quickly before the idiot woman could blurt out information that might get the whole family killed. "Just tell me what's happened," he added quickly in what he hoped was a soothing tone.

"Oh, yes, I forgot. This might not be a safe call. I read that in one of—"

"What's happened to your sister?" he asked, barely masking his impatience.

"Steve ran away—early this morning…"

Sergeant William Patowski was not having a good day. Not even ten in the morning and all hell had broken loose. "Pat" had red hair going gray, what was left of it, a slight paunch tugging at world-weary shoulders and a cynical face with pale blue ice chips for eyes. The homicide detective slammed the door of his dark blue Chevy and walked toward a cluster of green-striped white Miami-Dade police cars parked in front of a small marina on North Bayshore Drive just east of Biscayne Shores Park.

The sky was clearing after an early morning drizzle common in south Florida. A brisk breeze whipped his ketchup-stained tie away from the rumpled suit jacket he never buttoned. He'd eaten a rushed breakfast in a diner at dawn after pulling an all-nighter, something his ex-wife had never gotten used to. The uniforms were holding back civilian gawkers and a couple of TV news cameramen across the street—for the moment.

"We got two floaters, Sarge," an old officer named Arnold said the way most guys might announce they'd fished a quarter out of a crack in the sidewalk.

"ID?" Pat asked, knowing already that they were Russian Mafia, but which side?

"Two of Pribluda's guys. Our Mikhail's being a very naughty boy these days. Must be real pissed the Brighton Beach crowd offed his kid."

"How'd they die?" Pat asked.

"M.E. just got here. Nothing official but we saw what was left of them. Pretty ugly."

"Ain't it always with a mob turf war," Pat said impatiently, knowing an officer with Arnold's experience could describe the M.O. as accurately if not as technically as an M.E.

"Back of their heads blown off, close range, but not before some real creative snipping with a bolt cutter. 'Ace is the place' as the helpful hardware salesman says. Oh, their knee caps were worked over real good, too, and—"

"That's enough," Pat interrupted him. "Mikhail's sending a message to New York to get out of his territory."

"You think Pribluda'll pull out?"

"You believe in the tooth fairy?" the sergeant countered. Then he saw Special Agent Inez Gomez striding across the street toward them. At least this time he'd beaten her to the scene. That was something. "Who found the bodies?" he asked Arnold.

"Guy down there on the Sea Ray. Cleaning up his boat when he looks over the side and sees one of the poor suckers bobbing under the pier. Just as he's dialing 911 the second stiff washes out and he really freaks. Took the operator a few minutes to calm him down, figure what the hell was going on."

Gomez was an attractive woman, tall with smooth olive skin and a deceptively inviting smile that never reached her cop's eyes. Before she got halfway across the street, one of the reporters slipped under the barrier and stuck a microphone in her face. Pat smiled inwardly. Let her handle it. She was good at damage control. He only hoped none of the reporters put these killings together with two others yesterday—or Alexi Renkov's explosive demise.

Last night there had been another murder near one of Renkov's strip joints in South Beach and another that afternoon in the Grove. Both victims had been part of the defunct Nikolai Benko's organization. Neither murder was in Pat's jurisdiction but he was cooperating with the Beach and Miami PDs. And the FBI. What nobody down here wanted was for the CIA to become involved. Or Mikhail Renkov would never spend a day in jail.

The turf war between Renkov and Pribluda would soon make national headlines—the very thing he and Gomez were trying desperately to prevent before they made their case. Then he'd get to collar Mikhail and the Bureau could bust up the two competing Russian mobs with operations ranging from Miami to New York. But none of that would happen unless they moved fast.

He waited as Special Agent Gomez smoothly ditched the newshounds and approached him, nodding a curt good morning. "You look like hell, Sergeant. Sleep in that suit?"

"I wish. Didn't get to sleep at all." He filled her in on last night's killings, then asked, "Anything on the wires yet?"

"Renkov's playing real coy. Like he knows he's being bugged. Or, he's just smart and never talks on a phone. Pribluda's boys in Little Odessa aren't quite so clever. We just found out last night that they have a mole here in Miami, buried deep in Renkov's organization."

Patowksi whistled. "Who?"

"Don't know that yet, but whoever it is just spilled Ren
kov's CIA connection to Pribluda. The Brighton Beach crow
isn't exactly pleased about a fellow countryman reporting il
legal nuke sales to the Company."

"Cuts into their business," Pat said with a grunt.

"Big-time," she replied. "That's why the Company cover
for Mikhail, the SOB."

"If we can nab that mole, we'll be able to squeeze info o
both mobs from him."

Gomez changed the subject abruptly. She did that a lo
Pissed Pat off. "Your ex-cop friend still have that nosy re
porter on ice?"

"She's handling him okay," he said, hoping like hell it wa
true.

"She find out if he knows where Tess Renkov is hiding
We could learn a lot from her, I'd bet anything on it."

"So would I, but from what Sam's told me, the widow an
her son have gone into hiding. Not even Granger knows whe
they are now, but he's in contact with her by cell."

"Tell her to get me some numbers. We can track the cal
and pinpoint her location."

There were days when you were the dog and days whe
you were the hydrant. Right then Patowski felt like a dirty re
hydrant with its paint peeling off…which made Gomez th
dog. He smiled inwardly at that slight comfort as they walke
down the pier to the M.E., who was kneeling beside th
bloody remains of two bodies. Pat wondered if they'd waste
a lot of time and trouble bringing Sam Ballanger in on thi
The last case she worked with him had nearly cost him h
pension. It had gotten her dismissed from the force.

He muttered beneath his breath, "Now she's a hotshot P.
The only one who'll come out ahead on this gig, dammit."

* * *

"Tess is looking for Steve now," Jenny said now that Matt had calmed her down enough so she was quasi-coherent. "We just discovered he was missing when the girls got up. He always plays with them and they couldn't find him anyplace. He must've slipped away in the middle of the night or near dawn."

Matt's gut clenched. "Were there any signs of a struggle— like someone kidnapped him?"

"No. We have a small cottage. He was in the same bedroom with his mother, sleeping on a rollaway. He even packed a few things, you know, his favorite T-shirt, a pocketknife his dad gave him, stuff like that, sort of like he'd been planning to run away, then he must have taken off during the night after everyone else was asleep. He's been acting kind of strange—upset, you know, ever since he listened to the TV news the day we got here."

"What was it—the part about his mother being wanted for questioning in his father's death?"

"No, it was when Lori Barrington—you know that really smart newscaster from Miami, the one everybody says had plastic surgery?—well anyway, she tried to interview that bimbo wife of Mikhail's about the death of her stepson."

"And Steve reacted badly to Nancy Renkov?" Matt said, trying to focus Jenny. A hopeless task.

"We didn't even know he was watching. Thought he was out on the beach playing with Mellie and Tiff. This place has—"

"Did he hear about his mother being wanted or just the part about Nancy?" Matt asked, clenching the cell almost tight enough to crush it.

"We didn't see, but I don't think he heard what the police sergeant, Patterson or some Polish name like that, said about

Tess. She had already explained the reasons we were hiding to him and he seemed to take it okay. He knows his mother would never kill anybody, even a rat like Alexi. But we caught him watching the TV from the doorway because he gasped when Nancy shoved her way past the news crew. Some of Mikhail's nasty entourage were with her and she was really rude."

Sam listened in as best she could while the flaky woman explained about the runaway boy. How close would a kid be to his grandfather's trophy wife, a woman the same age as his own mother? It didn't make sense to Sam. She'd make book Nancykins never asked Steve to call her grandma. The boy probably didn't even like old Mikhail all that much. She scribbled her thoughts on the motel notepad for Matt to read as he quizzed Jenny.

Matt's mind raced as he tried to figure a way to find Steve before his grandfather got his grubby hands on the innocent boy...or something worse happened. "We'll have to come back," he started to say when a loud commotion from the other end of the line cut him off.

Sam could hear Mellie and Tiff squealing Steve's name. "Tess must've found him," she said with great relief. The thought of a missing child always gave her nightmares. She'd seen too much since the days when she was a cop.

After a moment's pandemonium on the other end of the line, Tess came on, her voice obviously tight with stress. "Yes, Matt, Steve's here with me. I found him hiding in a deserted shack about a mile down the beach. We're in a pretty isolated area, so I was lucky...."

Matt signed off after a moment. "She's got to get the boy calmed down and then she'll call us back. She knows something she doesn't want to talk about in front of her sister or the kids."

"Then he's okay?"

"Seems so, but I didn't like what she hinted at."

"You mean he knows something ugly about Grandpa and his sweetie of a wife?"

Matt nodded. "Mikhail picked her out of one of his strip clubs. Nancy Lee Dobson, formerly of Twin Pines, Oklahoma. She was working as one of his high-priced call girls, on special assignment to the boss whenever he wanted her. Somehow, she got the tough old Ruskie to marry her. I've been trying to dig up a reason he'd do it, but so far, bobkes."

"How long since his first wife died?"

Matt laughed without humor. "About six years ago, back in Russia. He left her behind and took Alexi to America when he defected. Sent her a pittance to live on. Probably starved to death."

"You are thorough," Sam said, impressed with his investigative skills. Reporters and cops had to do much of the same kind of legwork.

He studied her as he gathered up scattered clothes and dressed. "I vote we catch a quick bite while we're waiting for Tess to call back. Then we have to make some big decisions."

"We passed a McDonald's back a few blocks. I could go for a couple of Egg McMuffins."

Tess's call came just as they approached the drive-through. Sam placed their orders while Matt spoke on the cell. By the time she'd driven past the order window, paid and deposited the hot food on the console between them, he was done and he looked grim.

"So, what gives? Is Steve okay?"

"He's physically all right, but he saw something pretty ugly. That's why he ran away."

All thoughts of food deserted her as she pulled away from the drive-through. "Talk to me, Matt. What happened to set the kid off?"

"Steve used to spend afternoons now and then at his grandfather's place in Aventura," Matt explained while Sam pulled into an empty parking space on the lot and fished out the two tall coffees, handing one to him.

"Pretty fancy digs. Crime pays," she said. The small municipality was one of the most exclusive places to live in south Florida.

He took a scalding sip and went on, "Kid was supposed to be watching videos with Grandpa but the old man got called away. Apparently that happened a lot. Tess always took him on those command visits or insisted Alexi take him and stay there."

"Let me guess. Alexi took off and left his son."

Matt nodded. "Housekeeper was there and Steve liked her, so he asked her if he could take a swim in the pool while she was fixing him lunch. She could see the pool from the kitchen, so she agreed. The layout must rival Windsor Castle, the way Tess described it. Anyway, Steve fooled around in the water for a while until he got bored, then went into the cabana at the opposite end of the compound to get a towel.

"A boat had pulled up to their private dock, but the housekeeper couldn't see it because the cabana blocks the view from the first floor. Anyway, it must've been a fairly fancy rig. Tess said Steve thought it was a Tiara of some kind. Over forty feet. With the right engines, they can go pretty fast."

"His dad was a powerboat nut. I can see why the kid'd want to check it out."

"Yeah, well before he could, he saw Nancy slip out of the cabana and climb aboard."

"She didn't see him in the cabana?"

"Place is bigger than my condo from what I could tell," he said, grateful to feel the caffeine hit his system. "Steve waited a while. Grandma Nancy had never exactly been friendly, so he slipped up the dock and peeked through a porthole…"

"And?" she prompted.

Matt sighed. "He saw her with a lover, both of them starkers, going at it."

"Bad scene, especially considering she's married to his grandpa," Sam said glumly. "Did he know the guy?" she asked, half-afraid it might have been the boy's own father.

"Didn't get much of a look since the interior of the boat was dark. I know what you're thinking. Considered the same thing myself. Alexi."

Sam nodded.

"Steve never said a word about what he'd seen to his mom or anyone. When he started acting withdrawn the past weeks, she thought it was because of tabloid coverage of his father."

"When he fessed up now, did Tess ask him specifically? He might not have wanted to volunteer a thing like that for fear of hurting his mom," she said.

"I tried skirting around that, but Tess knew it wasn't Alexi, although she suspected the two of them had been an item a while ago."

"Uglier and uglier. Poor kid, he might have worried that Gramps would whack Nancy if he said anything. If he knew about his dad's exploits, he might have known about his granddad's criminal background."

"Well, I guess when Grandpa's always nice to you, lots of stuff can seem unimportant, especially if he pays more attention to you than your own father does," Matt said. "Oh, yeah, one thing Steve did notice. Nancy's lover had an odd tattoo on his thigh. That's about all the kid saw of him."

"What kind of tattoo?" Sam was immediately interested. That could be a solid lead.

"An infinity sign with some kind of letters beneath it. Too dark to make anything out. Know anybody in the skin trade thereabouts?"

"I might. Worth a try if we can't turn anything else quick."

Matt nodded agreement. "I can see why she thought it was her father-in-law trying to kill her, but now the playing field is wide open."

"It was logical. She files for divorce, then thinks Mikhail's the one trying to off her so he gets her son."

"But our pals Vassily and Yuri were hired by someone they didn't know and told to kill Tess *and* Steve," Matt said.

"If Nancy knows Steve saw her, that sure as hell gives her a reason to want them both dead," Sam agreed. "But it still doesn't add up. Why go to the trouble and risk to frame Tess with the cops—you know, the insurance policy, the switched cars..." Sam wanted to spit coffee across the dash the minute she realized what she'd just said.

"I didn't tell you anything about an insurance policy, Sam," he replied in a measured voice.

Shit! Think fast. "Sure you did," she bluffed. That usually worked with her brothers and dad...but never with Uncle Dec. Or Matt Granger.

"Sam, it's laundry day. Come clean." His eyes pinned her over the steam rising from his cup. He was starting to squeeze the Styrofoam ever so slightly.

"You'll burn the family jewels," she said, pointing from the clenched cup to his crotch, but he ignored the warning. She had the feeling the scalding coffee in his hand wasn't destined to end up in *his* lap.

"I'll burn the hide off your lovely keister if you don't tell me the truth—right now."

How could she explain without giving away Pat's involvement in retrieving her van? "I planted a bug under the Lan

Rover when you were at that first rest stop, then followed you back and listened in." Damn, she was good!

Matt looked skeptical. "You never mentioned you were into high-tech spy ware."

"Told you I was a cop. I worked on loan to the FBI for a few months on a drug surveillance team. We used all kinds of fancy stuff." Partially true, and Sam always felt it was best to stick as close to the truth while bending it as possible. "I removed the unit after you ditched the wrecked SUV."

"Show it to me," he demanded.

She had a couple of rudimentary listening devices packed in her bags, nothing remotely sophisticated enough to do the job on the highway with GPS that would be required for a car-to-car surveil. All she could do was hope he wouldn't know the difference. After all, he was a preppy kid who probably read Shakespeare. Did they offer electronics classes at Yale?

"I packed it away in the back. Right now we have more important things to consider—like who's trying to kill Steve and his mother, not to mention you. My vote's still for dear old Mikhail trying to frame Tess and get his grandson back. Granny Nancy would be the one who sent those two ex-Pribluda clowns after us, trying to kill the boy and anyone he might've told about her and her pal."

Much as he hated to admit it, she was probably right. "The only way to find out is to head for Miami and dig."

Just what Pat had hired her to prevent, but if she delayed their arrival, then kept him posted about their progress, the sergeant should have his collar before the *Herald* broke Matt's story. Worst case, she lost her money and the FBI put him on ice until the deal was done. She needed to check back with Pat to see when the Bureau planned to make their move. They supposedly were monitoring Renkov and Pribluda, tails, bugs, the whole enchilada. Then Matt cut into her thoughts.

"I want to make sure Tess and her family are safe. I don't trust Jenny to come in out of the rain, much less lay low while killers are searching for them. And we don't have time to drive. We'll fly home."

"You have any idea what airfares cost when you don't book in advance?" she asked, aghast.

He grinned at her. "Thought my aunt was paying your way."

She huffed. "Well, she is, but I hate to waste a client's money. The shower damage at the Stratford Lodge's gonna cost her a bundle already."

"She can afford a bundle and then some. Head for the airport," he ordered her.

She took one look at his mulish expression and knew he'd fly home without her if she put up a squawk. And he had all her weapons, drat it. If she got left behind, it would louse everything up for sure. At least if she was with him she could keep tabs on where he stuck his nose. *And other wonderful parts of his anatomy. Stop it, Sam!*

Matt called Tess back to explain what they were going to do and make contingency plans for her safety and that of Steve.

As she drove, Sam turned over options. If they had the location, the FBI could protect the women and kids, but how to explain that to Matt? Then again, dealing with Russian mobsters like Renkov and his competitors, maybe bringing in the fibbies wasn't such a hot idea. Witness protection didn't always work. From across the console, Sam listened to Matt's side of the conversation with Tess.

"You have to stay put. Keep the kids inside pretty much. How'd you pay for that cottage?... Good... Keep using cash. You have enough to last a few more days? Provisions?... Don't let your sister go anywhere," he said, emphasizing the point. "Yeah, We're flying back to Miami this morning...." He grinned and looked over at Sam. "I think I can trust her, but I'll be careful."

"So, you think you trust me, huh?" Sam muttered under her breath, acting miffed. *If only you knew, Matthew. Damn.*

He ignored her pout, listening as Tess spoke, before he responded. "That isn't a good idea. No, you'd just put yourself at risk and potentially your son, too." He paused, listening with a genuinely worried look on his face.

Sam waited as they talked some more, catching the gist of their exchange. Tess wanted to come to Miami and leave her son with Jenny and the girls. Matt and Tess argued about it until he convinced her to hold off, finally ending the call just in time to point, saying, "The turnoff to the airport's there."

"I've already got a crunched fender. If anything else happens to my van in that parking lot—"

"Aunt Claudia will replace it. Now are you happy?"

She turned in with a grunt. Sam was definitely not happy in spite of all the lovely money she stood to gain as his "bodyguard." What had come over her? She didn't want to consider the answer. They climbed out of the van in a deserted corner of the huge parking lot and grabbed their meager luggage.

As they started walking toward the shuttle, she said, "I don't like traveling without my stunner and .38."

"Airport security frowns on that kind of stuff," he said dryly. "You have a license?" At her nod, he added, "Just pick up more heat as soon as we land, then. It's not as if the Sunshine State is anti-gun, you know."

"I feel naked without—"

Her words were cut short when a black Lincoln came skidding down the narrow aisle of parked cars. They stepped quickly to one side but at the last instant, the driver veered directly toward them. They both jumped clear, throwing themselves on the hood of a Buick Roadmaster. The black Lincoln Town Car missed it by inches, then screeched to a stop.

"Not only did they get away but they kept their wheels, too," she said, recognizing the pug-ugly faces of Vassily Kuzan and his pal Yuri Garzenko as they climbed out of their big car.

Chapter 12

"Shit, they're armed," Matt muttered as he rolled over the side of the Buick. Sam had already hit the ground between the parked cars and was running in a crouch, fast as a crab skittering across the beach. He made a considerably larger target and couldn't move as fast, but the sound of bullets whizzing over his shoulders did wonders for his speed.

"How the hell did they get loose?" she snarled, trying to figure a way back to her van and the .38 in the glove compartment.

"Local yokels must've not run 'em because there were no witnesses."

She knew that would never have happened if the "local yokel fibbies" had arrived in a timely manner, but couldn't say so even if they weren't busy playing hide and seek with the Russian gunsels. "You gotta distract them while I get my gun back."

Another shot zinged over his head. "Want me to wave a white shirt and ask for a parlay?" he grunted, flattening himself against the side of a van. He watched Sam's eyes scan the enormous lot until she saw the airport shuttle a dozen or so rows over from them. "Think we can make it?"

"Maybe. If we split up."

"So will they. Then what?" he asked as they ducked and dodged again. At least with a shuttle in radio contact nearby, the goons had stopped shooting. But they were gaining ground.

As they moved, Sam rooted in her small carry-on bag and extracted a can of mace. "Almost forgot I had this little honey. I'd of had to leave it at security, but now it won't go to waste."

"You hope."

"Just listen up." She explained her plan to him. Not great but he couldn't think of anything better. He took off running in plain view, making a beeline for the shuttle, which was moving to his right about seven or eight rows up. Vassily, being the taller and quicker, followed him.

Being slower and squat, Yuri went after Sam. She spun to the left and ducked low, then kept moving too fast for him to see where she was. Counting on that, she made a fast circle around two rows of cars and came up behind him as he hunkered down, trying to listen for her footsteps on the concrete. But Matt's yelling provided sound cover as she made a mad dash toward Garzenko's back.

By the time he turned around she was two feet from him. "Hi ya, gorgeous," she said, macing him directly in the eyes before he could bring his Glock up to fire at her. He let out a yowl of Russian curses and tried to fire anyway, but she kicked the gun out of his paw, then dove after it. He tried to grab her but working completely blind, he couldn't stop her from scooping it up and dashing after Matt and Vassily.

Desperate after hearing his compatriot's curses, Kuzan raised his weapon and aimed at Granger, no longer concerned with the shuttle or the car cruising a few aisles over looking for a space. Like Matt, he was tall. Sam had a clear target as she yelled, "Drop it, Vassily!"

He whirled around, his narrow face grimaced with steely loathing when he saw the small woman standing with Yuri's automatic in her hand. The stance and steadiness should have warned him to comply with her command, but after the humiliation at the motel, he was blinded by rage. He raised his .45 to fire. Sam shot first and the impact of the .9mm slug knocked him backward against the door of an Impala sedan.

The instant Matt heard her yell, he turned midstride and started back toward them. Her bullet hit Kuzan in his left shoulder. He raced up behind the crumpling thug who was still determined to get another shot at Sam. She ducked behind a Jetta and yelled, "No use, Vassily. Drop it or I'll have to kill you."

That was all the distraction Granger needed before he tackled the injured man from behind, knocking him to the pavement. Sam dashed toward them, unable to shoot as they struggled for Kuzan's gun, but Matt had thirty pounds and an inch or two on the wounded Russian. He used it to good advantage, landing a solid punch to his foe's injured shoulder. The Russian's high-pitched scream was abruptly shut off as Matt hit him in the throat. Vassily dropped the gun, which Matt quickly scooped up.

Kuzan was out cold and bleeding pretty badly. Sparing him no more time, Matt stood up as Sam catapulted into his arms.

"Can't leave you alone for a minute without you getting in more trouble. I told you to wait until I got Yuri's gun," she said. Then she kissed him, still clutching the Glock in her hand.

He returned the embrace, holding Vassily's weapon in his hand. Coming up for air, he said, "We'd better ditch the guns and get the hell out of here before the local cops decide to detain us."

"Keep the guns but run," she said, taking the lead. "God only knows how these guys got away last time. I don't want to find out how much influence the Russian mob has in Vegas these days."

As they loped away from the shuttle, using cars for concealment, they could see the shuttle driver talking animatedly into her radio. "Great. Hope she can't give an accurate description to security in the terminal," he said.

"One thing's sure. We don't dare go inside and risk getting arrested. We'll have to drive," Sam replied.

They took a quick detour and slipped back into their van, watching for the Russians, but since they had Kuzan and Garzenko's guns, it seemed unlikely the two men would try another attack. Matt hid under a pile of gear in the back of her van. The shuttle driver would more likely have seen a tall man than a small woman running across the lot when shots were fired. He hid while she drove carefully to the booth and presented the ticket to the attendant.

Sam quickly paid the parking fee and turned onto the service road away from the airport. "You can come up now. I don't think that guy at the booth knew anything about a shooting. Wonder if security caught our pals," she speculated.

"They seem to have the devil's own luck. I bet they'll get away."

"Vassily's bleeding like a stuck pig."

"Those Ruskies are tough as they come. They hack off their enemies' forearms with axes, castrate them with rusty knives, bury them up to their necks in dirt and then start pulling teeth with pliers."

"I get your point," she said dryly. "He'll wrap his shoulder up tight and keep on keeping on just like that big pink bunny. And they'll have to report to whoever hired them sooner or later." She looked in her side-view mirror. "Aw, crap, not pink. Black. You can climb out of the back now—and bring the guns."

The black Lincoln was gaining on them as Sam hit the gas.

"How the hell did they follow us so quick?" Sam asked rhetorically. "They aren't smart enough to bug my van...or have I underestimated our boys?"

"How hard can that be?" Matt asked as he climbed over the seat and checked his side mirror. "I've seen it on TV a hundred times. They're gaining on us."

"Yeah, big surprise considering I have a Ford van and they're in a big Town Car. But, one thing nobody ever counts on." She hit the gas again, this time really tromping it hard. "Thank you, Uncle Dec," she said as the Econoline suddenly peeled away leaving the smell of burned rubber on the pavement.

Matt was thrown against the back of his seat before he could get his belt fastened. "What the hell—"

"My uncle switched out the engine and modified the drive train."

She started explaining a lot of car jargon that might as well have been Swahili for all he understood, but the bottom line was, they were suddenly outdistancing the Lincoln.

"Sometimes—not often—I get chased by irate cult members. Dec thought I should be able to get away clean and easy," she ended up saying.

"Why aren't you getting on the highway?" he asked as houses and strip malls on the narrow service road blurred alongside the freeway.

"I want to hide, not be pulled over by the state patrol."

Right on cue, a road to their right took them into an oasis of trees and high stone fences, an upscale new development. She took the corner on two wheels, then made a series of dizzying twists and turns through the winding streets that would've done Mario Andretti proud.

"Hey, you're good. You lost 'em," he said, looking behind them for the Town Car, which had disappeared about a half-dozen blocks ago.

"Not for long if there's a bug on this car. We gotta get inside someplace they can't get at us and check it out."

Just as they turned another corner the iron gate to one of the big estates swung open about a half block ahead and a plumbing repair truck glided inside the high stone walls. Sam did another wheelie and followed it.

"We'll never make that!" Matt yelled.

"Piece of cake," she said, pulling on the wheel, then gunning the engine while the gate started to close. The Econoline made it inside an inch from impalement. They followed the plumbers along the circular drive until the Econoline couldn't be seen from the road. The truck in front of them kept on going around the house to the rear entrance.

"The owners will call the cops on us," he said.

"We'll be out of here before any security company bozos come around. Trust me, it's unlikely anyone's even home to notice us. These gates are automated to let vehicles in at set times and anyone can get out by just driving up and waiting." At least, that was a common practice in upscale burbs with homeowners who both had to work to make the exorbitant payments on these kinds of digs.

"What if you're wrong and we're trapped in here?" he asked.

"Would you rather keep playing Coyote and Road Runner with Yuri and Vassily on our tail from here to Miami?" she asked reasonably, as she jumped out of the van and crawled beneath it.

Matt followed suit. "Okay, what are we looking for?"

"You're a reporter and you never used a bug or tracing device of any kind?" she asked, incredulously. "A small metal or plastic housing, about so." She used her hand to give him some idea of its size. "Magnetized on the bottom. Stuck on some flat surface where it obviously doesn't belong."

Matt had no idea what "belonged" on the underside of an automobile, but grunted and started crawling around, peering at greasy machinery and pipes, pretending he did. Rizzo had taught him to change his oil and that was about all. The only reason he could shift a standard transmission was because he'd been given a Corvette by his great-uncle as a high school graduation present. After he went on his own, spurning the family money, he bought practical, used cars and paid a cut-rate mechanic to repair them.

He crawled toward the back, reasoning that the two thugs weren't all that bright and would probably have placed the magnetized device somewhere easy and quick to reach—like inside the rear bumper. Sure enough, he felt a small lump and pulled on it. When it popped off in his hand, he held it out to her under the car, asking, "This it?"

"Matthew, you're a genius!" She framed his face with two greasy hands and planted a big, wet kiss squarely on his mouth. He raised up and bumped his head on the gas tank. He saw stars, but it didn't matter—she tasted so damn good.

If not for the two goons cruising around the neighborhood, probably with backup hardware now loaded and ready to use on them, Matt and Sam might have considered prolonging the kiss. But they broke apart reluctantly and scooted from under the van. She took the device and dashed around the house to where the plumbing truck sat parked, its occu-

pants now inside. The plumbers apparently never even noticed
the van behind them slipping in. Probably too in awe of the
fountains and gabled wings of the garish house. It looked like
a combination of old-time movie theatre and mausoleum to
her.

She quickly slid the device under the side panel of the van,
then sprinted back to where Matt stood waiting. "Now, we
take off."

"How the hell are we going to get away? Our friends are
probably sitting somewhere down the street, waiting for us
to come out."

"Count on it. But that little baby isn't exactly high-tech.
They don't know exactly which drive we'll come out of.
When we shoot out, they'll follow. Then I double back and
lose them close to here."

"And while we take off down the highway, they keep driving in circles until they figure out the van's parked somewhere
nearby. Then they park and wait." He grinned at her. Damned
devious woman. She could definitely be dangerous for his
peace of mind…not to mention his health. But, what the hell?
He was already onto a story that put him crosswise of the Russian Mafia and he'd never let that go. Sam just might be a big
help—if she didn't drive him crazy first.

Sam peered over the wall, standing on Matt's shoulders
and located the Lincoln down a block to their left. Luckily,
the gate opened when the van approached, just as she'd hoped.
She gunned the engine and headed directly toward the Town
Car, passing it before Yuri and Vassily could do more than
blink.

"I think you caught them by surprise," Matt said dryly.

She shot around the corner on the curving street, then
slowed just enough so the Lincoln caught sight of them after
it made a U-turn and took off in pursuit. They played cat and

mouse for some of the longest minutes of Matt's life. "You said you have an uncle who's a trucker. Any of your family into stock car racing?"

Sam was concentrating on her driving, but she could see his white knuckles on the door handle and his legs braced stiffly. "Never tried it. Too risky," she replied.

"Too risky! You snatch nutcases out of cults and drive like a Mexico City cabbie!"

He probably rolled his eyes, but she couldn't take her eyes off the road long enough to see. "Now, they're falling behind...after...this next...curve..." She chewed her lip in concentration, remembering the open drive on this street. A private park for the complex, and just close enough to where they'd left the bug, so that when the goons lost them, they'd think to check the tracking device and return to wait—for the plumbing truck. By the time they figured out they'd been had, she and Matt would be miles down I-15 nearing I-40 heading east to Miami.

"I don't see why we couldn't go with Mr. Granger," Mellie whined.

"Your aunt explained it to you all," Jenny replied.

"But he was so much fun to tickle," Mellie said in a sulky voice, slurping a Sno-Kone Jenny had bought her at a beachside stand.

"He was kinda neat," Tiff admitted wistfully.

"You got a crush on him?" Steve teased his younger cousin. It was one of the few smiles Jenny had seen on his face in weeks. She felt vindicated for bending the rules just a little bit.

In spite of Matt's warnings and Tess's promise to keep them inside, Jenny found it impossible to endure the girls' complaints and pouting. She also wanted to cheer up her nephew. This seemed harmless enough. They walked along the deserted beach until they ran into a stretch of smooth white sand—and lots of tourists baking themselves in the sun. Cabanas sold T-shirts, sunblock, souvenirs and cold treats. The kids had spotted it en route to their rental several days ago and her girls had never stopped talking about how neat it would be to visit.

While her sister was taking a nap, Jenny took them out for fresh air and a little fun. Hopefully, they'd be back before Tess awakened. Once she saw how much happier Steve was, Tess would forgive her. Jenny thought of swearing the kids to secrecy, but knew Mellie was too young to keep quiet. Besides she'd already dripped cherry ice on her blouse. Oh well.

"Mom, that man's staring at us," Tiffany said, tugging on her mother's shirt. She knew some bad guys were after them and they were hiding. Even the police didn't know about the trouble they were in, and for some reason having to do with Steve's grandpa, couldn't be told.

"Where?" Jenny asked, suddenly afraid. "Don't point—" she quickly added.

"I see him, too," Steve whispered. "By the Sno-Kone stand. He's talking on a cell phone or something."

"We're going back, right now," Jenny said, ushering her brood toward the curving beach. "We'll take the shortcut across the highway." It was a far more public place, safer if that man decided to follow them with ill intentions. All he'd done was look at them for a moment, then talk on a cell phone. They were probably all being paranoid, but the way everything had gone the past weeks, who wouldn't be?

Chapter 13

Sam and Matt were about fifty miles east of Kingman, Arizona, heading east on I-40 when his cell beeped. His eyes still watching the side-view mirror for a black sedan, Matt opened the phone. "Granger."

Sam saw him sit up straight, reading the tension in his body language. It was Tess and the news didn't sound good. She listened as he questioned her. When he signed off, her gut tightened. Why did children always have to get caught in the middle when adults screwed up their lives? Pat was right. Teresa Albertson Renkov had married a rich golden boy and paid the price. Sam only hoped Steve and his little cousins didn't have to pay for her mistake, too.

"Renkov got the kids, didn't he?" she asked.

Grimly, he said, "That's the best we can hope for. At least I don't think he'll hurt Steve's aunt and her daughters. That damn Jenny has the brains of a starfish!" He cursed and pounded the dash. "Looks like she took them to a public beach while Tess was sleeping. Poor woman's trying her best to hold it together."

"How long have they been missing?" Sam asked.

"Tess laid down just after lunch. When she woke up and they were gone, she figured out what must've happened. Jenny's girls had been nagging her to take them to a place where they sold Sno-Kones that they'd seen, but she'd said no."

"But with Jenny Baxter no never means no for long," Sam replied, remembering how ineffectual the woman had been in dealing with her spoiled daughters.

"Yeah. Tess waited for a half hour, figuring since she'd napped for forty-five minutes or so that they'd be back shortly. When they didn't show, she took their old clunker and went searching at the beach. Several people had seen them leave...and a guy following them."

Now it was Sam's turn to curse. She pounded the wheel. "She can't call the local cops."

"I convinced her of that, thank God. But she insists on meeting us in Miami. She's sure Mikhail has them and she intends to confront him."

"She'll be arrested and he's home free," Sam said.

"Tried to tell her that, but the best I could do was to get her to agree to wait until we can meet her there and work on this together. Cut down I-93 to Phoenix. We can catch a flight from there."

"Does she have cash to buy a ticket so Renkov won't have advance warning she's coming?"

"Yeah. At least that's something. I told her we'd meet her at a bar I know in the Gables."

"I don't like this, Matt."

"I'm not crazy about it myself, but if we don't meet Tess in Miami tonight, she'll tackle Renkov on her own."

Sam sighed in capitulation. She knew what her own mother would do if she or any of their family were in danger. There would be no stopping Tess, either. Sam didn't like rushing into a dangerous situation like this without a plan. Hating the thought of it, she knew she'd have to place a call to Patowski when they reached Phoenix. The bills were skyrocketing for Aunt Claudia…if she was ever able to collect from Matt's moneybags aunt. Right now, unbelievably, that was the least of Sam's worries.

Nancy Renkov walked across the ankle-deep snow-white carpet in her bedroom, too upset to enjoy the excellent job her decorator had done. The walls were ice-blue and the elaborately carved Louis IV furniture inlaid with gold and mother of pearl gave just the right touch of class. That's what she always dreamed of being—a class act. Even if it meant marrying a pig like Mikhail to have the money and fast life she craved.

God, how she hated him! He was big and brutish, but possessed considerable cunning. She knew how dangerous it was to cross him. He'd gone off the deep end ever since Alexi and the car bomb. She and her darling "stepson" had become lovers last year. They had been bored and Mikhail had been in London. It was fun because both of them got off as much on the thrill of the forbidden as they did on each other—not that he was a bad lover…

She sneered, thinking of that wild man in bed with his uptight suburban wife. But she scarcely mourned Alexi. It was his son Steve who concerned her now. Mikhail had kidnapped his grandson and was having the brat hidden until he could locate Tess, whom he planned to kill so he could groom the

boy to take his father's place in the family business. But
Nancy was determined that Steve would die with his mother.
If Mikhail found out what the boy, and most probably Tess,
now knew, her husband would kill her.

They'd been careless. No, that wasn't entirely true, she admitted to herself. She had been too eager and insisted on the
dangerous tryst. Who could know that nosy brat would follow her to the yacht? They'd sent men to dispose of Mikhail's
daughter-in-law and Steve, but so far they'd botched the job.
Now her husband was eagerly awaiting the arrival of his
grandson. He'd never believe Tess, but he would believe Steve
if the nasty little nerd accused her.

She had to find out where Mikhail had hidden the boy so
her lover could get rid of him before he destroyed them both.
Then Mikhail could kill Tess and the rest of her stupid little
family. She paused at the full-length Girandole mirror filling
half the wall and stopped to admire her face and body, reassuring herself of her power over the vile, deadly man she'd
married.

Her nerves were badly jangled. She really needed a boost,
but that would have to wait. She headed directly for her phone
on the escritoire. Right now, she needed to find out if those
men of Benko's had finally taken care of that reporter and the
woman with him. If so, it might take the edge off of Mikhail's
wrath when he found out his grandson was dead, too. She always tried to avoid him when he received bad news, be it
about business or family.

When she reached the voice mail auto-response, she
slammed down the phone in frustration. *Where the hell are
you!* She dared not leave a message. Frustrated, she took consolation by gazing into the mirror. "Not bad for thirty-six,"
she murmured, running her fingers over her surgically enhanced curves, clearly revealed through the diaphanous beach

wrap she wore over a string bikini. Her hair was a pale white-blond, cut in a fashionable shoulder-length style. Her deep tan and dark green eyes contrasted dramatically with the pale mane. Of course, the color was also enhanced.

When the phone rang, she picked it up immediately. A gravelly voice said crisply, "I thought we agreed you'd never call me from your house." Nancy could detect some kind of device that distorted voices so no one could recognize them. If anyone would be in danger, it would be her, not her partner, who added, "Is he home?"

"Yes, but I have to tell you—"

"Let's say the usual this afternoon…" There was a pause as the party on the other end of the line consulted an itinerary for the day. "Around three. I'm making final arrangements. Everything should be in place by then. Be prompt and be certain you aren't followed."

As they hung up, Nancy huffed angrily. She knew her lover had her surveilled whenever they met. If she was followed, she'd receive a call on her cell and their meeting would be aborted. It had worked every time until their impulsive tumble aboard the yacht, right in Mikhail's own backyard.

The vile old gangster thought his money bought her body and soul. Well, it gave him the right to paw over her when he wanted, but not for much longer. All they had to do was collect the payoff. Then she'd never have to look at Mikhail Renkov's big, ugly face looming over her again.

And to think those fools in Hollywood had told her she couldn't act!

Downstairs at the opposite end of the vast palatial mansion overlooking Dumfounding Bay, Mikhail Renkov paced, ignoring the stunning view of sunshine reflecting on the water and sailboats skimming over light waves. Extending to the top of the cathedral ceiling twenty feet above his head, the whole wall fronting on the bay was made of glass. Bulletproof glass.

Outside, carefully concealed in the lush subtropical landscaping on the rolling lawn, armed guards patrolled unobtrusively. None of his neighbors in the exclusive Aventura neighborhood had any idea that he conducted illicit international deals, drug trafficking with Colombians, running strip clubs and prostitution rings up and down the Florida coast, or that his most profitable venture of all was smuggling Russian billionaire industrialists out of their homeland—for a sizable cut of their wealth.

To casual acquaintances, the tall, stocky man with thick graying blond hair and heavy Slavic features was just another foreigner who ran a successful import-export business. The CIA helped with that cover and turned a blind eye to his unsavory past and present dealings in return for his assistance in stopping nuclear proliferation.

If the Italians knew where all the bodies were buried, Mikhail Renkov knew where all the "misplaced" nukes inside the former Soviet Union were buried. He had a network of contacts spread around the globe who informed him of weapons shipments. Renkov in turn supplied this invaluable information to highly placed people in the American government.

For the past decade, life had been good. But in recent months, things had started to shift seismically, all for the worse. Valentin Pribluda had reached his long arm south from Brighton Beach to muscle in on Renkov's turf. Somehow Pribluda had found out that the Renkov organization was behind many interdictions in their weapons trade. Mikhail had ordered Nikolai Benko captured and tortured to find out who had betrayed them to Pribluda, but the man had died before revealing anything.

Someone in his own inner circle had to be involved, but who? Alexi had caught Tess eavesdropping here and told him that she might cause trouble. At the time, he'd thought it far-fetched. Now he wondered if his American daughter-in-law had sold out the family to Little Odessa in New York.

Alexi had always been too much the playboy and his wife objected. He'd told his son to be more discreet. The last thing they needed was an ugly divorce scandal in the papers. Obviously, that hadn't worked. The bitch had filed for divorce—after taking out a huge life insurance policy on her husband. Then she'd killed him. Teresa Albertson would pay dearly for that, but first he would have his grandson back.

He smiled, thinking of the boy. Stefan was on a private jet which would land shortly. Tess's fly-brained sister and her daughters were an added bonus. They would provide additional leverage to bring Tess back to Miami.

Then he'd have her. To save her family, she'd tell him everything about her contacts with Pribluda. Then he would personally kill her. At length he looked out over the bay and allowed a rare smile to curve his wide mouth.

Stefan would grow up to take Alexi's place at his side.

As soon as they arrived in Miami, Sam hailed a cab outside the airport and gave directions to an address on NE 110th just off Highway 1.

"Are you nuts? Why take a chance on going to your place? Let's head for my condo. I have a car there," he said.

Sam shook her head patiently. "Matthew, Matthew," she scolded, climbing into the back of a battered Crown Vic whose driver slouched indolently to one side of the wheel, waiting for the big fellow to get inside.

"I'm not going home. I'm going shopping. I can get a car—one that our pal can't trace. Neither can the cops," she added in a whisper, although she felt certain as long as they paid the fare and tipped decently, the cabbie wouldn't care if they were escapees from Raiford State Pen.

The driver cut across town and headed north, leaving I-95 to angle east until he hit Biscayne Boulevard, Route 1. In a few more minutes he turned into a run-down neighborhood where rusted washers and automobile engines were considered yard decor. From what Matt could see in the twilight, the houses were mostly cinder block with shingle roofs, single story, once painted in Miami's ubiquitous pastel colors, now faded by sun and mildewed by rain into dingy shades of gray, yellow and tan-green.

"Charming ambience. The machine gun turrets on the roofs are a nice touch," he commented as the cab slowed.

Sam didn't spare him a glance as she said, "I figure a Yalie type like you for Bal Harbor, maybe the Grove."

"Happens I live in South Beach, close to the Art Deco district."

"Hmm, artsy. That figures, too." She leaned forward and told the driver, "Pull up at the rose-colored house there."

Calling the bilious hot-pink rose-colored was beyond charitable to Matt's way of thinking, but at least the house sported a fresh coat of paint. The rest of the place was pretty much in the mode of the neighborhood. Except the occupant appeared to be in the used car business. He doubted whoever it was had a dealer's license.

As they climbed out of the cab, Matt paid the driver and watched as Sam picked her way through weeds that hadn't felt the cruel cut of a lawn mower in at least a tropical month. She paused at a ratty dark green Dodge Charger that was old enough to qualify as vintage—except that the body contained more bondo than metal and the driver's door had survived collision with a truck or an artillery round.

"Ah, Senorita Sam, welcome back. I can make you a deal on the Charger. Or that fine Oldsmobile," a wizened little man with a gray crew cut said. A genial smile revealed a full set of white teeth as he bowed before Sam. He gestured to a '74 Olds that gave new meaning to the first three letters of its name. If the odometer hadn't been rolled back, it had to have a quarter of a trillion miles on it.

"That bucket of bolts would fall apart in a dozen blocks—if the engine even turned over," Matt muttered to her.

"Senor Obregon, please meet Matt Granger. He's not from around here," she said dryly.

"Mucho gusto," the little man said, pumping Matt's hand as he craned his neck up to look him in the eye. "You, too, Senor Granger, would like a car?"

Matt shook his head. "Nope, thanks just the same. This is Sam's show."

He stood back and watched them haggle in a mix of Spanish and English over the price for the Dodge. Rental only. She explained about leaving her van in Phoenix and needing a car immediately but for only a few days. First she examined the engine and kicked the tires. They reached terms after Sam got Obregon down to half his original price. *Sam, you could squeeze a penny into a copper bracelet.*

Matt chuckled to himself. But after Obregon handed her the keys, Matt almost jumped out of his skin when she reared back and planted her foot square on the driver's door handle with a hard kick. Obregon stood by calmly as the door popped open, nodding approval.

Turning to Matt with a grin, she explained, "Only way it works. I drove it before on a couple of cases. Good engine and transmission—four on the floor that can move out, but it has a few quirks."

"A few quirks?" he echoed in amazement.

"You have to keep one foot on the gas when you stop or else it'll die," she explained as she climbed inside. "Carb's got a flat spot. Engineering flaw from '72 to '78. Oh, yeah, and third gear's missing, so you kinda have to play it by feel when you shift. Get in. Your door works the usual way."

"After hearing all that, I'm not sure I want to ride in this bucket of bolts," he muttered, doing as she said.

Meanwhile, Sam walked over to Obregon and they started up again. She gestured as they conversed in Spanglish. Matt couldn't catch all the words but he recognized her bargaining mode. What now? The guy disappeared into his "bunker" and returned in a moment, waving what looked to be a Smith & Wesson .38 caliber Chief's Special. Matt squeezed the bridge of his nose between thumb and forefinger.

When Sam climbed into the driver's seat, he asked, "Buy or rent?"

Sam looked surprised by the question. "Rent, of course. I've got a perfectly good piece in my van."

Granger nodded. "Of course. I forgot. Say, how does Obregon charge? Flat rate plus unlimited bullets? Or maybe so much an expended cartridge? Or—"

"Stuff it, Granger," she interrupted, turning over the ancient engine with expert skill and backing out of the yard.

Before they turned the first corner, he could see what she meant about babying the carburetor. Matt couldn't help but admire how she downshifted while keeping a steady feed of gas through the engine. Most men he knew couldn't manage it and he was pretty sure he didn't want to try. There was something about having a woman driver show you up that nudged ever so slightly at his male ego.

"I hope we don't have to get in any more high-speed chases driving this junker," he said.

"Once you let her rip on an open road, she's a beaut. Yo

can lay rubber on a U-turn with this baby and wave bye-bye to whoever's after you."

"I fervently pray we don't have to put it to the test," he replied with a shudder at the vision of bondoed fenders flying every which way—and him with them. "You forgot to mention the seat belt on the passenger side jams when you try to open it."

"Hey, you got a door that opens. Want egg in your beer, too?"

"I just don't want to die trapped inside this coffin on wheels."

Her reply was a derisive snort. She jumped from second to fourth with only a slight lurch. His hips strained against the seat belt as she took off at warp speed, weaving in and out of heavy traffic on southbound I-95.

Chapter 14

The Ficus was large and crowded, an easy place to hide in plain sight. Matt often used it with sources who had to remain anonymous. Just off Ponce de Leon Boulevard, it catered to well-heeled businessmen who wanted to relax over drinks. The place was dark and semi-posh with marble floors and lots of big potted palms and ferns concealing the hidden alcoves where men and their mistresses held discreet liaisons. Out front at the big mahogany bar, a younger group was in full meat-market mode.

Sam eyed a balding man guiding a blonde less than half his age toward a side exit. "Wanna bet? Five gets you ten he'll have a heart attack before he finishes the night with her," she muttered. "You pick up women here, too?"

"No, yes and no, to answer your remarks in order," he replied, scanning the area for Tess. "We're a little early, but I hoped she'd be here already."

"Don't sweat it. She flew into that hicksville airport you recommended on the hop from Tampa. No way could Renkov's goons have found her." Was she trying to reassure him or herself?

"If only she'd been willing to wait for a later flight, we could've met her in Tampa and driven back here together."

"Hey, her kid's in trouble, and her sister and nieces. What can you expect? You keep an eye out. I have to use the ladies' room."

Sam scooted away as he took a seat at a centrally located table. He'd stuck to her like Velcro ever since they landed, damn the man! Not a spare minute to call Pat. If she hadn't been afraid of making their plane crash, she'd have tried using her cell from the restroom during their flight.

Once safely inside the neat tile stall, she speed-dialed Patowski's number. He picked up on the second ring. She knew he had caller ID and her cell number. "Pat, we're in trouble, big-time."

"Where in hell have you been? You got Granger back to the land of beans yet?" he asked, ignoring her opening remarks.

"Not gonna happen. Too complicated to explain right now. We're back in Miami."

An inventive series of curses followed that announcement as he'd expected, but it was time to fess up and take her lumps. If only Tess and her family were safe, it would be worth it. "Look, Pat, Tess and her sister followed us and kidnapped Matt, but I got him back. That's where I got the info I gave you earlier. Incidentally you didn't warn me about how big this whole enchilada was when I agreed to snatch Granger—but I forgive you."

"I'm relieved to hear it," Patowski said testily. "I hope you're riding herd on that newsman. If he messes up this investigation I'll—"

"Taken care of," she interrupted quickly. "I'll keep him out of your way, promise. But considering what we've found out and the connections Tess has, we may be able to help you and the fibbies. You might want to check into Mikhail's trophy wife. Seems she's having a fling. Young Steve Renkov saw them."

Pat whistled. "That'd blow the old man's mind."

"And cook her goose, pretty blond feathers and all. She's a good candidate for whoever hired those Ruskie thugs to kill us. Matt and I've been ducking and dodging them since Vegas. The fibbies in Utah screwed up. They should've had Kuzan and Garzenko on ice."

"I'm three thousand miles away, Sam. No damn way could help that, but I'll check out Nancy Renkov," Pat said.

"We have one complication and it's a beaut. Our Russian Godfather has his grandson, the boy's aunt and two little girls—at least we hope he does. If not, they're likely all dead. The widow is on her way here."

"I want her in protective custody right now," he demanded.

"Not until you're up-front with me, Pat."

"You weren't so interested in the details of this deal before—just wanted the money we arranged for you to receive."

"Things have changed. I met the people involved and now I can't feed them to the wolves—your guys or the Russian mob. Either way, three kids and two innocent women could end up dead."

"Speaking of 'involved,' you haven't fallen for Mr. Tall, Dark and Handsome, have you?" he asked suspiciously. He'd seen pictures of Granger. Even the SOB's driver's license photo looked good.

Like he could read her mind! Sam fumed but replied calmly, "You know me better than that, Pat. I intend to collect my money when this is over. Period. I made a new deal with his aunt to act as his bodyguard, so don't sweat his getting in your way."

"Why is it I'm not reassured?" he asked sarcastically.

"Level with me. How close are you to closing the net?"

"No details on the phone. We need a face-to-face."

"Any idea who snatched the woman and kids?" she persisted.

"We didn't know about the kidnapping, but we've staked out all the old man's haunts. If they show, we'll find them. I don't want to talk anymore on an unsecured line."

"Okay. Once I decide on a plan, I'll be in touch," she reluctantly agreed.

Sam didn't feel reassured by her conversation with Pat, but felt some of the weight on her shoulders slip away when she saw Tess Renkov sitting beside Matt in a dark corner. She slid onto a chair beside Tess, who looked pale but remarkably composed considering how she must be feeling. The two of them were deep in conversation. Sam didn't interrupt.

"So I called Mikhail and asked him if he had Steve. I know he tried to trace the call but I was in Chicago, waiting for that hop to Tampa. That ought to throw him if he was able to make a trace."

"Does he have them?" Matt held his breath until she nodded.

"Then I told him about Nancy and her lover. I'm not certain if he believed me. He pretended not to, but he's too arrogant to admit it might be true. I didn't say it was Steve who saw it. I don't want that old bastard frightening my son any more than he already has by questioning him about it. I also told him I didn't kill my husband and I knew nothing about the insurance policy. He said we could talk about it, that maybe he'd misjudged me. He knows that I know he'd never harm Steve, but Jenny and her girls don't mean anything to him."

"You can't walk in there. He'll kill you," Matt said. "Then where would your son or your sister and her kids be?"

"I know," she said wearily. "But he'll do it. One of them.. at a time." Her voice broke.

"Did you demand to talk to your son?" Sam interjected.

"Yes, but he put Jenny on instead. He's keeping them separated. Doesn't want his grandson to know what a monster he is," she said, shivering. Her hands clutched the cup, white as the heavy crockery she held in a death grip.

"Where would he keep them—his place in Aventura?" Matt asked Tess.

Sam's mind raced. What if Pat could get a warrant? Before she could go any further with the idea, Tess said, "He has places all over south Florida where he could hide them. It took him a minute to patch me over to Jenny, so I'd bet she's not with him."

Sam's heart sunk.

"Did he give you a time limit?" Matt asked.

"I told him I couldn't get a flight to Miami until tomorrow. I think he bought it."

"And that buys us a little time. Good thinking, Tess. We'll get your family back." Matt tried to sound positive, but things didn't look good. They discussed the two Ruskie goons who had been chasing them. "Someone hired them to kill you and Steve. Obviously not Mikhail."

"It's Nancy. Who else?" Tess replied. "I only pray Mikhail's keeping him someplace where Nancy can't get near him."

Sam interrupted then. "I made a quick phone call to a cop friend of mine." She could see that piqued Matt's interest sharply. Ignoring his narrowed gaze, she went on, "There's another set of candidates for Alexi's death. The Brighton Beach crowd is trying to muscle in on Renkov's action in Miami."

"It fits with Kuzan's story. I might buy that but why try for 'ess and Steve?" Matt asked her.

"Gotta be Nancy," she replied.

Matt nodded. "The big question right now is what do we o to find Tess's family and get them away from Gramps?"

"I think Kit Steele might help," Tess interjected. "She's al-ays been decent to me. I don't know for sure that she's in-olved in Mikhail's illegal stuff, but she's his tax accountant id he treats her like a serf—oh, a well-paid one. He lets her ve in a house down the road from the one Alexi and I have Indian Creek Village.

"Mikhail owns both places. I know she resents the way he minds her that everything she has is his and he can take it way any time he wants. He did that with everyone, even lexi. He'd be sly about it with us, just hinting about all we wed to his successful business.

"But once I overheard him tell Kit that she could either do he told her or lose the good life on the island and all the great erks he gave her. They had an angry exchange and she ormed out. I think he was asking her to do something illegal. Iaybe it was the first time and she was shocked. I'm not sure."

"Let me do some digging on her before you contact her." Iatt jotted down the spelling of her name. "She could be a eak link we can use. We need some way to trace that call to lexi threatening him if he didn't throw the tournament, too," : added, explaining to Sam what she'd already overheard.

"I have a friend who might be able to do it. Can you re-ember the exact date?" she asked Tess.

"It was the day before Steve's birthday and I'd just brought corations for the party to his grandfather's house. Mikhail ways insisted on all celebrations being held at his place. ay 11th."

Sam made some notes. "Good, that'll help a lot."

"I know a guy with the state insurance board. Did a piece on them a couple of years ago. He might be able to help us with the origin of that mysterious three-mil life policy you supposedly killed Alexi for," Matt said.

"I don't know how to thank you both," Tess said, feeling a little better with Matt and Sam on her side. "Mikhail and Alexi used to talk about how they outsmarted 'business competitors.' They used scramblers on their digital phones, fitted with silicon chips that encrypted the transmissions. Expensive but I have a friend in Marin who works in the field. He had two of them delivered express-mail to me the day before Steve and…" She stopped and took a sip from the cup of coffee before she could go on. "Before they were taken."

She fished in her handbag and gave a small, ordinary looking cell phone to Matt. "With these, we can talk and Mikhail can't know what we're doing."

"Next order of business is to put you under wraps while we work," Sam said to Tess.

"I can't just sit still while my family is in that man's clutches."

"No other choice," Matt said gently, taking her icy hand and squeezing it. "Let us work. There's a slew of hotels around here. Right now we're going to tuck you in one and you have to swear you'll stay put. Deal? Remember, Jenny decided a little stroll on the beach wouldn't hurt anything."

Reluctantly, Tess nodded.

After they checked her into a Holiday Inn on South Le Jeune in Coral Gables, Matt and Sam returned to the Charger. As she started the car, he said, "Okay, level with me. You're working with the cops, right?"

"I'm working for your aunt. I just happen to have friends on the force. I gave seven of my best years to Miami-Dade PD, remember? My sergeant owes me. I can call in a few markers, that's all," she equivocated. She let out the clutch, then moved into traffic, making a few more jumps and lurches than she needed to as she shifted. He didn't look convinced about the cops.

"You think she'll stay put?" she asked, worried that Tess might do something foolish. Sam toyed with giving her up to Pat, but decided that was risky, too.

"Damned if I know, but if Mikhail gets her, she'd dead for sure and so are her sister and nieces. She knows that."

"Let's get cracking. First, I'll put my phone company contact to work. Then we should look into this Steele woman."

"I know a little about Kit Steele from doing background on all Mikhail's players when I started this investigation. She's Brit. An ex-pat who's worked for the old man for five years or so. Rumor has it she's his money-laundering expert. Lots of trips to the Caymans, that sort of thing, but no hard evidence," Matt said.

"I have a feeling when the cops finish sorting all of this out, she might end up in the slammer along with her boss," Sam replied, dying to ask Pat what was up with Renkov's "laundress."

"She might be a way into the organization," Matt said thoughtfully. He opened the cell Tess had given him and tried directory assistance, then made a face.

"Let me guess. Unlisted." Sam's grin was smug, as she took the phone from him and dialed Ethan Frobisher.

Matt listened as she spoke with the guy on the other end of the line, wondering if this Ethan worked a night shift at the phone company. It was after one in the morning and the guy was not only awake but apparently willing to start tracing the call to Alexi Renkov on the 11th. Sam gave him all the pertinent info. She also asked for Kit Steele's private number and address. That he supplied while she waited on the line.

"Pretty impressive."

"When I said he worked for the phone company I was stretching the truth a bit."

"You? Stretch the truth?" he asked rhetorically.

Sam ignored the jibe. "He's really a hacker. Bell South canned him a couple of years back for, er, extracurricular activities. Ethan's a real geeky type, a wizard with anything IT. We went to St. Stanislaus Elementary together. He's had a crush on me since sixth grade."

"Devious woman. You'd use any man to get what you want." He was only half-joking and they both knew it. "All my background notes on the Russian mob in Miami are at my condo in South Beach. I need them since those goons trashed my place in the Samaritan complex."

"Don't you think someone might just be waiting for us to show there?" she asked.

"We lost our two pals back in Vegas, remember? They might be tooling down I-40, looking for your van, but I doubt they're smart enough to admit they lost us even if their boss calls them again."

"Yeah. It might get them fired or iced for botching the job," she agreed, turning onto I-95 north headed for the MacArthur Causeway to the Beach.

Matt's condo was in a three-story pale green stucco structure just off Collins Avenue a little north of the Art Deco district. Each unit had lots of windows and a big balcony overlooking the street. Bougainvillea and variegated shiffelera spilled over one on the second floor. When they neared the front gate, he pulled a small electronic opener from his pocket and the iron fence glided sideways, allowing them to enter before it closed behind them. The parking area was open, beneath the elevated first floor of the building. Volvos, Beamers and other fancy imports were parked alongside an assortment of American cars and SUVs.

"Pretty upscale on a reporter's salary," she said, wondering if he used some of auntie's loot to pay for it.

"I bought it just after hurricane season six years ago. South Florida was a wreck, if you recall. Got it for a song and fixed up my unit myself. It isn't paid for and my aunt doesn't make the payments, either. I do."

Like he could read her bloody mind! Sam was beginning to get a complex. She must be an open book for Matt and Paskowski. What was wrong with her wily Irish wits? "None of my business who makes your rent, Granger. Just a passing comment," she said as she pulled in next to a jazzy sea-foam-blue Mustang convertible.

"Don't scratch the paint," he said as she put her shoulder into forcing open the crushed door that was too close to the Mustang.

"Yours?" She raised one eyebrow. "Don't tell me. You found it at a junkyard and restored it."

"I know the dealer. It's five years old and I bought it used, for crying out loud."

Sam snorted as they headed for the stairwell.

"If you don't want to climb steps, there's an elevator. I'm on the second floor." He was already heading for the elevator.

Just to spite him, she started up the stairs. "Gotta keep my girlish figure. Meet you at the top."

She made it to the second landing when she heard heavy footsteps behind her. Something about the grunt coming from the man made her look back. Vassily Kuzan grinned like an ape as he raised yet another automatic and aimed it at her. Sam ducked and sprinted for the next floor, while reaching into her fanny pack for her "rental" .38. His shot ricocheted off the concrete wall, gouging a nasty hole in the surface. She didn't take time to examine it, just fired one quick shot in his direction to slow him down.

If Kuzan was after her, where was Garzenko? "Matt!" she
yelled at the top of her lungs as she yanked open the door to
the second floor just as the elevator opened.

Chapter 15

Sam flattened herself against the wall at the top of the stairs, behind the partially closed stairwell door. She waited for Kuzan to appear while searching desperately for Matt. The elevator was on the opposite side of the hallway. She had a clear view of it when the doors whooshed open. No Matt. She could hear Kuzan huffing his way up the last of the steps after her, but he did not step through the door frame.

Desperate to know if Garzenko had Matt, she began to slide soundlessly along the wall toward the back of the hallway, gun poised ready to fire. Before she could go back downstairs, she had to deal with Kuzan. The hallway made a sharp turn, revealing a narrow passage to what looked like a janitor's closet about six yards away. She turned the corner and hid, praying for Kuzan to show himself.

A faint squeak behind her distracted her. She turned just as the door of the closet opened and Garzenko raised his

Glock, aiming at her. She jumped around the corner, caught in a crossfire when Kuzan leaned through the exit door and fired, missing her by an inch. She could hear Garzenko moving toward the corner. No place to hide.

The best defense was an unexpected offense, Uncle Dec always said. She lowered her head and barreled around the corner toward Garzenko, butting him directly in the stomach. He let out an "oomph" as her head connected solidly with his solar plexus. Before he could lower his gun to fire at her, she shot him in his left side, angling the barrel so the slug went through lung, into his heart.

He crumpled over her, pulling her down with him as he died. She could hear Kuzan closing in and knew she was in trouble. These guys didn't exactly possess loyalty enough to hold their fire to save a comrade. Sam tried to untangle herself and free her gun but Garzenko held on stubbornly as the life drained out of him. Her weapon was caught beneath his arm. *He's taking me with him.*

When Kuzan neared their tangle of arms and legs, Sam made a desperate lunge for Garzenko's Glock, which he'd dropped when she shot him. But the gun had fallen a foot out of reach. She was braced for the smashing impact of Kuzan's shot when suddenly Kuzan went sprawling facedown on the floor. He landed hard.

Matt tackled him from behind with every pound he could put into it. A lot easier back in college when he'd been a running back. The Russian gasped for breath, trying to roll away from his attacker and get off a shot. Granger wasn't packing a weapon. He had to move fast. As Kuzan turned over and raised the gun, Matt knocked it aside with his left arm and brought his right fist down on Kuzan's throat with every bit of strength he had.

The training he'd received as an Army MP came back easier than the college football. He used his knuckles like a lethal weapon and it worked. The bright purple staining the Russian's face indicated that he'd crushed his windpipe, but Matt didn't care.

"Samantha, baby, are you all right?" He turned desperately toward the tangle of Sam and Garzenko's bodies and saw blood reddening the pale gray carpet beneath them. "Shit," he muttered, afraid to breathe as he seized Garzenko's body and shoved it against the wall, trying to free Sam.

"Did he hit you?" he asked, examining her for wounds. She was smeared with blood but it appeared to be the Russian's, not hers. Garzenko looked dead as Friday night's mackerel. Before she could get her breath back to answer him, he was on his knees between the two dead men, cradling her in his arms, rocking back and forth, never so happy to hear her heart beating solidly against his own, which was pounding frantically.

Sam turned her face up to him and he framed it with his big hands as they knelt. He leaned down to kiss her as a lopsided smile strained to break out on his face. "You iced him."

"Did a head butt first. Not much choice when you're caught in a crossfire," she said, still winded and a little more shaken than she wanted him to see. She looked down at the two dead men. "How'd you know they were here?" she asked, pleased with his fear for her but afraid to admit just how much that meant to her. Still, her arms remained tightly wrapped around his waist.

"Just as the elevator door opened downstairs, I noticed a big, black Town Car parked illegally on the condo lot across the street. I know everybody who lives there and none of them drive a boat like that."

"So you sent the elevator up empty and followed Kuzan up the steps," she said, admiring his guts. "Without a gun, it was a risky chance to take. Some tackle, too."

"I'm getting too old for football. Kuzan was a lot tougher than any of the linemen I played against in college," he replied, pulling her to her feet. He fished in his pocket and pulled out the gate opener. "Get the Charger ready to roll while I retrieve what I need from my place. I don't think we want to stick around and field questions about these stiffs when the Beach PD gets here. Lucky most of my neighbors are party animals, but someone's bound to call 911."

She nodded, knowing if the cops caught them here, it would mess everything up. She tiptoed up and planted a quick kiss on his lips. "I'll be outside waiting. Hurry up."

"Right behind you."

They could see the flashing lights of police cars coming down Collins through the heavy pedestrian and club traffic as they pulled out. Matt carried his laptop and a briefcase shoved full of documents he'd obviously grabbed in a hurry. Sam calmly turned in the opposite direction and proceeded around the block before the police got near enough to spot her.

"Just in case anyone got a look at the plates, I'll need to change them first chance we have to pull over," she said casually.

He grinned at her. "How many illegal plates do you carry with you?"

Sam shrugged. "None. But I can make a switch with a car parked in a public deck in two minutes, tops." She could still feel the imprint of his lips on hers and the desperate sound in his voice when he yanked Garzenko's body off hers and checked her for injuries. Maybe he might forgive her...did she dare hope?

"How the hell did those thugs get back here and find us?" he asked in frustration.

"Sure as hell didn't drive like we hoped. They may no know who hired them, but I bet they had some kind of emer gency number to call," she said.

"And whoever it was wired them plane tickets back here, figuring we'd turn up and they could take us out of the equation. Probably provided the automatics, too. Good thing they didn't have time to get into my condo and destroy my research first." He riffled through the papers in his open briefcase as she drove across the MacArthur Causeway and pulled into the Bayside parking deck.

Carefully picking a spot where none of the security cameras could see her, she made the license plate switch with the dexterity of someone used to the drill. Matt watched in anxious admiration. *I'm going to have to break her of a lot of bad habits.*

The little Boston Irishwoman was beginning to get under his skin. Damn if he didn't admire her in spite of some maddening quirks in her personality. He remembered how the breath had been squeezed from his lungs when he saw her body, entangled with Garzenko's, and his unimaginable relief when she got up unscathed.

Sammie, where is this leading?

Before he could think of an answer, she climbed back into the Charger and pulled out, heading west toward Little Havana.

"I have a Cubano friend who'll hide us until morning. I think we could use some sleep and time to regroup."

"Fine by me," he replied. "As long as he has someplace you can wash up. Riding with a blood-covered woman might just get me arrested."

Sam looked in her side-view mirror and wiped a smudge of blood off her nose. "Look who's talking. Your pant legs are soaked, too." She drove the speed limit, keeping a careful eye out for police.

When they reached Roberto Clemente's shop on Calle Ocho, it was three in the morning and he was just closing up.

Although no relation to the baseball hero of the same name, he ran a combination Santeria, tourist tchotchke and collectibles shop, and sold Cuban sandwiches, pastries and coffee on the side.

"Samantha, *hijita,* what has happened to you?" a chubby little man with a round, grizzled face asked, pulling her into the shop. The place was crowded with everything from baseball cards and T-shirts to black candles and odd-smelling jars with murky contents that Matt figured he'd rather not know about. Religious paraphernalia and Cuban cigars lay side by side.

In the front of the store, the window from which he sold food and coffee had been rolled down for the night, but the spicy rich aromas of fried pork and sweet coffee still lingered. Roberto gave her a quick hug, then examined her to make certain she was not hurt, although in a far more fatherly way than Matt had earlier.

The little man had a receding hairline framed by kinky gray hair that he wore in dreadlocks. He said the hair assured his customers that he was an authentic believer in the Caribbean voodoo blend of mystic religion. Around his neck hung several heavy gold crucifixes and assorted charms enclosed in pouches decorated with chicken feathers. Gris-gris. Powerful stuff, he'd assured her on numerous occasions.

Feeling the way she did, Sam didn't think she'd turn down any talisman he offered them for protection—provided it worked against the Russian mob. "Roberto, this is my friend Matt Granger."

The little man looked up at her tall companion and offered his hand. "You are welcome to my humble home," he said graciously.

"We need a place to hide out until morning," Sam said. "But first I have to tell you we're in trouble with Mikhail Renkov and his guys, maybe some other bad actors from Little Odessa in New York, too. And the Miami Beach PD wants to question us about killing two Russian goons who tried to take us out." She ticked off the damning list matter-of-factly.

"Sam never sugarcoats the medicine, does she?" Matt asked Roberto.

The rotund little man grinned, nodding. "She has always been honest with me." He turned to her. "But making enemies of the Russians, that is bad, very bad. So, did you hide your car behind the shop?" he asked, getting straight to business.

"I won't stay unless you say it's okay," she replied.

"Do not be foolish. You will stay as long as you need. What you did for my brother Rodrigo's daughter, I can never repay. Come, you need to clean up," he said, picking out clean T-shirts emblazoned with Little Havana logos in their sizes along with shorts from bins lining one wall. No one would pick Sam and Matt out of a crowd when they were dressed like tourists.

"I will lay out towels. You can decide who will get the first shower," he said as he led them up a dark, narrow flight of wooden stairs to the second floor where he lived.

Matt snorted. "As if I had a choice. Ladies first."

Sam turned to look at him.

"What? Did I suggest we should share? Even if it would save water," he whispered as Roberto puttered around digging out clean towels and other toiletry items from his bedroom while they stood in the hall.

"I know you were thinking it," she replied, not all that displeased at the notion. But not while Roberto was in the next room. She knew she was a screamer.

They cleaned up, one at a time, while their host prepared a feast of spicy pork and cheese pressed into sandwiches, an assortment of fresh fruits and, at Matt's request, lots of hot

strong coffee. They had to stay awake to work on the leads
Tess Renkov had given them.

Roberto left them alone in the small apartment's one spare
bedroom, which had bunk beds—for his grandchildren, he explained. He was a widower and they visited their grandpa
every weekend. Matt would've sworn the old man was wearing a hint of a grin as he bid them good-night.

Sam excused herself when Matt plugged in his laptop and
got on the Internet to dig some more on Alexi's golf schedule
on his most recent European tours. He'd already sent an e-mail
to his friend in Tallahassee about the insurance policy on
Alexi Renkov's life. "I'll wait for Frobisher's call downstairs,"
she said, turning off the ringer on the phone in the hallway.

"Now, why is it that I think it isn't just consideration for
your friend that makes you want to make your calls from
downstairs?" he asked.

"You could listen in," she said.

"You're gonna use your cell, not Roberto's phone, Sam, so
I can't listen in."

She pointed her finger at him as if it were a gun. "Gotcha."

He turned back to his laptop when she headed toward the
creaking steps.

"That's right, Christine "Kit" Steele. British. Is she by any
chance a laundress by trade?" Sam asked Patowski as she sat
munching on a chunk of smoked sausage.

He was cranky as usual after being awakened only an hour
after he'd hit the hay. "Ain't you the chipper one," he grunted.

She could imagine him sitting on the side of a rumpled bed
in his underwear, a cigarette dangling from one corner of his
mouth, as he jotted down everything Tess had told them about
Alexi and his father. Then again, maybe he slept in the altogether. *No, don't go there, Ballanger.* The thought of that
scrawny pale flab made her wince.

"I can only tell you she's under investigation. Does lots of hopping around from here to the Caymans and back, so it's part of what Gomez is working on."

"The widow wants to trust her, thinks the old man might have treated her bad enough that she'd turn on him. Maybe was forcing her to do some illegal stuff."

Patowski snorted an obscenity and coughed over the phone. "Right, and Nikolai Benko took a stroll off that dock after shooting himself in the back of the head." He paused, then asked, "You wouldn't know anything about two dead Ruskies. Usta work for old Nikki. Beach PD found them in the hall of your boyfriend's condo earlier tonight."

Sam knew he knew. Sighing, she said, "They were the same goons who tried to kill us out west."

"And of course, you couldn't stick around to explain any of that to the local authorities."

"We'd be in the slammer and where would that leave Tess and her family?"

"The way you draw shooters like a magnet, probably a hell of a lot better off," he snapped.

"Cover for us, Pat. You owe me that much. Please?" She nearly choked on the last word.

He cursed again and muttered, "For now, but you'd better keep your boyfriend's butt out of this or I'll roast it and your own sweet ass over slow coals." Then he slammed down the receiver.

She held her cell away from her ear. "No need to break the damn thing, Patty, sheesh," she said, closing it.

Down in the Gables, Tess Renkov lay staring at the ceiling in her hotel room. She'd tried to sleep for several hours and barely dozed before visions of her family awakened her. She imagined she could hear Tiff and Mellie sobbing and

Jenny trying to comfort them, Steve pleading with his grandpa to let him see them and being sternly refused.

Then she thought of Nancy. What if she found out from Mikhail where Steve was? She started to sweat and grow dizzy. Sitting up, Tess swung her feet onto the cool tile floor, pacing and trying to remember exactly what Alexi had said that day he and his father had fought. Something about "a clear channel straight to Pribluda." At first she'd thought it meant somewhere along the Intracoastal where he and Benko might've arranged to meet.

Then suddenly it hit her. She was almost certain, remembering the day before he and his father had their fight. "He'd been on his cigarette boat, working on…" Tess made a dash for the cell in her handbag and punched in Matt's number. It rang and rang. No one answered. Dread seized her. What if Mikhail had found Matt and Sam?

She had no one else to turn to…unless she took a desperate chance and contacted Kit Steele. "No, I'll wait and try again in an hour," she said, rubbing her icy hands over her arms and hugging herself.

Matt sat at his laptop, studying the printout his friend from the state insurance board had just sent. It paid to have sources in the capital, especially when they owed you favors. He'd kept Mel O'Donnell from going down with his boss when he broke a story about kickbacks on health and life insurance bids in the department last year. "Very interesting…but not funny," he muttered, his gaze narrowing on the printout.

Sam had been half dozing on the top bunk, her cell clutched in her hand, waiting for Frobisher and Patowski to call back. She turned on her side and hung her head over the bed rail. "What did you find out?" she asked, suppressing a yawn. So much for Cuban coffee. After spending the last days the way she had, a caffeine addict like her couldn't stay awake even if she injected the stuff directly into her carotid arteries.

"Guess who took out that three-million-buck policy on Alexi Renkov," he said.

"I give, who?"

"Alexi Renkov," Matt said thoughtfully.

"You mean our boy may have set up a phony murder scam to implicate his wife? That would mean—"

"Maybe he isn't dead?"

"But the autopsy—how could the M.E. make a mistake like that?"

Granger shrugged. "Guess we'll have to find out."

"Let me put the cops on this one. My pal at Miami-Dade will be hot to find that creep hiding in some sand trap."

"I don't know if I'd trust them with this until we know more," he said, still suspicious of her police contacts.

As they argued, neither one noticed the encrypted cell phone Tess had given Matt that lay on the cluttered table where he'd emptied the pockets of his bloody pants before showering and changing. During his tackle of Vassily, it had been damaged, but he had not used it and did not know it was no longer functioning.

Tess tried again. And again. Finally, as the sun barely began creeping up on the Atlantic, she made a decision. Her clothes were wrinkled and she looked haggard, but Kit Steele wouldn't care once Tess told her what was going on. If anyone could find out where Steve and the others were, it would be Kit.

In minutes she was outside the hotel flagging down a cab. Take me to Indian Creek Village. Yes, I have a pass card to

get on the island," she replied when the wizened little driver
eyed her quizzically.

She couldn't blame him. After all, people who lived on
such an exclusive private island did not normally stay in Holiday Inns.

Chapter 16

Sam was still arguing with Matt when her cell beeped. She picked it up, recognizing Ethan Frobisher's number—only because he allowed his number to be shown, she knew. He could trace anybody electronically and block anyone from finding him. Sometimes it creeped her out. "Hey, Fro, sweetie, what have you got for me?"

"Kinda weird and it took me a while. Sorry about that. Usually I can get this kind of stuff in half an hour, but it didn't make sense. Still doesn't."

"Tell me what you found and I'll sort it out," Sam said with a sudden premonition.

"Well, the call to the Renkov home on Indian Creek was made from another phone owned by—"

"Alexi Renkov?" she volunteered.

"Hey, you already knew." He sounded disappointed, just like when she'd turned him down when he asked her to the junior-high prom at St. Stan's. Before she hung up with him, Sam praised his genius, which always made Ethan feel good. One of these days when she visited her family, she'd have to look him up and take him out for a beer. They could talk about old times and get blasted at the Sam Adams Tap Room. Except Ethan didn't drink. Oh, well, he could have a Shirley Temple—if Burt Manion, Uncle Dec's best friend who ran the joint, knew how to make one. She sure as hell didn't.

Sam turned to Matt who was watching her intently. "Was that what I think it was?"

"Yeah. I think our pal Alexi has erased himself. Wanna bet it has something to do with the turf war between his pappy and Little Odessa?"

"I don't make sucker bets," he said, considering the ramifications. "The whole equation changes if young Renkov is still a player, you should pardon my pun."

She winced. "Jon Stewart you're not. I gotta call Patowski. We're in over our heads, Matt."

He threw up his hands. "Go for it."

She nodded and picked up her cell, which had gone dead because she'd forgotten to plug it in since this whole mess had started back in San Diego. Pretending that it was working, she went downstairs and used Roberto's phone. Sam wasn't about to admit to such a careless mistake.

Pat had obviously given up all hope of getting any sleep and went to his office. He answered on the first ring, his voice as gravelly as usual but alert this time. Still cranky as hell though. "You on a secure line?" he asked.

"None safer. I'm in Little Havana with an old friend. Believe me, no one taps his line."

The sergeant got crankier when she explained what they had just found out.

"Are you saying you already knew Alexi might still be

alive?" she asked, incredulously. "Why the hell didn't you tell me?"

"Because you were supposed to be driving Mr. Daisy back to bean land, not snooping in Miami. That damned newsman ought to be locked in a rubber room on Beacon Hill by now," he said. "It's what you were hired to do."

"No way could I stop Matt from getting involved after what happened in California. He feels responsible for Tess and her family."

Pat cursed. "Only because he led the whole shebang of Ruskies directly to them. This isn't your job, Sam. It's mine and the fibbies'."

"If he could find them, so could the mob and you know it. The FBI and Miami-Dade PD were the ones who couldn't, admit it, Patty. You used him as a stalking horse then. You can use him—and me—now."

"Don't call me Patty, dammit," he snapped. "I'm not a Mick."

"No, you're a Polack. So what's Special Agent Gomez's excuse for being dumb?" she shot back, her short Irish fuse ignited. Usually she and Patowski traded ethnic insults as casually as yuppies chatted about mocha espresso versus skim-milk lattes. She relented with a sigh. "Okay, it's been a long night. Let's agree to work together from here on, okay? Granger won't run his story until this whole mess is wrapped up. We have access to some sources you can't use," she added to remind him about Kit Steele.

"Between the two women, they know most of the places Mikhail might stash his prisoners. I can scam my way inside. You know I'm good at this. It's what I do for a living, for crying out loud. Just let me work for a few hours."

Grumbling, he agreed, giving her what they had on Alexi. Gomez ran the same check on insurance records and came up with the golden boy's policy trick, framing his wife. Made us suspicious, so we got a court order for the phone records. I won't ask how you got 'em."

"Good thinking," she said succinctly.

"The body in the car matched his dental records, but those can be substituted. We're checking that now. The DNA is trickier, harder to switch, but not impossible."

"If the body is a close blood relative?" she asked.

"Who? Nobody was missing when his car exploded."

"What if Alexi had some other kin back in the motherland he lured over here?" she asked, thinking out loud.

"That's awfully long-range planning for a playboy like Alexi." Pat sounded dubious. "But we'll check it out."

"Yeah, he took out that insurance policy, didn't he? With a fortune from the New York mob, he could sit on a beach somewhere surrounded by bimbos. Tess takes the fall for his fake death and Mikhail's organization loses big-time to Little Odessa. He's out from under daddy's very big thumb. Let me put Granger on that angle. He's got sources all over the place." Matt had a personal stake in this one, and now so did she, although she'd never admit it to Patowski.

"Look, just because you're boffing the guy doesn't mean I have to trust him—or you."

"I am not having a relationship with a man I was hired to snatch," she said adamantly. "It's a violation of professional ethics." At least the last part was true.

"If I didn't know how much coin that old lady was paying you, I'd never believe you. Keep me posted on what you find out," he added gruffly.

"I will if you will," she said. The line went dead. She fished her cell out of her pocket, intending to charge it. But then she heard Matt stomping down the steps into the shop. He had a cold, hard gleam in his eyes that made the hair c the back of her neck stand straight out. He hadn't looked like this since he'd come at Yuri and Vassily with that gooseneck pipe.

"Your cell's dead," he said conversationally.

"You listened in on the upstairs phone." She tried for indignation, failed miserably. "Look, Matt, I can explain."

"I think your cop friend already explained things pretty well. This was a setup from the get-go to keep me on ice until the local cops and FBI made their case against Renkov while keeping the CIA in the dark. My aunt was suckered into paying your exorbitant fees and I was suckered into believing you gave a damn about Tess and her family." *And me.* He didn't have to say that. He knew she knew it, damn her soul.

"You're wrong, Matt. It only started that way."

"Yeah, that's right. Once I got hold of the guns, you had to try another tack, so you convinced her to hire you as my bodyguard. I wonder if she knows bodyguards screw the guys they're supposed to guard." He tried for a sneer but it came out more a grimace. *Damn your mercenary little soul, Samantha Ballanger!*

Sam deflated. He was too mad to reason with. She couldn't blame him. "I'm sorry, Matt. I never should've become emotionally involved with—"

"Ah, but you aren't—remember what you just told your copper. 'No relationship.' Nice touch with the 'professional ethics' shtick. Lady, you wouldn't recognize professional ethics if they were emblazoned across Key Biscayne in neon letters!"

He turned around and took the steps two at a time. She quickly followed, hoping their yelling hadn't awakened Roberto. If it had, Roberto was too discreet to open his door. She watched as Matt packed up his notes and laptop. "Where are you going?" she asked in a small voice.

"To pick up Tess and figure out how to rescue her family.

I got them into this mess. I'll get them out. No help from you needed, Ms. Bodyguard."

"Matt—"

"Sorry about your deal with my aunt. Maybe you can bill her for the hours we spent on the road. Maybe not. The old broad's pretty savvy."

She watched him leave. This was even worse than her last day on active duty with Miami-Dade Homicide. A rookie blew a clean takedown with Patowski and their team. The kid turned the blame on her and it stuck. Everyone knew she was a hotdog. After a brief Internal Affairs investigation, she was kicked off the force. Pat suspected Graham of lying and tried to prove it but Sam, who had trained the kid, wouldn't turn on him.

Watching her career go up in flames had hurt, but not nearly as much as losing Matt Granger. Sam grabbed her fanny pack and took off after him. It was daybreak in Little Havana and everyone was driving in their usual "suicide salsa" style, rushing to work. Not a cab to be had. He started trudging west on Calle Ocho. Sam quickly retrieved her Charger from the back and followed him for a couple of blocks, watching him try unsuccessfully to hitch a ride.

No sane woman—or man, for that matter—would give an unshaven, disheveled six-foot-six stranger a ride. She let him walk off the worst of his temper, then pulled up alongside him. His long legs ate up the pavement pretty fast, but people in Miami never believed in cruising below sixty mph on city streets. The beeps were deafening but she ignored them, yelling out to him over the din, "You figure on walking to Coral Gables?"

He didn't answer but lengthened his stride even more until the press of people on the sidewalk began to slow him down. Fresh flower and fruit vendors, shopkeepers and bak-

ry deliverymen ducked the big guy carrying an armload of
aper and a laptop.

"Come on, Matt, no matter how you feel about me, you
eed my wheels—and my connections. We can help Tess to-
ether a hell of a lot better than working against each other."

"And, you get paid. Don't forget that."

"Yeah, I won't. Now, get in."

He considered giving her the finger, but in spite of his
ruised ego and an achy area somewhere in his chest, he knew
he was right about helping Tess. Muttering an expletive, he
anked open the passenger door and climbed inside, then
ulled out the encrypted cell Tess had given him. He started
unching in numbers before he realized it wasn't working.

"What's wrong?" she asked, weaving expertly through the
ad rush of traffic toward Tess's hotel.

"Damned phone's dead. Cracked on the back," he said,
rning it over. "Must've done it in when I tackled Vassily.
Ve landed pretty hard."

Sam had hers plugged in the charger on the console but it
vouldn't work for another quarter hour or so at best. "We'll
e in the Gables before I can call," she explained, speeding
p even more, which minimalized the beeping behind her.

"I think I left my old cell at Roberto's place," he said, an-
ry with himself now as much as with her. Almost.

When they reached Tess's room, the maid was cleaning it.
ess was nowhere to be seen. A clerk downstairs indicated
at she'd called a cab and taken off an hour ago.

"Where the hell could she have gone?" he asked, pacing
cross the lobby.

"Maybe she got a call from Steve?" Sam suggested but
idn't believe it herself. Then it hit her—and him—at the
ame time. "Kit Steele!" they both said at once.

In rush hour they made amazingly good time heading north

on I-95 and cutting over the Kennedy Causeway to threa
their way toward Kit Steele's exclusive address in India
Creek Village. The only problem was that it was a private i
land and security was impossibly tight. No one without
pass card could get inside unless a homeowner vouched f
them.

As Sam drove, Matt pored over what he'd learned abo
the woman who was probably a money laundress for Mikha
Renkov, even if an unwilling one. "I only hope her gue
about this dame was right," he said. "Steele might figure
score points with her boss by turning Tess over to him."

"My cell's charged. Let's see if you can raise her," Sam sai
She'd been watching the console signal as she drove. She hand
him her phone and he dialed. After a three rings, Tess pick
up. "Are you with Kit Steele?" he asked without preamble.

"Yes. We're searching Alexi's racing boat. I tried to ca
you but you didn't answer. Matt, I was sure I'd figured o
where he hid the information he threatened Mikhail with."

"And?" Matt prompted.

"I was wrong," she said in a weary voice. "Kit and I to
the radio apart. He'd said he had a 'clear channel to Pribluda
The Top Gun Cigarette is his favorite, the one he was alwa
tinkering with. I was sure he meant he'd put the material i
side the radio compartment. For good measure, we even too
apart his big Tiara's radio. Nothing."

"Can you get your friend to let us in?" he asked as the
drove up the bridge to the security gate where a very ster
looking man in uniform stared at them from behind a wi
dow in a brick building that looked strong enough
withstand a direct nuclear hit.

"We're here to see Kit Steele," Sam said hopefully into t
speaker. "Sheesh, should I have ordered fries with that?" sl
muttered to Matt as they waited anxiously.

The speaker barked something that sounded like, "Proeed," and the barrier in front of the visitors' gate raised. Sam idn't give the guy inside a chance to reconsider. The harger's tires squealed as she took off across the arched ridge and followed the twisting labyrinth to the address Frosher had given her.

"Some digs," she said, as she pulled her beat-up vehicle to a circular drive surrounded by palmettos, bougainvillea, ntana and all sorts of elaborate flowering and evergreen ndscaping. The house was a stone split-level, with lots of lass and open decks spilling off the sides.

"Yeah, but she doesn't own it."

"If everything Tess said about Kit was true, then Mikhail oes."

"Ditto her yacht—" he glanced down at his notes "—a Jag nd a Bentley."

"She must be very good at her job."

When they climbed out of the Charger, Tess was waiting the front door with her hostess. Kit Steele was a striking edhead whose naturally pale English complexion had been ade golden in the warm, moist tropical sun. Her hair, a deep uburn, was streaked with sunny golden highlights and worn a sleek French twist that accented high cheekbones and inged eyebrows over wide blue eyes the color of a cloudss south Florida sky.

Her smile was an orthodontist's dream. No "English teeth" ere, Sam thought as she took the beautifully manicured hand f the tall, slender woman. She was a couple of inches taller an Tess, who was taller than Sam.

"I'm ever so happy to meet you, Ms. Ballanger, Mr. ranger," she said in a crisp upper-class British accent. Won't you please come inside?"

"It's Matt and Sam," he said as they followed her into a

huge foyer with a polished marble floor. His aunt wouldn'
have sniffed at the Oriental area rug lying on it. He never coul
keep Chinese period pieces straight, but it looked like a Min
vase on the Henredon Circa East table. Either Kit Steele ha
grown up with serious money or she'd hired one hell of a dec
orator.

Sam only smelled money as she looked around, unable t
put names to the expensive-looking furnishings. Art and inte
rior design were not subjects she'd studied in college. Kit cha
ted pleasantly as they made their way down a wide hallwa
past a sunken living room toward a patio at the rear of the hous
where a servant was laying out breakfast on a glass table.

"Marguerite, please set two more places. You will join u
for breakfast, of course?" she offered them as the maid scur
ried off to do as she was told.

"Some coffee would be good, thanks," Matt replied wit
a smile. He turned to Tess. "How're you holding up?" H
hadn't the heart to scold her for doing something so poten
tially dangerous. What if Steele had been in on the conspir
acy? Tess would be a hostage along with Jenny and her kid
now and neither he nor Sam would have a shred of proof tha
Kit had been within a mile of them.

"We don't have much time until I'll have to confron
Mikhail," Tess said tightly. "All I can think of is where he'
keep them. Kit and I talked about it while we took apart th
radios on Alexi's boats."

Sam looked over at the woman who was politely motion
ing for the maid to begin serving fresh fruit and croissant
"Did you come up with any ideas?" she asked.

Kit Steele placed her delicate china cup back in its sauce
"A few. He owns some strip clubs in the South Beach are
but I don't think he'd want the boy to see that side of his bus
ness. It's a bit sordid."

British understatement? Sam wasn't sure. "Where else?"

"There are several ways into the house in Aventura that I oubt the police know about. It seems to me that he'd want teve to feel as safe and at home as possible."

Sam and Matt both looked at Tess. Had she told Kit about 1e potential danger from Nancy? Tess answered that indi- ectly. "We agreed that he'd think it was too risky."

"Mikhail knows the police and federal authorities are vatching him," Kit said. "He's admitted as much to me re- ently. Ever since this dispute with Pribluda's people began, 1ikhail's been even more paranoid than usual. Losing his son as only intensified it. No, he'd take no chance losing Steve."

"But he has places, yachts, a condo in Key West, even a each house on Key Largo. More that we may not even know bout," Tess added, leaning her head in her hand wearily.

"The bottom line is that it would take days to search them ll and if he learned what we were about, he'd just have Steve 1oved," Kit replied.

"What about Jenny and her daughters?" Sam asked. "I an't imagine he'd care where he stashed them as long as they ere secured.

"The places in South Beach and even up toward Bal Har- or would work for that," she said, consideringly.

"Is there any chance you could find out—either about teve or his aunt? I know you handle his taxes and money ansfers. Surely that database includes real estate," Matt said • her.

"Thank you for being tactful, Matt. Yes, I am what you anks call a money laundress for a criminal, but unfortu- ately, Mikhail has always kept his dealings very compart- entalized. I know he has other homes in the vicinity and, deed around the world, but very few actual addresses un- ss they're involved in business cash flow."

She hesitated, as if considering how much to tell them then added, "I've been looking for a way out for several years Mikhail was my green card to America and a whole new life I met him in London five years ago when I was newly divorced and quite down on my luck. He posed as an international import-export dealer and told me he was looking for hard workers who wanted to better themselves. I jumped at the chance when he said he had an opening for an accountant. Of course, I didn't have the proper certification, but I was fast to learn…"

"And then when you found out the truth you couldn't quit Matt supplied.

"Again, kind of you. But, no, at first the money and benefits—" she gestured around the lavish house and sparkling water beyond the manicured lawn "—made me willing to overlook where my good life came from. I told myself that was simply transferring funds, not killing people."

"You've never seen Mikhail change from a charmer into a monster. We have," Tess said quietly.

"I imagine the invasion from Little Odessa didn't exactly bring out the best in him," Sam said. "Do you have any idea what kind of information Alexi was going to peddle to Prbluda?"

"I would imagine a list of his contacts in the drug business—Colombians and their intermediaries," Kit said. "Some Middle Eastern ones, too."

"Does Mikhail have a guard posted at Tess and Alexi house?" Sam asked.

"You mean, could you get in and search the place without him finding out about it?" Kit asked.

"We were already on the premises to examine Alexi's boat Our house is only two doors down from Kit's," Tess said. "We just hopped on her Jet Ski and rode over to our dock."

"Dangerous," Matt said.

Tess smiled gamely. "I wore a blond wig. No one would've ecognized me as other than someone Kit knew. She's in harge of selling Alexi's toys for Mikhail."

"I know it sounds frightfully cloak-and-dagger, but I keep isguises here that I use upon occasion when I travel on busi-ess."

"I don't think it's such a hot idea to stick around right now," am said. "Who knows if some of Mikki's goons might not how up after seeing you with a stranger, especially if you vere snooping around Alexi's boats."

"Even if they're not on the island, they could be keeping abs on the place from across the Intracoastal with a high-ower telescope," Matt agreed.

"The boathouse is large and no one could see inside. As ess said, I've been showing his boats, Jet Skis and cars to erspective buyers for the past week or so. But you could be ght about Mikhail utilizing high-tech surveillance," Kit re-lied.

"The joint could be wired," Sam speculated as she looked ver at Tess, who paled.

"I should've thought of that. Mikhail's ever so devious," it said. Her porcelain English complexion turned decidedly llow now.

They rose from the breakfast table and everyone moved to-ard the front door with Sam in the lead.

"We'd really appreciate it if you could think of any possi-lities for where Jenny and her kids might be stashed," Sam id.

"I can access a list of Mikhail's strip clubs. Just give me a inute to print it out." She made a quick detour into a room lled with expensive electronic equipment and sat down at a eyboard.

Her fingers flew as she typed and punched in codes, so swiftly that neither Sam nor Matt could have followed the even if the monitor had not blocked their view. Almost immediately the printer started spitting out pages. Kit quick scooped them up and handed them to Matt.

He whistled low. "One's only a couple of blocks from where I live."

"And you think I live in a bad area," Sam said. "At least no one's tried to kill me in my own place."

"Someone tried to kill you?" Tess asked, appalled.

"Several times now," Sam replied calmly. "We'll explain about our adventures on the ride," she said to Tess. Without explanation, she gave the Charger door a karate kick and hopped inside. If Kit was surprised by the demonstration, she didn't show it.

Tess took Kit's hands. "Somehow, we'll all get out of this and see Mikhail behind bars. I swear it."

"I do so hope you're right," Kit replied.

"You think it's a good idea to stay here?" Sam asked. mean, if there's any chance Mikhail has bugged the joint and knows you're working with us?"

"Now that I consider it, I doubt he has. My anti-bugging system is pretty sophisticated, but I'll run a scan just to safe. If anything's amiss, I'll get out quickly and call you She looked back at Tess. "Now, get on with you, and do keep safe."

She stood in the drive as they pulled away, then turned back to her gilded cage and disappeared inside.

Chapter 17

am drove quickly to the gate, which lifted without delay.
A lot easier getting off this island than getting on," she mut-
red.

Matt skimmed the printout from Kit. "I know most of
ese places. I'll attract less attention snooping around than
ou would," he said to Sam.

"Yeah, especially if you keep your hands in your pockets,"
e shot back. "Let me put in a few calls to some tattoo joints
d see what I can come up with on that angle." She looked in
r rearview at Tess in the backseat. "Steve saw an infinity
gn? No idea about what those other doodads under it were?"

"I—I don't think he wanted to look any closer. He was
ocked and afraid. Not that Nancy had ever been the least
nd to him, but she was married to his grandfather and he
ally loved the old man. Damn Mikhail! Now he's destroyed
en that illusion for Steve," Tess said through clenched teeth.

"Tess, I know how high the stakes are for you, but you have
to let us handle this and stay where we put you," Matt said
gently. "His goons have orders to kill you. Once you're out
of the way, nothing's going to keep your sister and her family alive."

"And he'll have my son all to himself." She shivered and
bit down on her lip until it bled. "I was frightened when I
couldn't reach you, but you're right, it was poor judgment to
run off on my own. I was so sure about one of those damned
boats having Alexi's papers hidden on it."

"You took them apart stem to stern?" Matt asked. "Remember, we could be looking for something as small as a computer
chip."

Tess shook her head. "I doubt it. Alexi hated computers.
He was always getting ours bollixed up and Steve had to
show him how to retrieve whatever he'd lost. He was a genius as an athlete, but he had no patience to sit still."

"Then we're talking paper," Sam said. "Easier to find."

"Only if you know where to look," Matt replied thoughtfully.

He and Sam exchanged a glance, trying to decide whether
or not to tell Tess that her husband might still be alive. He
shook his head ever so slightly. She nodded imperceptibly.
*Damn, we operate on the same wavelengths. Pretty scary
stuff, huh, Ballanger?* She was going to get hurt if she wasn't
careful. Who was she trying to fool? She was already in way
over her head. The only consoling thought was that Matt
seemed to be, too.

Maybe he'd even forgiven her for working with Patowski...maybe.

"I have a friend who owns a Sea Ray at the South Beach
Marina. I know she'd let us borrow it for a couple of hours.
We could tie up at the Adkins place next door to our house

They're on vacation in Greece and their home is empty. A caretaker checks on things Tuesdays and Fridays. Then we could slip across and search. Alexi may have hidden the material somewhere inside our house."

"The cops have gone over that place with a fine-tooth comb," Matt said dubiously.

"I don't think your friend will want to get involved in B and E. Technically that house doesn't belong to you anymore. It's Mikhail's," Sam said.

"Brenda and I have been friends since grade school. She works at the marina to help pay upkeep on her boat. When I tell her what's happened, I know she'll let us have it," Tess replied.

"One other problem. Who drives the boat?" Sam asked.

"Don't look at me," Matt said. "I sculled back in college. I sail, but I haven't a clue about big powerboats."

"I can handle any kind of boat," Tess said. "Alexi adored speedboats and big flashy yachts. I learned how to operate every one we ever owned."

"Okay, looks like we have a plan," Sam said. "Matt, you use that list Kit gave you and look for Jenny and the girls while Tess and I try scavenging up Alexi's top-secret list in his house—and we'll go over that boathouse again, too."

"What if Mikhail knew his son's drunken threat was already a plan? He might have found the info and destroyed it," Matt said. "Or Alexi has it," he mouthed silently to Sam.

"Yeah, it could be gone," Sam admitted. "But looking is worth a try. Our time's running out."

Tess used her encrypted cell to call Brenda. After a brief exchange, she signed off with a smile. "She's there and said we can have the Ray for as long as we need it. It's all gassed up and ready."

"Tess, how long do you think Mikhail will wait for you to show in Miami?" Matt asked.

"I told him late afternoon. The plane supposedly arrives at five forty-five. If I tried for anything beyond that, he'd have known I was lying."

As they talked, Sam picked up her newly charged cell and started hitting speed-dial numbers. "Yeah, an infinity sign. No, it's kinda like a figure eight laying on its side." She hung up from the third call with a sigh. "There are a few more upscale places but I don't have them on my list," she said.

Matt raised one eyebrow. "Why doesn't that surprise me," he muttered rhetorically.

"Just look on the backseat floor, Tess. Last time I used the car, I left a couple of yellow-page books. Jorge doesn't clean up much."

Tess dug around and fished out two fat, badly dog-eared phone books. "They're here."

"Give the *J* to *Z* one to the Yalie." She handed it to Matt who started thumbing through it.

"Try checking under *T*, you know, for tattooing."

"Funny, Samantha." He dialed several numbers as Sam drove to a marina in Bal Harbor. "Zip," he reported disgustedly. "At least they knew what an infinity sign was, even did a few."

Sam snapped her fingers. "Look up a number for me." She gave him a shop name in the Brickell district. When he found the number and dialed, she took the phone, talked for a minute to a guy named Burt, then hung up glumly. "He remembers his shop doing one with some kind of letters around it."

"And?" Matt prompted.

"It was on a woman, several years ago. He couldn't remember much since he didn't do the job. Said she was a knockout blond."

"Well, that's a waste of time," Tess said.

"Maybe," Sam replied thoughtfully. "Pretty unusual comb

If she got one, maybe she had a friend who got one, too, and Burt didn't notice. He only pays attention to the chicks."

"His and hers. Possible," Matt admitted as she swung into the marina parking lot and stopped the car with an abrupt lurch.

"Sorry about that. I wasn't paying attention to sliding into second gear. Now, let's see your friend about a boat," Sam said to Tess. Turning to Granger, she said, "Be careful with the Charger...and yourself. We'll meet you back here—" she paused, checking her watch "—say, three."

"At least keep that 'rental' gun loaded and ready," Matt cautioned her.

Sam studied him, trying to read whether he really cared about her or was just concerned that she keep Tess safe. "Hey, snooping around mob strip joints isn't exactly the safest way to spend an afternoon, either," she replied flippantly. "Watch yourself."

"I'll try. Not easy driving around in this death trap on wheels," he said.

"Remember, if I don't bodyguard you, I don't get paid. You said Aunt Claudia's a savvy old dame." There was a dare in her eyes as she met his steady gaze.

"I'm a big boy, which I hope you've noticed by now. I can take care of myself," he said, chucking her beneath her chin.

Something loosened in Sam's chest.

"Take my cell, in case you find Jenny and the girls and need help," Tess interjected, handing him a phone to replace the smashed one.

"Good idea," he said. "Thanks." He and Sam exchanged another long searching look, then he climbed into the Charger and turned the ignition. It sputtered to life on the third try.

He couldn't quite make the transition through the gears.

Sam grinned at him in the rearview as the perverse machine died at second. Gritting his teeth, he started it up again and departed the marina lot in a series of teeth-rattling lurches.

Sam stared after him as Tess asked, "You're in love with him, aren't you?"

Sam blinked. Was it that obvious? "Yeah," she admitted with a sigh. "Guess I am, but it's complicated."

"It always is," Tess replied softly.

Thinking of Alexi Renkov, Sam said nothing as they walked to the office. Granger might be a handful, but at least he was one of the good guys, not an international playboy gangster.

"You are not happy here, Stefan?" Mikhail Renkov asked his grandson, who sat picking at a pile of fries smothered in ketchup just the way the boy liked them. The old man had his grandson smuggled from his beach house on Fisher Island back to his home in Aventura as soon as he was certain the police had no idea the boy, his aunt and cousins had been kidnapped. "I have Kiski make all your favorites—hamburger with all trimmings, Cokes, even we have ice cream. Double chocolate chip for dessert."

His cajoling tone and thickly accented English, which usually brought a smile to Steve's face, now only elicited a shrug. "Guess I'm not hungry, Grandpa. Where's my mom? And Aunt Jenny and Tiff and Mellie?"

Mikhail sighed. "I have explained this. The police would arrest your mother and aunt for your father's death. We both know they could never do such a terrible thing. I have your aunt and cousins safely hidden until I can find the men who did this to my son. Your mother is with them now."

Steve had overheard bits and snatches, a lot more than his mom or aunt thought he knew, about his dad's death and his grandfather's involvement in some kind of illegal dealings. They said he was part of the Russian Mafia and Steve knew that was bad. He suppressed a shudder, thinking of what such a man might do to Nancy if he found out about her lover. She had been off for a day of shopping at Bal Harbor when he was brought here this morning. He would never tell on her but he didn't want to face her, either.

"It isn't safe to talk to Mom because the police might have your phones bugged and find them." Steve repeated the story he'd been told over and over again by his grandfather and all the staff here. He did not believe Mikhail or his employees.

"*Da,* yes, that is right," the old man said, tousling his grandson's hair affectionately. "I will always protect you— and your mother. You must have faith, Stefan. Only faith. Come now, finish your lunch. Kiski will be hurt if you do not eat."

Steve forced down another bite out of the burger and ate a few fries to humor his grandfather. He even ate a small portion of his favorite ice cream to keep the old man happy. If he suspected his grandson was trying to escape, Mikhail would never relax his guard over him. The boy knew his grandfather's big house and the grounds around it as well as he knew his own home. He also knew several places where his mom and aunt and cousins might be held. He was going to find them.

"Now, it is time for your schoolwork, is it not?" Mikhail asked. He had arranged for the boy to have a private tutor while he was "visiting" his grandfather and could not attend his usual classes for gifted students. Before lunch, Mr. Mathis had given him chemistry and English assignments to complete for tomorrow.

Steve thought it was just another way to keep track of him without making him feel as if he was a prisoner. "Yes,

Grandpa," he said, glad to get away from the old man who he had once loved unconditionally.

Matt drove along a particularly unsavory section of Washington Avenue in the South Beach area, searching for a parking place. Sam would skin him if her classy rental got sideswiped—or just plain swiped, although given the profusion of Hummers and Jags to choose from, a smashed-up ancient Dodge didn't seem a likely target for thieves. As for being sideswiped? How could she tell?

He pulled into a public parking deck and resumed his search. So far, it had yielded nothing. He started at the top of Kit's list of clubs owned by the local mob, but had struck out at the first three he'd visited. After taking some pretty dicey chances sneaking into the back rooms, he only found discarded pasties and rats chewing their way through cardboard cases of booze. No prisoners, however. Deciding to try his luck farther south, toward the Art Deco district, he chose the Blue Dragon, even though it wasn't next on the list. It took up nearly a city block and was surrounded by dense, poorly tended tropical vegetation. It looked seedy and overgrown, perfect for hiding kidnap victims behind the barred windows on the second floor.

"But how the hell do I get upstairs?" he muttered to himself as he ambled into the dimly lit interior. At once cigarette and other less legal smoking aromas assailed his nostrils. Since quitting the cigs five years ago, a real battle for a newsman, he'd grown to hate the filthy habit. The air was heavy with human sweat and cheap liquor. He could feel his sternum vibrate from the mind-numbingly loud music blasting across the big low-ceilinged room.

The usual weekday lunch crowd of tongue-lolling perverts had assembled to watch an exotic dancer make whoopee with a neon pole on an elevated platform behind the U-shaped bar. He slid into a corner booth near a door leading, he hoped, upstairs. A waitress wearing more jewelry than clothing slithered over to take his order. She offered a lap dance to go with his beer—for a substantial additional charge.

He smiled at her and settled for the seven-dollar draft beer. Nursing the tall glass until he was sure no one was watching him, Matt slid out of the booth and tried the door. Locked. He cursed silently, then headed for the men's room. The doors along the narrow, barely lit wall were unmarked except for restrooms. Pretending to be drunk, he staggered against one, then a second, attempting to turn the knobs. On the third at the end of the hall he struck jackpot. A genuine drunk lurched out of the men's room just as he was closing the door but paid no attention to him.

Matt saw a narrow flight of stairs leading up and another down to the basement below. He hesitated for a moment but the sound of someone coming from the upper landing made the decision for him. He ducked down and descended into stygian darkness, flattening himself against the wall until the sounds of a conversation in Russian died away.

Flicking on the penlight he always carried on his key ring, he followed the cold stone steps to a dirt floor. The smell of mold and rat droppings wasn't much worse than the cheap perfume and hormonal slobber upstairs. A long corridor stretched before him. The walls were thick stone blocks and the doors looked like they were padlocked. Possibilities. He started cautiously toward the first door, calling softly for Jenny.

They might be drugged. Or worse. He refused to consider the possibilities. Poor scatterbrained Jenny and her two bright kids didn't deserve such a horrible fate. Besides, Tess had spoken with her sister only this morning. No, Mikhail would keep them alive until he got his grimy paws on his daughter-in-law. At the third door, he whispered again, "Jenny?"

A faint whimper seeped through the heavy wooden door. Looking over his shoulder at the stairs first, he tried again, this time louder. "Jenny? Is that you?"

"Mr. Granger?" a hoarse voice replied from inside. "Oh, we prayed someone would come—the police, that bounty hunter lady or even—"

"Shh," he cautioned, hoping her increasingly louder voice didn't bring uninvited company from anywhere in the vicinity. "Just sit tight until I can find a way to pry the lock open. Don't make a sound."

"Mom, is that Mr. Granger?" Tiff piped up.

He could hear Mellie sniffling in the background. "It still smells icky in here and I see another big mousie."

"That's not a mouse, dummy, it's a rat," Tiffany corrected her.

More wailing followed as their mother tried ineffectually to shush both daughters. Matt searched for something to use on the padlock. He found a small ice pick sticking in a wooden slat on a pile of crates across from the door. It was rusty and thin but better than nothing. He flicked open Tess's cell and hit 911, giving his location and circumstances quickly and quietly, then set to work on the padlock.

It might be wiser to wait for the cops, but they could be dead before the Beach PD arrived. The pick's tip snapped off when he tried using it for leverage against the rusty padlock. Great. Now he didn't even have the sharp end to serve as a lock pick. Not that he possessed any skill at the art.

Sam would have this open in a heartbeat. He cursed and tried again. Fat chance. That's when he noticed the wood around the lock. The door was heavy but very old. Years in Miami's damp mildew-drenched subtropical climate had partially rotted it.

"I think I might—" He stopped suddenly. The sound of voices drew near the stairs. They were speaking Russian. "Someone's coming. Be quiet," he whispered, then slipped behind the jumble of crates, praying that he wouldn't knock them all tumbling around him.

As usual, the little dragons did exactly the opposite of what they'd been told by an adult. Both Tiff and Mellie started squalling like banshees on a bender. Maybe he should've promised them Happy Meals. It'd worked for Tess.

The goons, two of them, shambled down the hall using a heavy cell flashlight to illuminate their path. They headed directly toward the racket, laughing and jabbering in a polyglot of Russian and English. One carried a tray. Lunch? Or something to drug their captives into silence. The other carried what appeared to be a damned artillery piece. Matt thought longingly of the wonderful arsenal back in Sam's van in Phoenix.

Shit, what I'd give just to have the stunner! The mobster packing the cannon tucked it under his arm and opened the padlock. The door swung wide and Mellie stood in front of the hulking brute, screaming her lungs out.

Then suddenly, the younger sister stepped aside and Tiff appeared out of the darkness, running directly toward him. Her head connected with a delicate part of the Russian's anatomy. He folded like an accordion.

But his companion dropped his tray and pulled a long-barreled revolver out of his jacket, aiming it at the little girls.

Chapter 18

Matt figured he had only one chance. With the dull, none-too-sturdy ice pick in his fist, he lunged toward the gunman, who started to pivot at the sound of his approach. Then the thug heard a noise behind him. Jenny appeared from behind the door with a length of pipe in her hand. The Russian was left with two choices—either deal with Granger or face the woman. He chose to deal with Granger, raising his Ruger six-shooter to fire.

It was a bad mistake. Jenny swung the pipe like Babe Ruth swatting one over the right field wall at Yankee Stadium. Before he could squeeze the trigger, her blow connected solidly with the back of his head, pitching him toward Matt, who gratuitously punched him in the face with everything his six-six body could put in it.

"Mommy, the bad man's getting up!" Mellie screeched.

The second thug had struggled to his feet, preparing to grab the little girl and use her as a shield when her sister intervened, sticking her leg out to trip him. Tiff gave an ineffectual push, but it was Matt's big tackle that sent him back to the ground. Granger then grabbed his gun hand, trying to seize the weapon from him as they rolled around on the floor.

A dim beam from his penlight, dropped during the altercation, suddenly moved and Matt felt a sharp pain in his left shoulder. "Ouch! That's me, dammit," he grunted as a second blow from Jenny's pipe glanced off his ribs.

"Oops, sorry, Mr. Granger," Jenny said, poised over the two men as they fought.

"Get...the other one's...gun," he managed to grunt as he pinned his opponent's gun hand to the floor. The instant he finished the sentence, he would've kicked himself if he'd been able. Put a gun in Jenny Baxter's hands! Was he completely crazy?

Sheer desperation drove him to pin the thug to the floor and smash his fist into his throat, ending the contest before Jenny could obey orders. He swung around, gasping out, "Don't touch the gun! For Christ's sake, don't touch the gun!"

Still clutching the penlight, Jenny backed away as Matt crawled toward the downed man in the hall. Granger snatched up his weapon. *Oh, my God...a MACH 10, fully automatic, large-pistol-size machine gun!* He checked the action. Yep, safety off. She could've shot the whole lot of them—him and the girls, the thugs, the strippers upstairs, everybody! By the time he got up off all fours, he was shaking from a combination of adrenaline, pure terror and disgust for his own stupidity.

"Did we do okay, Mr. Granger?" Tiff asked.

Taking a deep breath, he patted her shoulder awkwardly. "You bet, Tiff. You all did just great." He bent over and picked up the other unconscious man's weapon, then asked Jenny to shine the flashlight directly into their faces. "Now you should be able to identify two of your kidnappers in a lineup." He knew for damn certain he could. "Let's get out of here before someone upstairs hears the commotion and comes to investigate before the cops arrive."

"They'll arrest you," Mellie accused him.

He could've sworn there was a hint of a grin lurking behind those guileless six-year-old eyes. "That'd be very bad for you and your family," he replied, scooping up the tyke as Jenny took Tiff's hand and followed him. Surprisingly, Mellie didn't protest but laid her head against his shoulder as they went up the steps.

"We can't go out there," Jenny hissed, knowing what kind of a place lay on the other side of the door to the lounge. The sound of loud music and stink of tobacco surged through.

"Yeah, Mikki's boys might object, too," Matt said, turning toward an exit sign across from the steps. "Here we go. Be ready for a loud noise," he warned them as he pushed the bar down and an alarm began to screech. "I doubt anyone inside will even hear over the racket, but this might plug into some kind of system," he said, shoving Jenny and Tiff through, then closing the door.

They were in a narrow alley filled with garbage and delivery vans. He led them behind the cover of a beer truck before a couple of Renkov's gunsels burst through the door. Handing Mellie to her mother, he whispered, "Stay behind the wheels so they can't see your feet." Then he moved quickly to the front end, hiding behind the cab as he watched the two men looking up and down the alleyway. They conferred in Russian and obviously decided to split up, but just as one took a step toward the truck, police sirens sounded from down the street.

Both men turned to each other, perplexed expressions

shifting to alarm. One took the initiative of yanking open the door and ducking back inside. The other quickly followed. "Bet they'll try to wake up their buddies before the cops find them and start asking questions," Matt said to Jenny. "Let's get out of here."

They avoided the commotion out front of the Blue Dragon where half a dozen Miami Beach police cars had blocked off the street, escaping before the cops were able to cordon off the alley and surround the building. "Where are Tess and Steve?" Jenny asked anxiously as they entered the parking deck and reclaimed Sam's wreck.

"Steve's with his grandfather. Don't worry. The old bas— man," he quickly corrected himself when Tiff gave him one of her narrow-eyed looks, "Mikhail won't hurt his only grandson. Tess is with Sam. They're searching for some evidence that might send Mikhail to prison for a long time."

When he applied the usual "unlocking technique" to the driver's door, Jenny and the girls looked at him as if he'd lost his mind.

"Is that thing safe?" Jenny asked.

He jerked the door open with a loud screech. "Runs like a champ," he lied, reaching over to open the passenger doors from the inside so they could climb in.

"I don't like it. It's a piece of junk," Tiff said, eyeing the backseat cover that was regurgitating upholstery in unsightly tufts.

"Now, mind your manners, young lady," her mother admonished her.

With a snort of indignation, Tiff climbed in and made room for Mellie, who dug her small hands into the grey cotton mess and started pulling more of it out. "This is fun," she squealed.

Matt decided little kids liked anything they could destroy.

"Knock yourselves out," he said, then turned to Jenny. " I'l
stash you and the kids somewhere safe, then join your siste
and Sam."

Distracted from dismantling Mr. Obregon's backseat, Mel
lie said, "I wanna go along. Tricking those bad men was fun."

"Mom and I figured out the plan," Tiff said proudly.

Feeling the bruises on his shoulders and ribs beginning t
form, Matt wasn't altogether certain the plan had been exactly
what he'd call "fun." Jenny must have noticed him wince a
he shifted into First, because she said, "I'm sorry I hit you in
stead of that Russian but it was so dark and you were mov
ing so fast…"

He grunted a noncommittal agreement as the Charge
lurched forward.

"Can't you drive better?" Mellie complained.

Nancy desperately required the bolstering courage from
hit of coke. Mikhail thought she'd gone shopping at some o
her favorite places in Bal Harbor, but once she learned he'
had that brat grandson brought to their house, she was to
afraid to go home. The servant she'd spoken to sounded as i
all were well, but she could never trust any of Mikhail's staf
She was certain the boy would tell everything he'd seen an
her husband would kill her.

It was time for them to get away. The deal was suppose
to go down this very afternoon. All her lover had to do wa
give the information to Pribluda's men in Miami, pick up a
those cool millions in negotiable securities and they wer
home free. The thought made her smile as she sniffed mor
of the lovely white powder from the glass tabletop wher
she'd carefully arranged it into long, neat lines.

She'd been careful, changing taxis twice before picking u
a car registered with false ID that she kept at a private garag

on Collins. It was only a ten-minute drive from there to this trysting place, a small, very discreet hotel in Bal Harbor where her lover kept a suite. Nancy leaned back on the white velvet sofa and let the room spin lazily around her, finally enveloped in a haze of contentment. Soon they'd be on their way to Bimini on that lovely big Tiara that Alexi had rebuilt. She chuckled as she leaned down and took another hit. He worshipped speed.

Nancy looked down at her Cartier watch, glittering with diamonds, squinting to focus her eyes on the time. The deal should be done by now. She knew her lover hated to see her using. Only one small line left. "Oh, well, might as well get rid of the evidence," she said with a low chuckle and inhaled the last of it. She felt calmer, but knew vaguely that it was only because of the drug. Mikhail could be looking for her right now.

They had to leave the country soon. Nancy stood up on unsteady legs, then stumbled at the edge of the low glass coffee table and nicked her shin. Damn, that would leave an ugly bruise. Holding on to furniture, she made her way into the bathroom to freshen up. "Have to get straight," she muttered, deciding a good warm bath would help. She turned the tap on hot and poured a generous dollop of perfumed oil into the large round tub, recalling the last time they had used it.

"We'll have one custom built on a tropical island," she said, pulling off her clothes and pinning her hair haphazardly atop her head. She dipped a toe in the water, smiled and climbed into the tub.

He could see the trail of designer clothes from the sitting room to the bath and heard the roar of the tub. Nancy always did favor hot tubs, especially when she was spaced out. He grinned sharkishly and headed down the hall. He never disappointed a lady...but then, his darling Nancy was no lady.

Leaning in the doorway, he crossed his arms and cocked his head so a lock of straight blond hair fell across his forehead. He knew it made him look like a young version of Don Johnson. "Hello, Nancykins."

"Damn, I left my cell in the car," Sam said to herself. She watched Tess steer her friend's boat into the Intracoastal heading north toward Indian Creek Village. "Were you happy here when you first married Alexi?" she asked Tess.

"It seemed like a fairy tale. A gorgeous husband who was famous, a lovely home and a father-in-law who treated me like a princess. Then, when Steve was born, everything was too good to be true…and it was. It took me a while to realize that Alexi was playing more than golf when he traveled without me, but I had my son and, you might find it hard to believe, but Mikhail, well, he seemed so supportive. Like the father I never had." She gave a sad, ironic laugh. "And now he believes I killed his son and he wants to kill me in revenge."

Although she and Matt had agreed not to tell Tess about Alexi, Sam decided his wife should know about their suspicions, rather than face the shock if he did turn up alive. "Alexi might not be dead, Tess," Sam said over the roar of the engine.

Tess's head whipped around. "What do you mean?"

Sam explained what they'd learned about the insurance scam and phone calls. Tess stared straight ahead now, steering the Sea Ray with whitened knuckles. Finally, she murmured so low Sam could barely hear her, "I never knew he could be so vindictive. He hated his father's life so much he'd do anything to get out—even sacrifice his own son in his place."

"We don't know for sure, but—"

"I know. Now it all makes sense. Alexi is alive." Tess drew a ragged breath. "Let's find that information and get Steve back from Mikhail. Then I hope the old devil does kill Alexi!"

* * *

Steve sat at the computer, gazing aimlessly at a periodic table of elements on the screen, trying to concentrate on his chemistry assignment. He had been in special accelerated classes for gifted children ever since he was tested in early grade school. His grandfather had insisted, over his mom's objections, that he be sent to an elite academy and have private tutoring. He'd liked the advanced placement classes in the public school system and hated losing his friends, but he'd done as his grandpa and father had insisted.

His grades had always been outstanding...until the last few months when they started to slip. Moving to California to hide with his aunt, he had missed a lot of classes, but after everything that he'd learned and all that was going on right now, he just couldn't concentrate. Still, unless the chem assignment was completed, he wouldn't be allowed to swim or do anything around the house that might enable him to slip out and search for his aunt and cousins.

He focused on the jumble of letters, searching for the ones he needed when suddenly, it hit him. "Ohmigosh," he breathed, putting the two elements together to form the lettered design that fit beneath the infinity symbol on that awful tattoo he'd seen. It all made sense now in a weird sort of way. He was almost certain who was with Nancy on that yacht! *Grandpa would go crazy!*

But who could he tell? The old man would have them both killed and his mom and her family would still be prisoners. He gulped. No, it would be worse than that, a fact he'd been trying not to think of until now. No, he had to find another way. The computer in his room was not hooked into the system downstairs. He had no Internet access for the same reason the phone had been taken away.

That got him to thinking. He couldn't convince any of

Mikhail's employees to let him near a phone, but since he
was assigned to do homework, maybe he could get Kiski or
Reena—both Russian women adored their boss's grandson—
to let him use a linked computer to complete his chemistry
assignment. His fingers flew over the keys as he began eras-
ing all the tables and charts from the program on his computer. Grabbing up his books and papers, he headed
downstairs.

His grandfather was out for a meeting in the Brickell district, so he wouldn't interfere. Several of the big men with obvious bulges in their suit jackets watched him as he made his
way toward the kitchen. Steve knew if he tried to go outside
they'd follow him. He gripped his books and papers like a du-
tiful student and said in Russian, "I need a snack. Homework
makes a guy hungry." One of the thugs glowered at him but
the other grinned and practiced his broken English.

"Yes. Books, they are hard work. Go, eat."

He smiled back and struggled to control his breathing as
he walked down the hall to the kitchens. Kiski, the old cook,
disliked computers so she wouldn't know what he was doing,
but she was too shrewd and knew him too well. He couldn't
fool her. But Reena, her assistant in the big Renkov kitchen,
was young and sweet—fresh off the boat from St. Petersburg.
He put on his best worried expression and walked into the
small cubicle where she was making up grocery lists for a big
dinner party her boss planned for next week.

Matt tucked Jenny and her agile little dragons in a motel
off Biscayne, threatening them within an inch of their lives
if they so much as peeked out the broken blinds at the deserted
parking lot of the joint. "I have to meet your sister and let her
know you're safe. She's worried sick and might do something
really crazy if she thinks Mikhail still has you. Understand?"

"Oh, please, Matt, I know I made a really dumb mistake back in California, but I swear I won't do it again." She looked over at the girls with the sternest expression he'd ever seen on her face and said, "Tiff and Mellie will stay quiet until this is over. Won't you, girls?"

Something about the tone of their mother's voice—or the life-and-death struggle they'd experienced in that rat-infested basement—had taken a little of the starch out of them. "We'll wait here," Tiff said grudgingly. "But I still don't see why we can't come and help you. If it hadn't been for us, you'd of never been able to beat those two big men."

She had him there but he was damned if he'd encourage her. "I appreciate the diversion, but right now the best thing is for you to stay safe. This'll all be over in a little while. I promise."

"Soon?" Mellie piped up. "This place is icky and the television doesn't work."

He looked at the dingy room and wondered if it wouldn't have been wiser to spend the last of his waning cash on fancier digs for them. But cash in a good hotel raised flags that he didn't dare chance. Sam had figured it right. She always used cheap flops like this when transporting "patients."

Sam. Clever, devious woman. *Not the time to be thinking of that, Granger,* he reminded himself. He knelt down in front of Mellie and promised solemnly, "Soon. Just wait here. Okay?" When she nodded, he grinned and added, "You might try using the beds like trampolines." She brightened at once.

Jenny threw up her hands. "They always do that every time I take them on a trip."

"From the looks of these beds, I don't think they're in any danger of hitting their heads on the ceiling," he said dryly.

Matt left the girls giggling on their dandy new toys under Jenny's watchful eyes, wishing fervently that her brains were as good as her vision. He walked back to the Charger and gave the door a good kick. Still stuck tight as a stripper's ass. Why was it that a little thing like Sam could whack the damned lock into submission and a big guy like him couldn't? "Because I don't drive pieces of crap," he muttered with a dandy oath, dealing the recalcitrant door another smashing blow.

This time it popped open. He climbed inside and struggled with the ignition, cursing Obregon's mechanical genius and worrying about being late when the women returned to the marina. What if they took it into their heads to do something as dumb as Jenny might? Like try a face off with Mikhail Renkov? No, Sam was too smart for that.

The damn junker finally turned over. He put it in Reverse. The trouble came when he tried to move it through the missing gear. He just didn't have Sam's touch. A teenage kid wearing raggedy cutoffs and high-tops sniggered as the car choked to a stop. He was joined by a second boy with enough body piercings to set off a metal detector at half a mile. As Granger struggled to get the car away from the motel, he hoped they'd remember the dumb Anglo who couldn't drive and not the women and kids he'd checked into the room.

He was just pulling into the marina when the encrypted cell Tess had given him beeped. Opening it, he expected to hear Sam or Tess's voice. Steve Renkov was the last person he would've guessed to be on the other end. "Where are you?" he asked, cutting short the boy's inquiry about his mother.

"At my grandpa's house in Aventura. He's away and sneaked a cell phone from Reena's office," the boy whispered. "Are my mom and Aunt Jenny and the girls safe?"

"I just got your aunt and cousins parked in a safe place. Your mom's with Sam. How the hell did you get this number?" Matt asked, worried that the boy was being set up.

"Oh, that was easy once I got on the Net. I just e-mailed

Uncle Jerry—he's not really my uncle but he's an old friend who works in silicon valley. I knew Mom would get phones that couldn't be traced from him. We have a code so he knew it was okay to send me her number."

"Good work. Your family's safe. All you have to do is sit tight until we wind this up and everything will be okay," Matt said with relief. This kid was the polar opposite of his fruit-cake auntie. "How about it?"

There was a long pause on the other end of the line. Matt could practically hear the boy take a deep breath and swallow for courage before he replied.

"Mr. Granger, I figured out who Nancy was with on that yacht…"

Chapter 19

"Well, I'll be damned." Patowski put down the phone and looked over to his partner's desk.

Ross Garten's expression shifted from boredom to interest as he shoved his chair away from the computer where he was filing a report on a gang-related stabbing just north of Liberty City last night. "What's our favorite fibbie done now, Pat?"

"Gomez struck pay dirt. Guess who arranged for his long lost brother from Russia to get into the US of A via Canada?"

"Mikhail Renkov has a brother?"

"Not him," Pat replied patiently. He knew he and Gomez hadn't kept Ross as up-to-date as they should have. Ross hated the FBI. "His son, Alexi. The brother was born to Mikhail's first wife. They divorced and Mikhail married the golden boy's mother, then took Alexi and left the old country, two wives and his first son behind. Some bad blood between them over the older son's mother."

"I doubt Mikhail Renkov was ever a model husband," Garten said dryly. "And I bet Alexi wasn't trying to patch up an old family feud when he slipped his long-lost bro into the country, either."

"It would give us an answer to the DNA question," Patowski said. "After he entered New York via Buffalo, he vanished like a puff of smoke. No proof he saw Alexi before he disappeared, but I bet he did—at least once."

"That's cold, man. His own brother," Garten said.

Just then the phone rang and Pat picked up. Immediately, his partner knew he was onto something even bigger than the news Special Agent Gomez had given him. "We have probable cause to search Mikhail Renkov's place in Aventura," Patowski said, hanging up and rubbing his hands like a ten-year-old itching to take his first punch in a schoolyard fight. He dialed the Dade County Courthouse for a warrant, then waited while he was transferred to Judge Morely's office. "We have that skunk now."

"How'd you do it?" Garten asked.

"I didn't. The old man's grandson just called 911 from that waterfront palace and told them he'd been kidnapped by his gramps."

They grinned at each other. "We gonna let the fibbies in on the arrest?" Ross Garten asked his partner.

Sam and Tess sneaked into what had formerly been her palatial mansion of a home in Indian Creek Village. If she was upset with losing all the material splendor of her old life, Tess didn't show it. Instead she determinedly walked through rooms already searched by the Miami-Dade PD and FBI task force.

"Any ideas about where Alexi might have stashed something that the cops missed?" Sam asked.

"Only one and it's a long shot. I stumbled on it by accident a couple of years ago. A hidden room."

"Jeez, you mean like in some kind of Gothic novel?" Sam was
intrigued as she followed Tess up the curving foyer staircase and
down a long hallway to what was obviously the master suite.

"Remember, his father built this place and he's Russian.
They're always paranoid, especially when they used to be
KGB. I don't think the authorities would've been able to find
this." She walked across the room, ignoring the huge cano-
pied king bed and went into one of the his-and-hers marble
baths at the other end. The urinal and workout benches told
Sam that this had been Alexi's domain. She watched as Tess
slid her hand along the edge of the slab of serpentine coun-
tertop at the side of the sink. When Tess hit the right spot, Sam
heard a slight hissing noise and turned her head to the floor-
to-ceiling mirrors lining the workout area.

One of the glass panels rotated neatly, allowing enough
room for a good-size man to slip through. "Open sesame,"
Tess said bitterly.

"How did you find it?"

"Alexi was always very secretive when he worked out in
here. I used to wonder why since he was such an exhibition-
ist in every other way. One day he didn't lock the door. I'd
come in to get a sweater out of my closet and could see
through a crack in his bathroom door. When I heard the noise
I came closer and saw him press that button and the glass
open. But then he saw me out of the corner of his eye and
closed it at once. We had quite a fight over that. He told me
it was something his father had designed, fireproofed to keep
important papers in for his business—which by then I already knew wasn't exactly on the up-and-up."

"Did he threaten you if you mentioned it to anyone?"
Sam asked.

Tess nodded. "Of course. It wasn't the first time he'd done that, either. I was too frightened for Steve to say anything."

"If he knew you knew about this place, I doubt he'd put anything you could use against him here," Sam said.

Tess's shoulders slumped. "That's what I thought, but since the boat lead didn't work out, this is all there's left. I'm sure the police haven't checked it."

Sam went first, fumbling until she found the light switch. The room was small and sparse—and made of solid steel panels lined with lead. "Old Mikhail sure went to some trouble to keep this place a secret. I bet his house in Aventura is filled with little nooks like this," she said as she began to pull open file drawers. "Shit! The stuff's all written in Russian," she said, slamming a drawer in disgust.

"I think he kept all his records in Russian. Most of the help is Cubano or Honduran."

"Not likely to read Russian," Sam said. "Not that most Anglos could, either."

"Steve does," Tess said with a catch in her voice.

"We'll get him back for you—and the rest of your family." Sam prayed that her assurances weren't false. She was worried about that big newsman, too. He'd taken on a really dangerous enemy and he wasn't even armed. Forcing herself to think practically, she said, "I think I'll give my old friend at Miami-Dade a call and let him know what we found. Patowski will find someone who reads Russian, you can bet the farm on it."

"But that doesn't give us the ammunition to get Steve back," Tess said desperately.

"You know yourself Mikhail won't hurt Steve. And Matt will find Jenny and her girls. Once the cops have this stuff, they'll arrest the old man and you'll all be reunited. Odds are they'll round up dear Nancy, too. I bet she's up to her bleached eyebrows in this mess."

"Wrong. Dear Nancy had an accident. She won't be talk ing to the police or anyone else. Neither will you," a low silk voice said from the edge of the revolving door.

"Alexi!" Tess cried. "You are alive, you bastard—you—

He slapped her with his right hand. "Yes, I'm alive an well, no thanks to you and your pals. He held a .9mm Beret in his left hand and it was leveled at her.

Sam remembered that he was a lefty. She could feel th weight of the .38 in her fanny pack, but getting to it wouldn be easy. How could she distract him? "So, you killed Nanc Were you the lover boy your son saw with her on that yacht she asked, hoping to strike a nerve.

He surprised her by laughing. "Not hardly! But she kne too much about our plans. I arranged a little drowning accide at her trysting place over in Bal. She's always been a cokehead

"So, an OD and she slips under the suds, huh?" Sam aske edging closer. No way could she get to her gun without di arming him first. Just like the Charger door. She focused the distance between them as she said, "It's pretty hard to fo the M.E. faking suicides, especially considering who she w and the ongoing investigation."

"In a couple of hours, it won't make any difference. I'll out of here…but you…well, my darling wife…" He caress the cheek he'd slapped.

"You really don't give a damn what happens to your ow son, do you, Alexi?" Tess asked.

"The kid'll be okay. Maybe after I get resettled, I'll se for him, who knows?" he replied indifferently.

Sam used the instant of distraction to edge closer. "You have to arrange another accident for us, I guess. Is your pa ner in crime making the deal with Pribluda even as we speak

His cold green eyes narrowed on her. "For some broad wl got herself kicked off the police force, you know an awful lo

"So does the task force that's going to take down your family and the guys from Brighton Beach," she replied.

"They can have my dear father. Even Pribluda's men—after they pay up. Then I'm home free."

"Going to cut out your partner after you collect from Pribluda's goons?" Sam asked as she prepared to kick.

His smile was frighteningly beautiful. Sam could understand why he'd been able to charm an intelligent woman like Tess Albertson. "I gathered all the information, risked my life in some of the worst hellholes of Eastern Europe and Russia to get it. God, how I hate that cold dirty place. Mother Russia," he sneered.

"Drug connections from Afghanistan?" Sam asked.

"That's only a small part of it. The really lucrative thing is the network. My father and I arrange to smuggle rich industrialists and their fortunes out of Russia and into the land of opportunity. You think Putin's government won't pay a fortune for that? After all, we've already sold Pribluda the locations of stockpiles of nuclear weapons scattered from the Black Sea to the Baltic. We'll sell it again to the stupid spooks."

"So that's why the CIA's been protecting your daddy's ass. He doles that information to them bit by bit."

"And who do you think has gathered that information for the past six years?" Alexi asked rhetorically, thoroughly engrossed in his tale now.

Sam tried to telegraph to Tess that she was going to make a move.

Tess seemed to understand. "Who's helping you double-cross your father if it isn't Nancy—or *was* it Nancy?" she asked.

"Nancy had her uses," he replied.

"You cheated on me and your own father with her, didn't you?" Tess accused angrily, balling up her fists.

Sam raised her foot in a lightening kick, directed at his le
hand, but he was a professional athlete, trained for instanta
neous response. He dodged the kick by a hairbreadth an
yanked Tess off balance before Sam could spin in for anothe
strike. He held his wife in front of him, choking her an
pressing the barrel of his gun to her head.

"Now, back away," he said through gritted teeth. "Yo
know, you're both really beginning to piss me off." To en
phasize his point, he struck Tess in the temple with the sic
of the Beretta. She stopped struggling. He let her fall to th
floor and stepped away from her, all the while glaring
Sam. "I'll bet you're packing, aren't you, bitch? Peel o
that fanny pack and drop it." The barrel of the gun neve
wavered.

He obviously didn't intend to shoot them outright or he
have done it by now, so Sam went along, unfastening the pac
and giving it an underhanded slow toss toward him. It lande
beside Tess's crumpled body. Wake up, Tess! Fast. He foile
whatever faint hope she had of Tess recovering the weapc
when he kicked the pack across the room.

"What kind of accident do you have in mind for us.
double drowning in his-and-hers baths would really stretc
credibility."

"No need. A fire will take care of everything. Who know
they may never find your bodies sealed inside this vault…
maybe they will, but the place will be gutted before anyone
the island knows. I turned the smoke detectors off and seal
all the doors and windows. Before anyone has an idea there
a fire, my father's airtight stronghold will blow sky-high."

With that, he stepped through the glass panel and clos
it from outside. Sam could hear nothing after that. The lea
lined walls were soundproof. But she could imagine him
an arsonist all too easily, a logical progression for a sto

killer. She knelt beside Tess and cradled her head on her lap. "Are you able to hear me?" she asked.

Tess blinked, then nodded, still dazed. "He got away, didn't he?" she asked, struggling to sit up.

Sam started to retrieve her snub nose from the fanny pack but immediately realized that it was of no use in the metal room. "In the movies you can always shoot the lock off the door or something like that," she muttered.

"I smell smoke," Tess said, crawling to the door panel.

Sam cursed. "The son of a bitch did it!"

"He set the house on fire?" Tess asked as she struggled to her feet.

"If there's a way in, there has to be a way out," Sam said, talking to herself while she began examining the walls around the door. "What if you were in here filing something and heard somebody come in the bedroom?"

"You'd have to be able to close the door from the inside if you didn't have time to slip back out and close it from the counter," Tess supplied hopefully.

"So you'd have to be able to get out from here," Sam replied, continuing to push and press. "You try the left, I'll go to the right."

The two women set to work as the faint whiffs of smoke became stronger....

Matt drove from the city across the Kennedy Causeway and headed north for Indian Creek Village. Traffic was snarled and every time he had to downshift the lousy old car stalled out. Not once while Sam had been driving had it done that to her. Sam. She and Tess were on their way back to the marina to meet him. He had no way to reach them since he had Tess's cell and Sam had left hers in the car. It was well after three. They should be safe, wondering where he was, worrying about him.

That brought a goofy smile to his face. Samantha worrying about him.

They probably thought he was dead in some alley in Sout Beach behind one of Renkov's strip joints. He grinned. H nearly had been. With Jenny and her kids safe and the cop on their way to rescue Steve, this just might turn out all righ after all. He'd told the boy to call 911 and turn in dear ol grandpa. The kid had done it and called him back to repo success, then slipped the filched cell back into his frien Reena's purse. Smart little dude.

If Sam's pal Patowski was as good as she said, he ough to have Mikhail and company cooling their heels in the locku by the time he reached his destination. What a piece of luc that a traumatized kid could put the pieces of the puzzle t gether. Boy, not only had he been fooled, but so had Sa Funny how his thoughts kept coming back to the maddenir woman. In spite of her avaricious soul—maybe because it—he was gone on her.

Might as well admit it, Granger.

The goofy grin returned as he imagined life with Sama tha Ballanger. There'd never be a dull minute. But he was ge ting ahead of himself. First, he had some evens to take ca of and a story to file. *Pulitzer, here I come!*

He approached the drawbridge to the island, knowing could not get in the way he had the last time. But he'd bee giving the problem some thought and had a plan. He pulle onto a quiet residential street several blocks away from t entrance to the private island, then parked the junker. If som one here in the high-rent district complained about the ey sore and had the cops towed it away, so be it. He'd be hap to pay Obregon just to get the menace off the road.

He carefully deposited the Ruger he'd taken from the Ru sian mobster in the watertight pouch he'd picked up at a scu place in Bal. He'd also purchased a snorkeling rig so he could swim underwater for a short distance. He strolled down the street like a tourist, watching the more modest homes around the area for a likely crossing place near the narrow channel separating Surfside from Indian Creek Village. When he found what looked to be a pair of houses with no one at home, he walked purposefully to the side door of one, then around the back.

Still standing between the houses, he slipped off his bermudas and T-shirt and stuffed them along with his shoes in the watertight pouch after removing the snorkeling gear. Hoping the landscaping along the waterfront would keep the security cameras at the access bridge from seeing him, he slipped the snorkeling rig on, then moved into the water, submerged and began to swim.

It took him about fifteen minutes to reach the other side and find cover. Matt tossed the snorkeling gear in some well-tended schiffelara bushes and pulled his clothes and shoes out of the pouch. He left the Ruger in the pouch and slung the pouch over his shoulder since he had no place to conceal the gun on his body, then began walking, feeling rather like "007" on a mission. He resisted the urge to dash flat out, knowing he did it might draw attention, something he certainly couldn't afford. Hell, he'd end up being the one interrogated while the bad guys escaped with a fortune.

He moved along the curving road, pretty much hidden by tall hedges and stone walls. Only one car, a Lexus, passed him the entire time. The lush vegetation on the island looked like natural tropical growth, but it was likely cultivated carefully to maintain that illusion while providing privacy to each estate. When he reached his destination, he slipped behind a tall boxwood hedge, using it as cover to reach the boat dock he'd seen from a distance earlier.

There it was. The fifty-foot Tiara. In a few hours it could take them to Bimini. He wondered when the deal with Pribluda would go down. Even the best-laid plans sometimes went wrong. Grinning sharkishly, Matt checked the house. No one was home. Maybe in town setting up their deal with Pribluda's agents? He hoped not, but there was only one way to find out for sure. He slipped down to the dock and climbed aboard the boat, then ascended the steps to the steering station at the top level. He took the Ruger out of the pouch and stuffed it in his belt. Time to get to work.

"It has to be here," he muttered to himself as he used the screwdriver he'd brought to pry open the radio compartment. Then he reached inside, shining a penlight until he found a small cylinder. "Jackpot!"

Matt pulled the tube out and sat back in the captain's chair to look at the list that the CIA and FBI had fought over. It contained the exact locations of several dozen nuclear weapons caches scattered around Eastern Europe and in the small nationlets around the Black Sea, once part of the former Soviet Union. A second page was filled with Slavic names and bank account numbers, mostly in the Caymans, a few Swiss. The total was hundreds of millions.

Completely engrossed as he put the puzzle pieces together, Matt didn't hear the soft footsteps of a man climbing to the steering station behind him. He whistled low as he figured out what Mikhail and Alexi Renkov had been doing. "I wonder what their cut was?" he murmured.

"Half," Alexi replied conversationally. "Now drop the piece from your belt—very carefully."

Matt spun around in the chair and looked down the barrel of Renkov's Beretta.

Chapter 20

Sam's eyes burned like she'd soaked them in lye and sweat poured from her forehead, adding to her misery. The heat was intensified by their metal cage, which had become a literal oven that was suffocating them even faster than it cooked them. Blinking back tears from the smoke, she continued groping along the wall, now more by feel than sight. Tess fell to the floor, coughing in dry breaths as she fought for consciousness.

"Don't...give...up," Sam rasped, "or we'll be Pop-Tarts." Her fingers continued pressing, moving—until suddenly she felt a smooth rounded bump behind the filing cabinet: She pushed it hard.

The panel whirred open, letting in a black billow of smoke. Of course, putting the switch beside the door frame would have been too obvious. She should have thought of that five minutes ago—five minutes that could still cost them their

lives. Sam reached down for Tess and started to drag he
through the door, but Tess struggled to her feet and stumble
out on her own, coughing desperately.

Flames leapt capriciously across the big room, setting th
canopy on the bed ablaze. "Soak towels for us," Sam tol
Tess, who seized two big bath sheets from an open shelf an
held them beneath the high arched faucet on the whirlpoc
bath.

While Tess was doing that, Sam checked the bedroom fc
a way out, wondering how Alexi had managed such a feat c
arson so quickly. Probably a contingency plan if the polic
ever closed in on the family and they needed to escape an
leave no evidence—some kind of accelerant handily stashe
in strategic places. A jug labeled as a cleaning product, tosse
empty in one corner of the bedroom, confirmed her suspicion

She scanned the room. The door to the hallway was a ra;
ing inferno. "The balcony," she whispered to Tess, who fo
lowed her across the master suite to a large set of Frenc
doors. The heavy brass knob refused to turn. Sam trie
again—and again with no more luck.

"It's the security…system. He…set it when he left," Tes
said, struggling to get the words out. "All the doors…windows.
locked tight. We can't get out…less I put in…code dow
stairs."

"That's not an option," Sam managed to cough out. Sh
grabbed a heavy chair from the front of what must have bee
Tess's dressing table. It weighed a ton, but as she'd alread
experienced on numerous occasions, when it was act or di
a person developed strength they didn't ordinarily possess

Rather than trying to break through the small panels on t
French doors, she took aim on the big picture window besid
them, closer to the fiery bed than she would've preferred, b
what were a few singed hairs compared to roasting alive? Sl

swung like Barry Bonds still on steroids and connected with the glass, jarring every bone in her body.

The window held. "Shit! Oh, shit!"

"Now, I'll take those," Alexi said after Matt had tossed his gun to the floor and Renkov had kicked it across the deck. He indicated the papers Matt had been reading. He moved in closer, the Beretta steady, centered on Granger.

"You don't look bad for a dead man," Matt said, holding the papers out so they fluttered in the breeze.

"Let them go and I shoot."

"Shoot and I let them go. Looks to me like we have us a little standoff here." Granger grinned.

Alexi didn't. He stepped closer again, just as Matt hoped he would. "I can't believe you and your girlfriend were dumb enough to use paper and not to make copies."

"Oh, these are the copies, all right. Just a little bonus to trade to my dear father's friends at the Company once I'm safe in South America. She sold the computer disk to Pribluda's agent in Miami this afternoon. I was ready to sail when your girlfriend and my darling wife interrupted." Seeing Granger's reaction to that, he smiled coldly. "I took care of them...and now, I'll take care of—"

Matt felt the breeze from the Intracoastal gust ever so slightly and let go of the papers. For an instant, Renkov's eyes wavered. That was all Granger required. One long leg shot out and connected wickedly with Alexi's right knee. Matt could hear cartilage pop as he came up from the chair and knocked the Beretta aside. A shot exploded, going wild as his fist landed squarely in Renkov's gut. When Alexi tried to fire again from his doubled-over position, Granger twisted the gun away with his left hand and chopped Renkov in the side of his neck with his right.

The golden boy of golf crumpled to the deck, out cold. Matt quickly stuffed the Beretta into his belt. The papers had not gone over the side but fluttered precariously near the stairs. Forgetting the Ruger, he lunged after the documents. But the fickle breeze whisked them in a lazy swirl down toward the deck below.

Matt jumped down the ladder and knelt to scoop them up. His back was to the dock as he grabbed the last of his prize. "So thoughtful of you, Mr. Granger," a cultivated voice said smoothly. "Now do be a dear and toss that Beretta of Alexi's overboard, won't you?"

Granger cursed beneath his breath as he complied. Once that was done, his latest nemesis heaved a heavy satchel into the boat, then jumped aboard. For the second time in three minutes, he was looking down the business end of a Beretta.

Sam swung the big chair, now minus one walnut leg, at the window again, concentrating on the crack that had appeared after her first effort. This time the glass flew outward. Tess covered her with a soaking towel an instant before the fire whooshed toward its fresh source of oxygen. Quickly using the chair to knock away jagged pieces of glass, Sam reached for Tess and they jumped through the fiery inferno onto the deck.

"Is there a staircase…" Sam paused to gulp in a long breath of clean air, then continued, "down from here?"

Still coughing and struggling to breathe, Tess shook her head.

"We'll have to climb down," Sam said, looking at the windows all around the big house. Flames were shooting out both stories. "Any shrubs, vines, whatever?" she asked as she checked the railing.

"No, just a couple of small mimosas over there."

Sam looked down at the fragile lacy branches. The top of the tallest one barely reached the deck floor. Then she saw a flower bed freshly turned for an early summer replanting. "Here we go. Just follow me."

She demonstrated, casting off the wet towel and throwing it onto the softened earth below. Then she climbed over the railing and lowered herself from the deck floor. Her feet were still a good five or six yards above the ground. She let go and dropped with knees bent to absorb some of the shock. Luckily, she didn't twist any joints when she landed, although she did lose her balance and hit the ground. Years of martial arts practice had taught her to roll in a ball and use her left arm to slap out and absorb the force of the landing.

"Come on, Tess. I can see the fire heading our way through the atrium windows," she yelled up.

Tess threw her towel down and did her best to emulate Sam. When she hit the ground, Sam was there to steady her before she tumbled backwards, but she let out a hiss of pain as her right ankle turned on impact.

"Let me help you," Sam said, throwing the taller woman's arm across her shoulder and practically dragging her clear of the burning house. They didn't get a few yards away before the glass windows of the sunroom behind them blew outward, sending shards of glass in every direction.

"We have to call the police and tell them about Alexi," Tess said. "I'm all right now," she added. Though her teeth were gritted in pain, she started to jog without Sam's help.

"Let's just get the hell out of here before he realizes he didn't finish us and comes back to try again," Sam replied.

"We can call from Kit's place."

Sam considered. It was logical. How far could Renkov have gotten? She hadn't been able to hear the sound of a boat or a car taking off through the soundproofed room and roar of the fire. He could be anywhere by now. "Okay. You sure you can make it?"

"I'd crawl through that broken glass over there just to see Alexi Renkov behind bars," Tess replied gamely.

The women ran around hedges and cut through lush landscaping on the waterfront estates until they could see Kit Steele's place. And Kit. She was at the dock, climbing aboard her fifty-foot Tiara yacht. She tossed a heavy satchel on the deck. Then Sam saw Matt stand up in front of her. He threw something in the water. Neither woman could tell what it was from the angle where they stood. But the weapon she was pointing directly at him was clearly visible.

"What on earth—"

"She's Alexi's partner in this scam," Sam said, cursing herself for not figuring it out sooner. She wished fervently she'd been able to retrieve her fanny pack with the gun inside. Of course there was the matter of wasting precious time in the black smoke looking for it when every second counted. Before she could think any further, Kit backed Matt into the lower cabin. Then she fired inside and slammed the door.

Sam's heart stopped beating. Had she killed him? No, Sam couldn't imagine it. Surely she'd know if Matt were dead. *Be alive, you big lug! I haven't told you I love you!*

Kit quickly climbed to the steering station and started up the boat. Almost immediately, they could see Alexi stand up beside her, rubbing his neck.

"He and Kit are quarreling," Tess said, afraid to venture what must have happened to Matt.

Just then, Kit Steele raised the gun she'd used on Matt, but Alexi twisted it out of her hand and gave her a hard slap. She fell backward a few steps, then dropped down. Almost instantly a small pop echoed on the water. Alexi crumpled back to the deck.

"Some lovers' spat," Sam said as Kit pulled the Tiara away from the dock and headed south on the Intracoastal. "She's making a run for it and Matt may be bleeding to death in that damned cabin! I need a phone to call the Coast Guard. Any neighbors around here likely to be home?"

Tess shook her head. "I doubt it this time of day, but she can't get away. Even with low tide, she can't make it under the Venetian Causeway in a boat that big. She'll have to radio ahead and ask them to raise the bridge. That could take a while if no other boats are in line."

"Given her situation, I doubt she's going to wait," Sam said grimly. "If she gets out to the open sea, Matt's as dead as yesterday's lunch meat. We have to catch up with her."

"We can! Alexi's Cigarette. Come on! It's a thirty-nine foot Top Gun Unlimited," Tess said, turning back toward her burning home. "The keys are in the boathouse. I know where he keeps them."

"Just get me close enough to the Tiara to jump aboard and I'll take it from there," Sam said. The two women made a run for the boathouse.

Once inside, Tess quickly retrieved the keys to Alexi's favorite speedboat and fired it up. "Hold on," Tess said as she maneuvered the long, sleek craft out onto the open water and let it rip.

"How fast can this thing go?" Sam asked, looking with frustration at the disassembled radio. Kit had done a good job throwing them off the trail when she'd helped Tess tear it apart, supposedly searching for papers she already possessed.

Tess grinned grimly. "In miles—eighty-five, maybe faster. Alexi had it specially outfitted, like I told you. He worshiped speed. We can catch that yacht, no sweat. She can't get under the Venetian, but what will we do then? She has a gun and we've seen she's willing to use it." If there was any regret for

Alexi's possible death, Tess didn't feel it. She tried not to think about the man she knew Sam loved.

"I'll figure out something. Just get me close enough to jump aboard," Sam replied, not all as confident as she made out to be.

The Cigarette took off like a rocket, flying over the gentle waves of the Intracoastal Waterway. Never a sailor, Sam held on to the seat for dear life. Although she could drive a semi down a mountainside at seventy-five, anything faster than a rowboat on water gave her the willies. But Matt was a prisoner on Kit Steele's yacht, maybe slowly bleeding…or even dying as she headed for the open ocean. Once Kit was in the clear, she'd get rid of Alexi and Matt. Dear God, Sam had to stop the bitch!

Some great bodyguard you turned out to be! For once in her mercenary life, Sam Ballanger was willing to let Aunt Claudia keep every damned cent of her fee if only she could see Matt Granger grin at her again. She said a silent prayer to St. Jude, even promised to start going to church again if the patron saint of impossible requests spared Matt's life.

Tess was good. She hadn't been bragging when she said she'd learned to handle all of her husband's customized toys. "Watch her make it under Kennedy," Tess said as the Tiara approached the first causeway she'd have to get past to reach open ocean.

The big yacht glided under the causeway with room to spare. Kit, too, was daring and skilled handling a boat, but the Cigarette was gaining on the slower Tiara in spite of its souped-up engines. The day was cool and slightly overcast. Few pleasure craft were out on the water. Kit didn't have to negotiate any traffic.

"Wouldn't you know it. Not a Coast Guard or Harbor Patrol boat in sight," Sam said with an oath as the two boats raced madly southward. Tess put the Cigarette between the pilings of Kennedy Causeway.

"Uh-oh, I think she's spotted us," Tess said as Kit turned around. In response, Kit throttled up and the Tiara lunged forward. They narrowed the distance gradually now, not as fast as when Steele hadn't known she was being chased. "Alexi had work done on the Tiara, put in bigger engines. It belongs to Mikhail and she used it to run errands for him."

"So, you still sure you can catch it?" Sam asked.

"Absolutely. He fine-tuned this baby, too," Tess replied grimly.

Sam leaned forward in her seat, willing their craft to catch up. Visions of Matt's bloody corpse made her shake. She forced the thought aside. They raced endlessly over the blue-gray waters as the sun and clouds vied for dominance. The wind whipped her hair in her eyes as she squinted at the yacht in the distance.

"She's coming up on I-95," Tess said as the big interstate causeway loomed ahead of them, filled with its usual stream of cars coming and going between Miami Beach and the mainland.

Again the Tiara made it through the pilings without incident. Sam tried not to look at the heavy concrete sides of the passage when their fragile craft shot through a few moments later. "We're gaining on her!" she said excitedly.

"Next comes the real test. She'll have to turn around at the Venetian," Tess said. "We can clear it but she can't. Somebody has to radio to raise the bridge. If she does and waits, we'll have her."

"Oh, I'll have her all right," Sam said, picturing her hands around that sun-gilded, elegant throat, choking the life out of Kit Steele.

"Damn!" Tess muttered as the bridge started to rise. A

small SeaVee 310 fishing boat had radioed to the bridge man. It waited patiently as the huge steel grated arms rose, slow and graceful. "She's crazy!" Tess yelled, appalled as Kit came flying directly behind the SeaVee, intent on cutting it off and making it under the bridge.

"I knew she'd try running it somehow. She's not crazy, just desperate," Sam said. "She's sitting on millions and just shot two men."

"She could crash and blow up both boats," Tess said.

"What's she got to lose?" Sam asked. But she knew what she had to lose. *Matt!* He was trapped below in the cabin, near the engines and gas tanks, maybe bleeding to death. He counted more than the fortune Kit had stashed aboard the damned yacht.

As Tess drew the Cigarette near, they watched the scene play out. The SeaVee, seeing the much larger Tiara bearing down on it at a faster rate than that kind of yacht was supposed to be able to run, tried desperately to get out of the way. It was clear that she intended to take advantage of the open bridge. Apparently the gateman also was aware of it and started to lower the bridge.

"Why the hell is he doing that? He could kill them," Tess said over the roar of the motor. She floored the racing craft, which was now bouncing more above water than on it as they watched Kit approach the causeway. The smaller fishing boat cut sharply to port and circled, bouncing like a cork in the wake of the Tiara as it flew toward the lowering drawbridge.

They watched in horror as the Tiara approached the narrow chute. Sam forgot to breathe. Living in Miami, she'd seen on television news what happened when a big boat with full gasoline tanks crashed at high speed. She alternately prayed and swore as Kit Steele buckled down to her deadly task.

Steele almost made it before the bridge came down. Then they saw why the engineer had lowered the gate. On the south side another yacht, an Azimut, drew near in a dissecting course. It had the right of way to pass by the causeway but Kit wouldn't veer from her break for freedom.

"They're going to crash," Sam breathed.

The Tiara hit the chute but could not quite reach the other side before the two halves of the bridge lowered into place. The heavy steel sheared off the top of the Tiara's flybridge. Big chunks of metal and fiberglass ripped away as quickly as an ape could peel a banana. The sunroof, GPS station and satellite television box flew in all directions, crashing against the pilings, plunking into the water. The impact of hitting the bridge threw the Tiara to one side where it sliced against the concrete chute. Sparks flew like fireworks on the Fourth of July.

"It could blow apart any second!" Tess yelled as they sped toward the causeway.

Sam couldn't close her eyes but she did pray harder than she had since she was a five-year-old girl in Boston and her grandfather lay dying. She watched as the Tiara cleared the bridge and kept on going—directly toward the Azimut. The much larger yacht pulled forward in a desperate attempt to avoid being broadsided. The sound of horns filled the air.

Chapter 21

At the very last second, the two yachts missed each other by a coat of paint. The Tiara held its course dead south but the Azimut's wake rocked the smaller craft. Sam and Tess could see Kit Steele fighting to hold the wheel. Then amazingly, she regained control and picked up speed.

"She doesn't have navigation or radio but I doubt she's taking on water, either," Tess said as they continued the mad chase.

"I can't believe that thing's still afloat," Sam said, swallowing hard and fighting the first bout of motion sickness she'd ever experienced in her life. Then she realized it wasn't the speed or the narrowness of the chute as they passed under the causeway that created her misery. It was fear for Matt, pure and simple.

"You think that guy who lowered the bridge will call the Coast Guard?" Sam asked.

"You bet, but they have a lot of water to cover and not enough manpower. If she slips south past the Rickenbacker, she'll avoid the Government Cut where their station is located. Whether or not they can catch her will depend on where their patrols happen to be right now—if one's even out."

"She'll head straight to Bimini. There's an international airport there," Sam said, thinking out loud as she held on to her seat while they flew across the waves.

"We're gaining on her," Tess said. "I know I can catch her, but what do we do then?"

"I'm working on it. Just get me to that bitch," Sam said.

Kit cleared the MacArthur Causeway in moments. To their right Bicentennial Park was a blur as they pursued her at breakneck speed. The Tiara crossed through the always-open railroad drawbridge south of it and flew around Dodge Island.

"She's avoiding the Government Cut, just like I thought, even though it's a quicker way to reach the open sea," Tess said.

"Then she'll go under the Rickenbacker and past Key Biscayne to lessen her chances of any water-patrolling boats seeing her," Sam replied.

"Yes, it's wide open. We'd better stop her before she rounds the tip of the key," Tess said, looking down at the gas gauge. "We're losing fuel. Alexi must've forgotten to tell Norge to repair a fuel tank leak."

"Great," Sam muttered. "Can you coax any more out of his toy before it gives out?"

In reply, Tess bore down. They were narrowing the distance as Kit followed the channel, veering east to avoid Brickell Key. The long sleek rise of the Rickenbacker Causeway loomed in the distance. "Okay, it's leveling out now. Maybe a faulty gauge. I can't tell."

"Just give it everything you've got. Matt's aboard and in
jured."

Neither woman would voice aloud the fear that Kit migh
already have killed him.

"I can trim time she can't risk. The Tiara draws deep
enough to force her to stay in the main channel. We don't hav
to with this little baby," Tess said.

"We've barely touched the water since this race began.
believe you," Sam answered, her mind busy turning over var
ious ways to board the yacht and keep Kit Steele from shoot
ing her like a sitting duck.

The Tiara shot under the last causeway and swung south
east to round the large man-made keys of Virginia and Bis
cayne. They drew within a hundred feet, fifty, twenty… Sam
came up with a plan—not much of one but all she could thinl
of—if Tess could pull it off.

"I don't think she can take her hands off the wheel lon
enough to turn around and use her gun. Can you pull along
side so I can jump on board? Then if you dart ahead and spi
across her bow, you could create a wake to occupy her whil
I climb the stairs to get at her."

Clutching the wheel of the Cigarette, Tess nodded grimly
"You betcha."

Sam climbed to the backseat of the long narrow craft an
waited her chance, her eyes on the Tiara when suddenly
Alexi reappeared. Sam's eyes widened as she saw him hol
up a gun, forcing Kit to let go of the wheel and knock his han
aside. The pair struggled over the gun while the yacht turne
erratically, then veered sharply to starboard.

Inside the cabin of the Tiara, Matt was thrown against th
shower stall in the head. What the hell was going on? Th
cabin started to spin like a dreidel at Hanukkah and he brace
himself, a hand on each side of the narrow compartment. H

ight side ached like someone held an acetylene torch to it, ut he'd been lucky. When Kit fired into the cabin, he'd anicipated her move and spun sideways just enough to keep the ullet from hitting dead center.

He'd spent the past twenty minutes of the insane ride alernately passing out, bleeding over the plush interior and attempting to locate the first-aid kit. He'd found it and, after everal tries, he'd made a temporary binding that slowed the leeding. Then he began searching the bedroom and kitchen. arlier, during his first bout of unconsciousness, he'd awakned to the scream of metal being torn off the craft and seen he flash of fire when they were nearly crushed under the Veetian Causeway.

He figured the Coast Guard or Harbor Patrol were in pursuit. Each time he was tossed against a wall or over a piece f furniture, that hope kept him searching for a weapon he ould use to break down the door. He'd tried his shoulder unl it ached like hell. The damned boat was built like a brick ouse and he was too weak from blood loss to make a dent n anything stronger than cellophane.

Hearing a struggle overhead, he decided to look out a portole and see if the authorities were closing in. To his horror, e saw Tess and Sam in a damned featherweight Cigarette ulling alongside. His desperation increased tenfold when he aw the way Sam was hunched on the edge of the backseat. he was going to jump aboard! Kit would shoot Sam before he could reach the flybridge. Sam appeared unarmed. He had o do something before she was killed! But what?

On the racing Cigarette, Tess yelled at Sam as she pulled ack, "I can't dare get closer or the Tiara could smash us to aste."

"One of them has to win—quick," Sam said, watching as lexi struggled with Kit for the gun. And it was looking like it was going to be Kit. Apparently Renkov had been injured gravely when Kit shot him. Now Kit smashed her fist into the bloody mass of Alexi's shirt and he crumpled with a scream of pain, dropping his gun. Sam could imagine what the woman was yelling at him by the ugly smirk on her face.

Steele followed through by pulling a gun from her belt and shooting him a second time. Then she seized the wheel.

Caring nothing for the playboy, all Sam could think of was the man locked below the deck. *Please be alive, Matt!*

As soon as Kit regained control of the Tiara, Tess slid alongside it and Sam, poised at the edge, sprung across the scant yard separating the boats. She barely made the jump, clawing desperately for the steel railing as the Cigarette left her behind. The small boat lunged forward to provide the hoped-for distraction.

Tess pulled a dozen yards ahead in a wide arc, then shot across the Tiara's bow, leaving a fierce wake that rocked the yacht. Kit looked back as Sam scrabbled over the edge onto the lower deck but she couldn't let go of the wheel to aim and fire her weapon. The Cigarette circled and came at the Tiara again. The second pass bought Sam enough time to reach cover where Kit couldn't see her without leaving the steering station. As long as Tess kept her busy making passes and creating fierce wakes, Steele wouldn't dare go after Sam.

But Sam had to keep Kit from shooting at Tess, who was an open target directly in front of her each time she cut across. The wildly pitching yacht and swift cuts of the Cigarette would provide quite a challenge, even for a good marksman—but Sam had no idea what other hidden talents Kit Steele possessed and wasn't going to risk Tess's life to find out. She waited until the next wake, when Kit was occupied with regaining control of the yacht, then made a mad dash up the stairs and tackled her.

They hit the bridge and rolled past Alexi's body, wrestling over the Ruger that Kit had pulled from her belt when she heard Sam behind her. The Tiara bounced and veered sharply in the choppy water, first to port, then starboard, tossing the two women hard against what was left of the steering station.

Sam had a death lock on Kit's right hand holding the gun, which she fired wildly into the air. She was taller than Sam with the long, strong physique of a woman who worked out regularly at her club. Sam worked out, too, but not in the kind of high-toned gym she was sure Kit frequented. Sam's skills as a black belt in judo were augmented by growing up the smallest kid in her class in the hard proving grounds of south Boston. She'd never let her brothers fight her battles for her, even when they got big enough to do it.

Instead, her uncle Dec taught her to fight…dirty. "To make up for what we lack in height, doncha know, colleen," he used to tell her.

Sam pinned Kit's gun hand against the captain's chair while avoiding the other woman's clawing nails aimed for her eyes and a knee to her pubic bone. Kit, too, had learned a few tricks in the mean streets of Manchester. Then, remembering the bulging satchel containing her loot, the Englishwoman grabbed it with her left hand and tried to swing it at Sam's head.

Sam ducked and the blow bounced painfully off her shoulder, sending a flutter of Mafia loot flying across the deck. Her legs were shorter but that gave her leverage to bend her knee just high enough to kick the tall woman's kneecap, eliciting an oath of pain. In that instant Sam shifted her hold on Kit's gun hand, catching her thumb and applying pressure to bend backward until Kit was forced to release the weapon.

It slid across the wildly pitching deck.

Below, Matt was knocked away from the door twice as the

Tiara raced out of control. He resorted to crawling on all fours with the ring of keys he'd spied concealed inside the glass control cabinet on the steps. He'd never have found them if the wildly pitching yacht hadn't knocked them from their hiding place and hurled them against the glass. Having no idea which key might work on the locked door, he desperately tried one, then another as shots rang out and the thumping noises of a desperate fight continued overhead.

Sam needed him! He had to get out of here and save her. Then one of the keys slipped in the lock and turned. The cabin door popped open. Directly in front of him, he could see Alexi Renkov crawling toward Kit's Beretta, which had just tumbled down the steps from the flybridge. Without thinking about his bloody side, Matt leaped through the doorway and landed on Renkov, who was, by the looks of it, injured far worse than he.

He flattened Alexi like roadkill, then slid across the deck toward the gun, but the wildly careening yacht sent it flying out of his reach. Doggedly, he crawled to the stairs, determined to save Sam.

On the flybridge, Sam rolled on top of Kit, delivering a chop to her jaw and pinning her to the deck. Steele still struggled but Sam grabbed a fistful of red hair and slammed Kit's head against the deck until she passed out. Sam held on to the chair, struggling to stand up as the yacht rolled onward, out of control. But when she pulled herself into the chair, she looked down at what appeared as confusing to her as an airplane cockpit's control panel.

"What the hell do I do now?" she yelled at Tess, who was approaching on the Cigarette once again.

But it was obvious the other woman couldn't hear her over the noise of the engines. Nor could Tess get close enough to jump aboard. Whatever happened, Sam would have to han dle it herself—and quickly. The yacht was headed directly for land and clusters of big yachts moored on the marinas surrounding the Coral Gables Waterway. She hadn't come this far to have Matt die in a boat crash because she couldn't stop the stupid yacht!

Sam swallowed hard. "How tough can this be after driving an eighteen-wheeler?" she asked to reassure herself as she took the helm. She began to turn the wheel while downshifting on the lever that appeared to control speed. It was a lot more complicated than it looked, but by the time Tess drew near again, she'd slowed the Tiara to a crawl and reversed the course in a more or less straight line headed away from land.

"I may be able to help you," Matt said as his head appeared at the top of the stairs behind her.

He was a mess with bruises covering his body and his clothes torn and reddened by his own blood, but he looked as handsome as a *GQ* model to her at that moment. She let go of the wheel and jumped over to help him up the last couple of steps.

"You've been shot! Are you okay? Dumb question, of course you're not," she said as she examined him to see how deep the wound was.

"I'll be a lot less okay if we run into that Azimut," he said between gasps of pain.

Sam turned instantly and seized the wheel again. "Yeah, sorry," she said, trying to straighten her course again.

"This isn't exactly a sailboat but the principles are the same," he replied, ejecting her from the seat as he plunked gratefully into it and took over. "We have to stay in the channels or we'll run ag—"

At that instant the yacht hit a sandbar hidden beneath the water, jarring every fitting on the much-abused boat. "Good, now we're stopped," Sam said with relief.

"Not exactly the way I'd of chosen, but I guess you're right," Matt said with a goofy grin, obscenely pleased that she was alive and unhurt except for some nasty scratches and a few chunks of hair pulled out. He cut the engines.

Alexi was down for the count, but Kit stirred. Seeing her move, Sam jumped over and scooped up the Ruger before the Englishwoman could reach it. "That's a no-no, Ms. Steele, or whatever the hell your real name is." She leveled the weapon on Kit, who lay stretched across the steering station, glaring at her victorious enemy.

"I doubt it's Steele, but the conceit of having it tattooed on her hip bone tipped us to her involvement."

"Huh?" Sam said.

"Pull down her shorts on the right side and take a gander," he suggested.

Sam yanked the shorts down with gusto, revealing the infinity tattoo.

As she looked at it, he explained. "Steve figured it out when he was doing his chemistry lesson."

"Is he safe?" Tess asked as she climbed up the stairs after running her Cigarette aground beside the yacht.

Matt nodded, grinning. "He's fine and so are your sister and the girls. Some family you have, Tess." He described the rescue of Jenny and her dragons, then went on to explain how Steve had contacted him. "He called the cops who by now have Mikhail in custody. The old man was dumb enough to bring Steve to his house in Aventura.

"Your son figured out that it wasn't a man he'd seen with Nancy but a woman. He had no idea at the time of the encounter because all he could see was her hip with that infinity sign and some letters below it. The tip-off came when he was doing his schoolwork at Grandpa's place. He recognized the periodic table of elements' symbols for iron and carbon. Fe and C."

"Iron and carbon make steel," Tess said. "And he's met Kit several times at Mikhail's house. She was always very charming to him."

"Check this out." Matt pulled the list Kit and Alexi had fought over from the control panel where she'd stashed it and handed it to Sam.

"The fibbies will turn handsprings over this," Sam breathed as she skimmed over the information.

"The CIA won't be too thrilled. Kit and Alexi already sold the info to Pribluda but they were planning a couple more sales. One to Putin's government so they could plug the holes in the dike for escaping Russian billionaires. Another to the Company, giving them the same info they already furnished Pribluda about stolen nukes he and his daddy had located inside the former USSR. Oh, that satchel and the documents spread across the deck here are probably worth quite a few mil. Negotiable securities if I don't miss my guess," Matt added with a grin.

"Wanna split it and make a run for Bimini?" Sam asked, only half-teasing as she looked at the size of the sack.

"In case you hadn't noticed, we're aground...and I do believe the Coast Guard is coming to the rescue even as we speak." Matt grinned at her and Tess as two cutters approached them from opposite angles.

"Rats, foiled again," Sam said with a sigh.

Tess chuckled a bit, then looked down at her husband. "Will he live?" she asked, not sounding as if she particularly cared.

"If he could take all the battering his ladylove here gave him, I expect he'll make it to stand trial with his daddy," Sam replied.

"Hey, I was the one who flattened him while you were busy beating up on poor Ms. Steele."

"Poor, my ass, she's twice my size, you big lummox—and you're twice the size of Alexi."

"Now, children, don't quarrel," Tess said with a grin.

Matt and Sam barely spared her a glance as the cutter pulled up behind them and a Coast Guard officer asked if he was Matt Granger. He identified himself, Sam and Kit Steele, then added, "And the guy down for the count is Alexi Renkov, alive and in person."

"Would you please drop your weapon, Ms. Ballanger?" the young Coast Guard officer asked her as he climbed to the flybridge. "We have instructions from a Miami-Dade homicide detective—"

"God help me!" Sam tossed him the gun. "Sergeant William Patowski will have my guts for garters if this busts loose." She looked at Granger, knowing what he was going to say.

"Oh, it's gonna bust loose—count on it. In a special edition of the *Herald*." He was grinning from ear to ear. "Pulitzer, here I come."

He rubbed his hands in glee. Sam just massaged her aching temples with her fingertips while the military men loaded Alexi Renkov on a stretcher and cuffed Kit Steele for her ride to the brig on Terminal Isle.

"There'll be one hell of a fight over jurisdiction," Matt said with relish.

Sam only sighed and started thinking about how she was going to explain to Pat about the local television station copter that was approaching. Garters, hell. He'd use her whole body for chum!

Chapter 22

"For dragons, they really aren't bad kids," Matt said as he sat on the gurney in the Cedars Medical Center, watching Tiff and Mellie hug their cousin Steve. The girls' shouts of glee drowned out the tearful reunion of Tess and Jenny.

"Good, I'm so glad you found them." Sam had heard the story of the unconventional rescue and the part Jenny and her girls played in the dangerous drama. "How the hell did you figure out where to look?"

"After trying a bunch of places on the list Kit so thoughtfully provided and striking out, I reversed order and tried going bottom up."

"So you suspected her from the get-go?" Sam's tone was decidedly dubious.

"Not exactly," he admitted, shrugging. Then he winced in pain as the raw slash across his midsection oozed more blood into the fresh pressure bandage the medics had placed on it.

"But after so many strikeouts up north, it made sense to move directly south. Besides, I was more familiar with the South Beach area."

"You go to strip clubs?" Sam hated the accusatory sound of the question the moment she uttered it.

Matt gave her a wide grin and waggled his eyebrows à la *Magnum, P.I.* "Only when I'm doing research for a story." At her skeptical snort, he protested, "Hey, where do you think I dug up the lead that led me to San Diego and that 'coconut commune' as my aunt so quaintly called it."

The mention of Aunt Claudia made her wince. "She'll be arriving in a couple of hours. Private jet. Said she'll see you in your private room, which she's already arranged with the hospital staff...then..."

"You've been summoned for an audience in her suite at the Biltmore." He knew the drill. The old bat would make sure he was safe, then get down to brass tacks with Sam. Lord, he'd love to see that interview but knew Claudia wouldn't permit it. Besides, he had his own plans.

"You should be lying down," Sam said, noticing how pale he looked. "You lost a lot of blood. Maybe you need a transfusion or something." She'd had to fight like crazy to get him to come to the E.R., even though his clothes looked like he'd just spent a day in a slaughterhouse.

"Anybody tries to put me in a hospital room will be the one needing the transfusion, not me."

"Tell that to your aunt."

"She isn't here yet." He started to climb down from the gurney.

"Are you crazy? You're covered with blood—your own blood!" Sam practically screeched at him.

That was enough to bring an earnest young nurse wearing

pink scrubs and a sun-damaged perm skittering across the busy floor toward him. "Sir, you can't move."

"Looks like I can," he replied as Sam tried to stop him.

"Get somebody here, real quick. He's been waiting for nearly an hour," Sam said in her toughest south Boston accent.

The kid bobbed her head and called out to a weary man slouching down the hall, "Oh, Dr. Dyer, sir, we have a problem here."

Dyer, an unfortunate name for a physician, had a face with more wrinkles than a folded accordion and shoulders that looked as if he'd been holding up the weight of the world for too many years to count. He took a cursory look at Granger's bloodstained clothes and said, "Put him in number three. It's empty...or at least I hope it is."

Sam stood forlornly watching as they wheeled their protesting patient into the examination area. Tess and Steve walked over to her. "He'll be okay," she said to Sam.

"My father was shot twice and he's going to live," Steve reassured her. "And Mr. Granger won't have to go to jail."

"I'm sorry about your dad, Steve," Sam said solemnly.

He shrugged bony preteen shoulders, already broadening, hinting at the fine physique he would grow into. "So am I, but I have my mom and Aunt Jenny and Tiff and Mellie."

Wanting to divert the sad conversation, Sam asked, "Where did they go?"

"When Tiff asked one of the orderlies if she could borrow his stethoscope and then Mom caught Mellie riffling through stacks of hypodermic needles, we figured an E.R. was too full of temptations," Steve replied with a grin.

"And sharp instruments," Tess added. "Jenny took them to that hotel you got me in the Gables. After the authorities have taken our statements, I think we'll probably all sleep for a week. We can't leave the area until everything is settled but once it is, I think we'll be moving back to San Diego to make a fresh start."

"California's way cool," Steve said, squeezing his mother's arm reassuringly. "And Uncle Hugo just got out of the hospital. He's waiting for us."

Somehow Sam knew they'd be all right once the dust settled and the shadow of the Renkovs was permanently removed from their lives.

Claudia Witherspoon was past ninety but didn't look a day over seventy—not that she'd even admit to being so much as Medicare age. She breezed into the medical center on a cloud of hundred-dollar-an-ounce French perfume, flicking cigarette ashes from a long holder as the automatic door whooshed open. Two aides approached her, pointing to the large No Smoking signs plastered everywhere.

"Very tiresome," she rasped. Like a queen humoring her pet peregrines, she wafted the platinum holder toward one glowering orderly, allowing him to remove the custom-rolled tobacco from it, leaving the disposal of the offending cigarette to the uniformed attendants while she strode to the information desk on Via Spiga heels.

Her hair was silver, smoothly coiffed in a French twist with a few discreet diamonds winking from the platinum comb that held it in perfect place. Everything about Claudia Witherspoon was perfect, from her tailored Bill Blass red suit with pearl buttons down the front to the pearl studs in her ears. Her posture was erect and she was decidedly tall for a woman her generation.

Sam saw her from across the room and knew immediately who she must be. "Stand your ground," she muttered as the storm trooper manning the desk immediately caved and ushered her into treatment room three to see Matt. They had permitted Sam to go with him. "Well, she is a blood relative," she reminded herself.

It still pissed her off.

In moments, Matt's great-aunt reappeared and walked directly toward her. Matt must've described the scratched and bruised short woman with clumps of her hair ripped almost as badly as the remnants of her clothing. She felt like a leper. No use trying to straighten her appearance at this point—as if she could.

"So, you're Samantha." Claudia's ice-blue eyes swept over her in one quick glance. "Matthew informed me—between bouts of cursing at the doctor—that you've been instructed to wait here for the police. When that's taken care of, please call me so we can have a civilized talk, face-to-face. I'm at the Biltmore, of course."

"Of course," Sam couldn't resist echoing as Claudia took a card from her Gucci bag and gave it to Sam, then turned and headed toward the doors.

Kit Steele and Alexi Renkov had tried to shoot her and burn her to death, but they weren't a fraction as frightening as the woman climbing into the stretch limo that waited outside the E.R. As it pulled smoothly away, she muttered, "Well, that went great. Cat got your tongue, 'Samantha'?"

"I never saw you so subdued in your life. Who was that dame?" Sergeant Patowski asked, sidling up to her from behind.

"Claudia Witherspoon, the one you and your fibbie pals tricked into paying me…if she still will."

Pat whistled low. "I was thinking of calling her in to answer a few questions."

"You just rethink the idea?" Sam asked sarcastically.

"Let's just say she has friends in high places. Thanks to you and your boyfriend, I already have half of D.C. ready to tar and feather me. Not to mention the director, twelve of the thirteen county commissioners and the county attorney."

"Only twelve?" she asked, curious who the lone holdout was.

Patowski snorted. "Don't think I'll tilt at any more windmills, at least until the dust settles. Come on, we gotta take a ride out 25th Street." The Miami-Dade Headquarters building was on the west side of the airport on NW 25th.

"Bet you can't offer me a stretch limo," Sam said.

"You're lucky I let you ride in front of the wire barrier instead of behind it," he snapped.

"Homicide dicks don't drive green and whites. You can' threaten me."

"I can arrange for one to take you in and book you in : heartbeat," he shot back as they left the E.R. and climbed i his plain blue sedan.

"Look, I know you didn't like Matt's statement to the tele vision news—"

"Oh, I friggin' loved the part about the *Herald* scoopin them in a special edition. That'll just make our day whe every detail of Renkov's ties to the CIA goes public."

"Hey, you and the fibbies were out to nail Mikhail and tl whole Russian Mafia—and the Company, too, so why l mad at Matt for breaking the story of his career? He was tl one who found that list, after all."

"We want Mikhail for murder, but the whole operation w supposed to be hush-hush until after we had all our ducks a row. We didn't count on a speed race down the Intracoas drawing every newshound in the Southeast. Television he copters." He spat the words like a curse. In Patowski's boc the only newshounds worse than newspapermen were broa cast journalists.

"Steele would've killed Matt and Alexi and gotten aw

with that list of nuclear weapons. Then she'd have turned around and offered them to the CIA, who would've bought them—only to find the Brighton Beach crowd already had the same list. She'd also have sold a copy to Putin's government. Can't imagine they'd be too happy if we'd let that happen. Besides, it was Tess's son who gave you probable cause for that warrant. Bet you found plenty at Mikki's digs in Aventura." Sam waited for him to reply, knew he wouldn't.

Instead, he shifted the topic. "The FBI has Mikhail Renkov on drug trafficking, money laundering and kidnapping. Alexi gets insurance fraud and several murders added to the indictments in his Christmas stocking. Oh, yeah, one of them's Nancy Renkov."

"He admitted drowning her to us before he locked us inside that lead-lined bake oven. Hey, I'll testify," she said, cajolingly.

He grunted. "Damn right you will. Maid at a Bal Harbor hotel found the body about an hour ago. Looked like she drowned in her bubble tub, but the M.E. has other ideas."

"Kit sent Alexi to do it, I'd bet, but why bother? They—or rather Kit after she killed Alexi—was making a getaway with millions to retire on. She had to know Mikhail would be after her for that."

Patowski shrugged. "Bureau's had a tail on Nancy for months. She may have known a hell of a lot about Kit Steele that Mikhail could've beaten out of her—or once she realized that Kit had used her, she might've told him out of spite. Whatever."

Sam nodded. "That makes sense. Kit already sold the list to Nibluda's man. That's where all the loot on her boat came from."

Patowksi's normally down-turned mouth actually inched into what might have been a smile. "Special Agent Gomez and her team nailed the boys from Brighton and retrieved their copy of the list," he admitted.

"If they'd caught Steele, I wouldn't have had to chase her down the Intracoastal." Sam knew she'd scored on that one.

He harrumphed into silence as he threaded his way north onto I-826, then finally said, "I wanted to nab her but Gomez insisted her guy tail the bitch. Thought she'd lead him to Alexi, but instead, she gave him the slip on Brickell."

"Never underestimate the resourcefulness of a woman," Sam said, rubbing her aching head. "She damn near snatched me bald."

This time Patowski actually grinned. "You gotta quit picking fights with people who're bigger than you. Didn't your uncle teach you that?"

She returned his grin. "Naw, Uncle Dec only taught me t fight dirty."

When they reached the glass-and-stucco headquarter complex, the parking lot was filled with unmarked vehicle either Bucars or fancier models reserved for CIA types. "A cording to Matt, his aunt has some clout with the spooks," sh said hopefully.

"Who you tryin' to convince, me or yourself?"

"You guys are the ones in trouble, not me," she said inge uously. She'd cut out her tongue before she told him abo her upcoming sweaty-palm meet with the Witherspoon dan

They walked into a conference room just off the main e try where a coven of FBI agents clustered at one side of t long table, male and female alike in gray suits with short ha cuts. They mixed uncomfortably with several Miami-Da cops Sam recognized from the old days. Two gave h thumbs-up grins but one who'd been a pal of the rookie s took the fall for appraised her with hard eyes. The kid h been canned for another screwup only weeks after she left force. The hostile cop believed, wrongly, that Patowski had set up the kid as a favor to Sam. The irony of that brought a wry half smile to her face.

The room was quiet. That didn't surprise her. Cops and fibbies never socialized unless forced by circumstances. At the opposite side of the table two men stood apart. "If they branded them with a giant *C* on their foreheads, do you think it'd be more obvious they're Company?" Sam muttered to Patowski.

"Let's just finish this before anyone gets to interview your boyfriend," Pat said doggedly.

Sam considered whether or not Matt would still be her boyfriend when everything was said and done. He'd been pretty mad at her when he found out that she had been working with the MDPD and the FBI—even more angry that she'd taken his aunt's bribe. She doubted he worried about poor Aunt Claudia. It was his being set up that got to him. His aunt apparently swam with the sharks. She'd take care of herself. Sam fingered the old lady's card in her pocket, using it as a good luck piece when Special Agent Gomez headed their way.

I'd rather have a double root canal without Novocaine than go through this debriefing. Sam assumed her most badass south Boston demeanor when Gomez introduced her to the fibbies and spooks. She was damned if they'd see her sweat...but glad the room was well air-conditioned.

They reviewed every facet of the case as it pertained to her involvement. Sam answered as completely and truthfully as she could, leaving out only her romantic liaison with the reporter she'd been hired to snatch. So much for her rep as a retrieval specialist if that fiasco got out!

After a couple of hours of grilling, punctuated by several sparring matches between the FBI team and the two CIA

men, things started to wind down. Then a tap on the door
brought disaster. Sergeant Cisneros slipped in and spoke quietly to Pat and Gomez. They argued in monotones for several
moments. The special agent must've won because Patowski's face was the same shade of red as the chairs around the
conference table.

Special Agent Gomez turned to the task force and held up
a newspaper. A special edition of the *Herald* with banner
headlines. Then she passed it to her FBI and MDPD col-
leagues. One CIA agent grabbed it and read aloud:

CIA COVERS FOR LOCAL MOB BOSS!
ALEXI RENKOV ALIVE, UNDER ARREST!

Sam couldn't see the byline, but she knew who the reporter
was. Intimately. Now she sat back in her chair and tried to
make herself invisible as the firestorm broke over the room.
How the hell had he done it? The man was hospitalized. He'd
been shot and lost a gallon of blood. Then she overheard a
FBI agent who'd just entered the room say, "Granger gave police security the slip in the E.R. and headed straight to the
Herald offices." He glared at Patowski—who glared right
back.

So much for worrying about Matt's health. He was no
doubt in his glory. One of the cops brought in a whole bundle of newspapers and she grabbed one, reading the first
person account of their encounters with Renkov's associates.
Sam skimmed down the front page, then skipped to the second. Everything except their personal relationship was out-
lined in detail. She hoped his aunt had as much clout as he
thought she did. Before the dust settled, he'd need Claudia to
keep the spooks from arranging an accident for him.

But he wouldn't need Sam. He'd left her at the hospital without confiding a word about his plan or asking her help making a getaway. *What, did he think I'd rat him out to Patowski?*

Obviously, yes. Her heart sank.

It was nearly dark by the time she walked out of the head-
uarters building, grateful not to be in federal custody. Sam
onsidered calling the *Herald* offices to see if Matt was there,
en decided against it. If he wanted to reach her, he knew
here she lived. Pat had the Charger brought to the building
o she'd have transportation home. Considering everything,
was a decent gesture. The cab fare from NW 25th Street to
E 110th would've broken the bank for her.

As she climbed inside the old wreck, she felt Claudia's
rd in her pocket. She'd been summoned. And no one dared
ow off Claudia Witherspoon. "Might as well end the day as
ell as I began it," she muttered, heading for the Gables.

The Biltmore Hotel had been a Coral Gables landmark
nce 1926. It's three-hundred-fifteen-foot central tower
andly overlooked an eighteen-hole golf course, ten tennis
urts and the largest swimming pool in the continental U.S.
e Spanish revival architecture with Moorish and Italian
cents was pure Gables schmaltz. Over the past century,
e grand old lady had an impressive guest list—the Duke
d Duchess of Windsor, Bing Crosby, Babe Ruth, even Al
pone.

And now it housed Claudia Witherspoon in a suite that was
ubtlessly larger than Sam's whole house. Although she'd
ed in Miami for years, she'd never set foot inside the mau-
leum before today. The vaulted lobby's massive columns
d marble floors dwarfed her as she passed several immense
ass-and-mahogany birdcages. Heading to the banks of el-
ators, Sam felt as if she belonged inside one of the cages—
a newspaper liner for the exotic plumed inhabitants.

Chapter 23

"She's just another rich old broad from Boston, for cryi
out loud," Sam muttered as the brass-and-mahogany elev
tor whisked her to the penthouse. Apparently, Claudia ke
the suite on retainer, like mob bosses kept sharpie lawye
always available when necessary. Thinking of mob boss
she wondered how Mikhail and Alexi were doing in the sla
mer. That brought a fleeting smile to her lips just as the e
vator chimed discreetly and its doors glided open.

If Claudia was trying to impress Sam, it worked. The ha
way was lined with huge marble urns overflowing with bi
of paradise and other lush tropical flowers in brilliant hu
She glanced at the card and the suite-number directory, th
headed for her confrontation. The old woman's wealth a
social position would not have intimidated a tough kid fr
south Boston like Sam...but her relationship to Matt and

shadowy power he'd hinted Claudia wielded in Washington made her nervous as hell.

What had begun as a profitable snatch in cooperation with the MDPD had placed her smack in the middle of an international conspiracy. Those spooks at headquarters hadn't exactly been happy with her. Aunt Claudia would protect Matt, but would she extend the courtesy to his abductor, especially considering that she'd taken the old bat's offer of money under false pretenses—and had done such a bang-up job acting as his bodyguard that he ended up gunshot and hospitalized?

"Might as well find out," she said, pressing the chimes on the massive wooden door.

Amazingly enough, "the old bat" opened the door herself. She'd exchanged the red suit for a silk lounging outfit in some shade of silvery purple that Sam couldn't identify. An expensive Cuban cigar's fragrant smoke wafted gently into the hall. Her hostess waved a fat Triangelo between two dainty fingers that winked with enough carats to keep all the rabbits in the state fat for a year.

"Please come in, Samantha. I've dismissed the servants for the evening and ordered hors d'oeuvres to go with our drinks." She turned and floated toward the onyx bar across a sitting room large enough for a Patriots' game.

Sam's shoes sunk into pale gray plush carpet as she followed, trying hard not to gawk at the retro decor, reminiscent of films set during the 1950s. A curving sectional sofa in soft black leather was flanked by chrome torchière lamps. A pair of blond wood chairs with charcoal upholstery sat with a low glass table between them. The appetizers Claudia had mentioned suddenly made Sam remember she hadn't eaten in nearly twenty-four hours.

"Name your poison. I used to be a fair bartender back in Berlin…or was it Paris? I forget now," Claudia said, pouring a generous slug of expensive gin into a container and adding a breath of vermouth, then shaking it and pouring the drink into a crystal glass.

"You wouldn't happen to have any beer, say Guinness?" There. *Might as well let her know where you come from.* After all, Claudia was the one puffing on the stogie.

Claudia laughed and produced one of the distinctive bottles from the mini fridge beneath the bar. She uncapped it and handed it to Sam. "Your uncle taught you to drink it when you were underage. Straight out of the bottle, no glass. Scandalized your mother."

"You do your homework," Sam said grudgingly, eyeing the cigar.

"I would've offered you one, but I know you quit smoking when you were—"

"Fifteen. I only sneaked Uncle Declan's Marlboros. Never tried a cigar."

"I acquired the habit during the twenties—not mine, I was only sixteen, but I was a flapper in the roaring twenties. Actually, the thirties were far more interesting. Do have a seat," she said, gliding into one of the Danish-looking chairs and raising her glass in a toast.

Sam sat and they both took a drink while eyeing each other like two poker players at a world championship game.

Sam broke the silence, intrigued in spite of herself. "What made the 1930s so interesting?"

"I met Charles Rochat in Berlin. He was a pianist, classically trained but playing jazz in a small club where I sang." Her eyes glowed for a moment but then turned cold. "Of course, my family was horrified that I'd abandoned my grand tour and taken up with an impoverished French musician. When I married him, my father disowned me."

"You were kind of a Sally Bowles?" Sam couldn't res

asking, never having imagined the daughter of Boston Brahmins with such a colorful past.

Claudia shrugged and took another puff on her cigar. "Weimar Germany was quite the place…until the Nazis took over. Charles and I worked for the resistance. My family was involved with the State Department and suddenly my connections abroad were useful. All was forgiven…after my husband was killed by the Gestapo." She paused and took a fortifying sip of her martini before continuing. "Paul and Julia broke the news to me. My father wanted me to come home and be safe. Of course I refused."

"Paul and Julia *Childs?*" Sam asked.

"We worked together until the war ended, remained good friends until their passing."

"Why'd you ask me to come here? I already know you're richer than God and pissed as hell about how the cops and fibbies tricked you into hiring me."

"Tricked *me?*" Claudia's mood shifted to amusement. She arched one eyebrow and smiled a Cheshire cat smile. "Samantha, no one has 'tricked' me in…well, let us just say a very long time. Do you honestly believe I'd think Matthew had been 'brainwashed' by some cult? Really. I tried brainwashing him for over twenty years without a modicum of success."

Sam suddenly remembered to close her mouth before her jaw hit the low glass table in front of her. "He did mention his family not approving of his newspaper career," she managed to get out.

Claudia chuckled. "Spurning his trust fund and refusing to take his place at Lodge, Asher, Witherspoon & Fiske made my brother go ballistic. I was secretly pleased to see my blood will out, not that I've let Matthew know, of course."

"Of course," Sam echoed, taking a long pull on her Guiness as Claudia continued.

"Within hours of that ridiculous call from my nephew's bogus editor, my sources had appraised me of what he'd become involved in. He is my only living heir and I do not intend to see him hurt. Ever. So, I investigated you since you came recommended by the Bureau. I was prepared to dislike you."

Sam tried to read the old lady's face but hadn't a clue. *Jeez, she's better than Uncle Dec.* "You ever play poker?" she asked incredulously.

Claudia threw back her head and laughed. "Oh, you passed muster. I decided to play along with the subterfuge as the most expeditious way of removing Matthew from danger."

"Yeah, but I let him get kidnapped and shot," Sam replied glumly.

"Ah, but you did save his life—at considerable risk to your own, I might add. I hired the best woman for the job, which you did without interference from your local flatfeet, the Bureau...or the CIA."

"I almost screwed up. If Tess Renkov hadn't been able to catch Kit Steele's boat, she'd have killed Matt," Sam confessed.

"I read my great-nephew's story in the *Herald*. I'm sure he considers you his heroine." Claudia eyed Sam over the edge of her glass as she sipped.

Sam had no clue where this was going. *Some heroine. He ditched me.* She changed the subject back to his aunt. "How'd you become a Witherspoon?"

"My second husband. Poor Hubert. Such a dry old stick, but at least he had the good grace to drop dead at the stock exchange a year after we were married. He was sixty-seven. I was twenty-nine. My father died during the war and my younger brother, very impressed with becoming titular head of the family, insisted I marry someone of my station. Since he was controlling the purse strings until I did, I chose Hubert Witherspoon.

In spite of everything, Sam couldn't resist a grin. "He was old and rich and let you do whatever you wanted."

Claudia nodded. "After I inherited Hubert's money, I invested it and made a tidy profit. Irritated the hell out of Matthew's grandfather and father."

"You hinted earlier about insider influence in Washington politics. Was that how you kept the CIA off Matt when he started investigating Renkov?"

"As I said, I contacted my sources," Claudia replied. "Caleb and I go back a ways."

"Caleb Ware, the former CIA director?" Sam asked, thinking of the distinguished elder statesman.

Claudia's Cheshire cat smile returned. "Men who're high in the inner circles of government can be very helpful—and sometimes excellent lovers. Perhaps Henry was right. Power can be quite an aphrodisiac."

"Kissinger." It wasn't a question. Who hadn't this amazing old lady had a liaison with?"

"A pity about J. Edgar's sexual peculiarities. He would've been very useful during the McCarthy era, but then he always was such an icky little toad...."

Sam was so fascinated by Claudia's sexual and political adventures she forgot the feast spread in front of her until her hostess took a water cracker piled high with Beluga caviar and popped it into her mouth. "Do eat or that stout will go straight to your head. I imagine you haven't had a thing but dreadful squad-room coffee for hours."

Sam wolfed down a couple of wafer-thin proscuitto roll-ups and some superb Roquefort cheese, then leaned back and looked Claudia straight in the eye. "Now," she said, wiping her mouth with a monogrammed napkin, "why did you ask me here? I know it wasn't to shock me with your colorful past or intimidate me with all the powerful men you've slept with."

Claudia threw back her head and laughed, a low throaty growl of delight. "I knew you and I would get on famously. No, I had no doubt that I could either shock or intimidate you. I want to make you an offer…"

Sam knocked on the door while glancing across the open hallway to Collins Avenue below her. The bright Florida sunrise illuminated the topiary phalluses standing guard at the entrance to the condo across the street. Somehow that seemed appropriate. But then this was South Beach, after all.

"Come on, Granger, where are you?" she muttered, leaning on the buzzer. He'd left the *Herald* offices around seven the night before, an ecstatic young clerk told her in awed tones. Right now everyone up to the managing editor probably thought Matt Granger could walk on water.

The door opened and the bleary-eyed subject of her thoughts leaned against the door frame. He didn't look the least bit buoyant as he said, "It's the crack of dawn. I was asleep."

She walked past him into the living room, trying to pull off Claudia's panache. Failing miserably. Nothing she could do but to be Sam Ballanger from south Boston. No class, just nerve. "You gave the fibbies the slip. Pissed 'em off," she said with a grin.

"Oh, they caught up with me at the *Herald*. Spent an hour grilling me. Your pal Patowski helped out."

"You still mad with me about him, working the deal to trick your aunt, I mean?" She had no intention of sharing what Aunt Claudia had told her in confidence. He didn't need to know.

Sam stood in the center of the meticulous living room. Plain masculine furniture in shades of brown and dark green, a couple of potted plants, end tables without clutter. The walls were filled, mostly with newspaper articles, some with his byline, more written by famous reporters. The plants were thriving and even the damn frames were hung straight. She ought to hate him for that.

Matt took his time replying. With all that had happened to him in the last few days, his mind was a touch on the fuzzy side. The charming interrogation by the local and federal constabularies hadn't been easy, either. When they finally released him, he'd taken a cab straight home and become one with his bed. But seeing Sam standing in the middle of the room, her toe tapping impatiently, hands on her hips, staring intensely at him made him forget his achy side and lack of sleep.

"I might be. You and my aunt have your little chat?"

"We talked. She's led a...dramatic life."

That elicited a snort of laughter. "Dramatic? That's like comparing Robert DeNiro's acting style to Gary Cooper's. She's been everything from a cabaret singer to a spy. Drove the family nuts. That's why it pissed me off so much when she insisted I stick to the straight and narrow after my parents died."

"She wanted you to be safe...to live to carry on the Granger name. Being a stockbroker's a lot safer than going for a Pulitzer."

"Ya think? Dullsville, though."

"She admits you've inherited her wild streak."

"Just not her penchant for making money."

Sam shrugged. "You always have the trust fund." He bristled. She grinned. "I know you don't want it, but think of all the security you grew up with, just knowing it was there."

"I guess a kid from the other side of the tracks might think that's a little weird." He appeared to consider the idea as if it had never occurred to him before.

"I don't think it's weird, Matt," she said softly, walking toward him and raising her hand to touch his beard-bristled cheek. "I think it's completely nuts—but," she cut him off when he opened his mouth to protest, "I forgive you."

Then she wrapped her arms around his neck and tiptoed up to insert her tongue in his mouth, coiling it with his in a hot, languorous kiss.

"You clean up pretty good," he finally managed when they broke the kiss. She had obviously showered and changed clothes. He nuzzled her neck, inhaling a faint scent of floral perfume. "Smell good, too."

She took him by the lapels of his terry-cloth robe and said, "Well, you don't. Into the shower, Mr. Granger."

"Isn't this where we started last week?" he asked, following her down the hallway.

"God, I hope your shower's cleaner than the ones in those motels." Looking at the immaculate state of his digs, she knew it would be. This might really work out after all…or not.

He cupped her derriere. "You gonna give me a good scrub off?"

She looked over her shoulder and grinned at him. "I even brought a blindfold and cuffs."

"No way. I intend to see and feel every inch of you."

"Speaking of inches…" Her voice trailed away when the tent pole under his robe prodded her in the backside. Taking the protruding "handle," she led him into the small bathroom and said in her best retrieval specialist's voice, "Now strip. I gotta check your wound before we do anything too strenuous."

"I'm okay for strenuous," he murmured with a small grunt of pleasure. "In fact, the doc told me to remove the bandages and shower this morning when I got up."

"Oh, you're up all right. But let's just make certain the stitches aren't seeping. I'm the health-care professional, remember?"

He untied the robe, then slipped it off his shoulders, letting it drop to the floor. Except for a narrow wrap of gauze around his ribs, he didn't have a stitch on under it. "Now it's your turn."

As he began to unbutton her blouse, Sam removed the bandage and checked the ugly gash on his side. Not deep but it had been a bleeder. She'd seen lots worse in her paramedic days but knew they had to take it easy. "Just lean back against the shower wall and let Nurse Sam do the rest, okay?"

"You're the health-care professional," he said without a hint of sarcasm this time, while his hands continued to undress her.

"And you're the get-naked specialist," she said as he unhooked her bra with two fingers. Amazing. Even more amazing when his big hands each cupped a breast and teased her nipples into pebbly ecstasy. "All the blood you have left in you's in one place right now. Look, I don't want you passing out in the shower stall like you almost did at the back of my van. I'm too little to carry a lummox like you so let's go slow."

Why in the hell had she started this without thinking about his physical condition? The man had been shot yesterday afternoon! Because the minute she'd seen him in that doorway looking disheveled and sexy as hell, all rational thought had fled. He wasn't the only one whose blood had settled someplace else besides his brain.

"Slow is good," he agreed, turning on the water, nice and warm. Steam quickly enveloped them.

Sam took the shampoo and lathered up his thick curly black hair, massaging his scalp while he held on to her waist, running clever fingers up and down her spine. He stuck his head beneath the spray and rinsed off as she applied soap to his chest and shoulders, being careful of the stitches. Obediently he raised his arms so she could scrub them. Then she knelt and washed his legs.

"Saving the best for last, huh?" he murmured over the rush of water.

When her soap-slicked fingers glided over his cock, Matt gasped in a mouthful of water and started coughing.

"Teach you to be a smart-ass," she said with a chuckle.

"It wasn't my ass I was thinking about, believe me," he said as she turned off the water and opened the shower door. Her hair, so carefully curled earlier, was drenched and hanging in her eyes. "You look like a cute little sheepdog," he said, cupping her face in his hands.

"There's no such thing as a cute sheepdog—or a little one, but thanks anyway," she said breathlessly, reaching for a stack of towels.

He took a huge tan bath sheet and wrapped it around both of them, holding her close. "Let's see if we can figure a way to dry us both at once…maybe a little friction…hmm?"

She intended to say she needed to apply a new bandage to his ribs, but the thought never moved from her brain to her lips. He already had them occupied. His erection probed her belly as he moved the soft towel sensuously around them. Overhead, a heat lamp glowed down, warming the room until her hair started to kink into the curly mass of ringlets she'd spent a lifetime trying to tame. They pressed their bodies together under the towel, moving in sync until he let it float to their feet.

"Dry enough?" he murmured, taking her hand and pulling her toward the door.

"Your side—I have to bandage it." She dug her bare heels into the bath mat, stopping him.

"Hurry up," he groused as she picked up the gauze and tape he'd been issued at the med center yesterday.

She'd done this so many times she couldn't count, but he

hands trembled when she picked up the scissors. *Damn, I'll probably slice off a finger.* She cut the package open and managed to unroll the bandage. "Hold up your arms." He complied as she moved in closer. It didn't help her concentration that he rained small kisses across her shoulders while she reached around him to wrap the gauze in place and tape it.

"Finished?" he asked as she backed away to inspect her handiwork.

Far from her most professional job but it would hold—if they didn't get too acrobatic in bed.

It held for three minutes.

But neither of them cared as they rolled around on his king-size bed until he pinned her beneath him and slowly penetrated her until they were both mindless with pleasure.

"Sammie, Sammie," he murmured against her hair as he thrust and she arched.

Sam called out his name as she climaxed, her nails digging into his shoulders, luxuriating in his shuddering release so close behind hers. Perfect.

Well, maybe. If the next part went the way she planned. Before she could gather her thoughts, he rolled to his good side and curled her against him, cradling her in his arms and kissing her softly.

"I could do this for days." He nuzzled her throat and splayed his hand through the mop of curly hair on her head.

"How about forever?" *Cool, Sam. Real subtle.*

"What've you got in mind?" he asked.

But by that time he had turned her over and started sucking on her breast. Sam forgot what she wanted to say. Matt forgot what he'd asked her.

They finally made it out of bed in time for lunch. Matt scrounged up some bagels from his freezer and a package of cream cheese to spread on the toasted rounds. They shared a pot of strong Cuban coffee as they ate…and Sam worked up her courage.

"About my visit with your aunt…"

"Yeah? She's a kick in the head, isn't she? Stormed into that E.R. and put the fear of God into Dr. Dyer. She said she was going to talk to you. Knew who you were before I described you. Damn woman knows everything," he said, wiping his mouth with a paper napkin. "Sometimes it creeps me out."

Sam took a fortifying swallow of caffeine and said, "Aunt Claudia and I agreed—"

"Already I don't like this," he interrupted.

She put her cup down and looked straight across the table at him. "We agreed the only way to keep you alive is for me to marry you. She's offered me ten K for every month we stay married, so I'm proposing and I won't take no for an answer."

He stared at her, his jaw dropping. "Well, I'll be damned," he finally managed on a croak.

Sam dared a cheeky grin. "I can have a custom straitjacket designed to look like a tux."

Matt grinned back and stood up. "Kinky. From Leather and Lace. I like it." He reached down and pulled her into his arms.

But Sam had the last word as he bent down to kiss her. "Oh yeah. No divorce. I'm not giving the money back, Granger."

* * * * *

Look for Sneak and Rescue *by Shirl Henke*
out in July 2008!

Keep reading for an exclusive extract from

High-Stakes Honeymoon
by RaeAnne Thayne,

*out in July 2008 from
Mills & Boon® Intrigue.*

High-Stakes Honeymoon
by RaeAnne Thayne

Olivia sighed, gazing out at the ripple of waves as she tried to drum up a little enthusiasm for the holiday that stretched ahead of her like the vast, undulating surface of the Pacific. She'd been here less than twenty-four hours and had nine more days to go, and at this point she was just about ready to pack up her suitcases and catch the next puddle jumper she could find back to the States.

She was bored and lonely and just plain miserable.

Maybe she should have invited one of her girlfriends to come along for company. Or better yet, she should have just eaten the cost of the plane tickets and stayed back in Fort Worth.

But then she would have had to face the questions and the sympathetic—and not so sympathetic—looks and the resigned disappointment she was entirely too accustomed to seeing in her father's eyes.

No, this way was better. If nothing else, ten days in another country would give her a little time and distance to handle the bitter betrayal of knowing that even in this, Wallace Lambert wouldn't stand behind her. Her father sided with his golden boy, his groomed successor, and couldn't seem to understand why she might possibly object to her fiancé cheating on her with another woman two weeks before their wedding.

It was apparently entirely unreasonable of her to expect a few basic courtesies—minor little things like fidelity and trust—from the man who claimed to adore her and worship the ground she walked on.

Who knew?

The sun slipped further into the water and she

sighed again, angry at herself. So much for her promise that she wouldn't brood about Bradley or her father.

This was her honeymoon and she planned to enjoy herself, damn them both. She could survive nine more days in paradise, in the company of macaws and howler monkeys, iguanas and even a sloth—not to mention her host, whom she had yet to encounter.

James Rafferty, whom she was meeting later for dinner, had built his fortune through online gambling and he had created an exclusive paradise here completely off the grid—no power except through generators, water from wells on the property. Even her cell phone didn't work here.

Nine days without distractions ought to be long enough for her to figure out what she was going to do with the rest of her life. She was twenty-six years old and it was high time she shoved everybody else out of the driver's seat so she could start picking her own direction.

Some kind of animal screamed suddenly, a high, disconcerting sound, and Olivia jumped, suddenly uneasy to realize she was alone down here on the beach.

There were jaguars in this part of the Osa Peninsula, she had read in the guidebook. Jaguars and pumas and who knew what else. A big cat could suddenly spring out of the jungle and drag her into the trees, and no one in the world would ever know what happened to her.

That would certainly be a fitting end to what had to be the world's worst honeymoon.

She shivered and quickly gathered up her things, shaking the sand out of her towel and tossing her sunglasses and paperback into her beach bag along with her cell phone that she couldn't quite sever herself from, despite its uselessness here.

No worries, she told herself. She seemed to remember jaguars hunted at night and it was still a half hour to full dark. Anyway, she had a hard time believing James Rafferty would allow wild predators such as that to roam free on his vast estate.

Still, she wasn't at all sure she could find her way back to her bungalow in the dark, and she needed to shower off the sand and sunscreen and change for dinner.

She had waited too long to return, she quickly discovered. She would have thought the dying rays of the sun would provide enough light for her to make her way back to her bungalow, fifty yards or so from the beach up a moderate incline. But the trail moved through heavy growth, feathery ferns and flowering shrubs and thick trees with vines roped throughout.

What had seemed lovely and exotic on her way down to the beach suddenly seemed darker, almost menacing, in the dusk.

Something rustled in the thick undergrowth to her left. She swallowed a gasp and picked up her pace, those jaguars prowling through her head again.

Next time she would watch the sunset from the comfort of her own little front porch, she decided nervously. Of course, from what the taciturn housekeeper who had brought her food earlier said, this dry sunset was an anomaly this time of year, given the daily rains.

Wasn't it just like Bradley to book their honeymoon destination without any thought that they were arriving in the worst month of the rainy season. She would probably be stuck in her bungalow the entire nine days.

Still grumbling under her breath, she made it only a few more feet before a dark shape suddenly lurched out of the gathering darkness. She uttered a small shriek of surprise and barely managed to keep her footing.

In the fading light, she could only make out a stranger looming over her, dark and menacing. Something long and lethal gleamed silver in the fading light, and a strangled scream escaped her.

He held a machete, a wickedly sharp one, and she gazed at it, riveted like a bug watching a frog's tongue flicking toward it. She couldn't seem to look away as it gleamed in the last fading rays of the sun.

She was going to die alone on her honeymoon in a foreign country in a bikini that showed just how lousy she was at keeping up with her Pilates.

Her only consolation was that the stranger seemed just as surprised to see her. She supposed someone with rape on his mind probably wouldn't waste time staring at her as if she were some kind of freakish sea creature.

Come on. The bikini wasn't *that* bad.

She opened her mouth to say something—she wasn't quite sure what—but before she could come up with anything, he gave a quick look around, then grabbed her from behind, shoving the hand not holding the machete against her mouth.

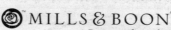

FREE

4 Books
and a su...ise gift

We would like to take this opportu...
Boon® book by offering you the ...
selected titles from the Intrigue seri...
offer to introduce you to the benefi...

- ★ FREE home delivery
- ★ FREE gifts and com...
- ★ FREE monthly New...
- ★ Exclusive Reader S...
- ★ Books available be...

Accepting these FREE books and g... p...
you may cancel at any time. even after receiving your free shipment. Simply
complete your details below and return the entire page to the address below
You don't even need a stamp!

YES! Please send me 4 free Intrigue books and a surprise gift. I understand
that unless you hear from me. I will receive 6 superb new titles ever
month for just £3.15 each. postage and packing free. I am under no obligation
to purchase any books and may cancel my subscription at any time. The fre
books and gift will be mine to keep in any case.

I8ZE

Ms/Mrs/Miss/Mr .... Initials ....
BLOCK CAPITALS PLEAS

Surname ....

Address ....

....

.... Postcode ....

Send this whole page to:
UK: FREEPOST CN8I, Croydon, CR9 3WZ